The l

She opened h
fleeting glimps
features. Her fingers felt along the bandage on her brow. "What happened to me?"

"You fell into the river and hit your head. Max and I pulled you out."

"Max?"

"My dog. Come, Max."

The Newfoundland eased his large frame between his master and Alexandra. She gasped in surprise—he outweighed her by at least three stone! She tried to sit up.

The man assisted her. "Easy now, lest you cause yourself further injury. Mayhap you should lie still." Impatience crept into his voice again.

She winced at his mild rebuke and lowered her gaze, only to realize she was clad in her bedgown. "Sir, has a woman been caring for me?"

"Nay." Amusement glittered in his eyes. "Women are not allowed on vessels. They bring bad luck."

Heat flooded her cheeks, but she forced herself to continue. "I'm—" She cleared her throat and tried again. "I'm not wearing my pink dress."

"Aye, that is true." He nodded, his expression unfathomable.

Sapphire and Gold

by

Penny Rader

*To Aunt Joan,
Happy reading
& thanks for your
support!! :)
Penny*

Sapphire and Gold

Cover Art by *Nicola Martinez*

The Wild Rose Press
PO Box 706
Adams Basin, NY 14410-0706
Visit us at www.thewildrosepress.com

Publishing History
First American Rose Edition, 2009
Print ISBN 1-60154-475-8

Published in the United States of America

Dedication

To my family—Thank you for your unwavering love & encouragement.

To Jo—Who made the shuttle driver pull over for me at my first RWA conference and became my first writer friend.

To Eva—Who helped me get the Wichita Area Romance Authors started. Rest in peace.

To all the wonderful ladies of WARA—I have learned so much from all of you.

To the Tuesday Night Group: Brandi, Denise, Jeannie, Rosalind, Sandy, Sharon, & Starla—What would I do without your critiques, brainstorming, nudges, kicks in the backside, and friendship?

Prologue

2 October 1752

Today I visited the waterfront again. What force keeps pulling me there? A dark-haired man aboard a vessel sailing into the harbor gave brisk commands to his crew. He turned; our eyes met. My heart thudded so hard against my ribs I scarce could breathe. My skin tingled as I imagined his touch in the whisper soft caress of the wind. He reminded me of a knight of old, the perfect rescuer. But what need have I for a rescuer?

Chapter One

Philadelphia, October 3, 1752

At the loud, incessant rapping, Alexandra Whittaker rushed from the sickroom to the side entrance and swung the door open. "Shhh! I've just settled an ill child down for a much needed rest."

The unkempt man before her removed his battered felt hat and shifted his weight from foot to foot. "P-pardon me, miss. This is for Mr. Bartholomew Taylor." He thrust a folded piece of paper into her hand and scurried away.

Although tempted to pretend the unexpected visitor had never arrived, she knew there would be no peace for any of them if Bartholomew learned she had neglected to deliver his message. She suppressed a shudder of dismay and resigned herself to the unpleasant encounter to follow.

Mindful of Bartholomew's penchant for neatness, Alexandra tucked the stray strands of ebony hair back into her ruffled cap and smoothed her long skirts. She held the smudged note by its tattered edges and proceeded up the two flights of stairs. As she reached the floor he occupied, she slowed her steps, loath to complete the unwelcome task.

Voices drifted through the open door a short distance ahead. Relief welled inside her. He was not alone. She would be able to deliver the note and leave without fending off unwanted advances. She continued down the long, shadowy hallway, anxious to be done.

"Alexandra's mine and mine alone! She will soon become my bride. This time no one will thwart my wedding."

Alexandra smothered a gasp with her hand and flattened herself against the wall outside Bartholomew's office. Wedding? This time? There had never been a first time.

"Sh-she wasn't abandoned, was she?" Henry Taylor's voice quivered.

Alexandra ceased breathing, then inched closer to the open door and listened with growing trepidation. "Mind your own business, Henry, or I'll forget you're my brother."

"D-did you take her from her family all those years ago?" Henry's voice shook. "Polly told me something wasn't right when you first brought her here, but—"

"No more questions. I'm all the family she needs."

The underlying menace in Bartholomew's tone sent chills slithering down Alexandra's spine. She tiptoed back through the hallway, crept down the narrow stairways, and fled to the sanctuary of the sickroom. All the while she tried to sort through the confusion jumbling her thoughts.

Perhaps she had misunderstood them. But even as she pressed her hand to Mandy Rourke's brow, Alexandra knew with bone-numbing certainty Bartholomew's statements did not bode well for her.

Polly Taylor bustled into the room and smoothed her graying hair in place. "How is the wee one?"

"She's asleep." Alexandra brushed dark tendrils from the child's pale cheek. "I dosed her with Peruvian bark earlier and her fever lessened."

The older woman rested her plump hand on Alexandra's slender shoulder. "You look tired. Perhaps you should go to your chamber and lie down."

"I'd rather stay here."

"You'll do Mandy no good if you fall ill as well. You watched over her all of last night and all of this day. I insist you rest. I shall look after her."

Alexandra knew it would be pointless to argue, so she placed a kiss on Polly's round cheek and left the room. Polly's heart might be as big as the three-story brick home she had inherited from her first husband, but once she set her mind to something it was easier to acquiesce right away. She inevitably persuaded everyone to do as she requested.

Everyone but Bartholomew.

Weary from the day's events, Alexandra placed her hand on the balustrade and mounted the stairs to the second floor. The conversation she had overheard tumbled back into her thoughts. Had she misunderstood Bartholomew's marriage plans? Maybe he had not meant he was going to wed *her*. He was old enough to be her father.

She paused mid-step. Henry had said she had not been abandoned, that Bartholomew had taken her from her family.

"Hello, Alexandra."

Alexandra froze, then schooled her features to reveal naught of her inner turmoil. She lifted her head and met Bartholomew's dark, penetrating gaze, a gaze devoid of warmth. A stranger might find him attractive, at least on the surface. He kept his black hair stylishly cut, powdering it upon occasion, and he wore clothes of the latest fashion. But she saw beyond the trappings. His moustache-topped smile did not fool her. His eyes revealed the true Bartholomew Taylor. Shaken by his sudden appearance, but unwilling to show it, she inclined her head and moved to step around him.

He blocked her ascent, then reached into his pocket and withdrew a crumpled piece of paper. "Did you drop this?"

Alexandra recognized the note and caught her breath. He knew she had been outside his office. Her knees grew weak, but she held her ground. "I know what you did."

"Do you now?" The corners of his mouth turned up.

"You stole me from my family. Who are my parents? Where are they?"

Bartholomew rested his shoulder against the wall. "I'm your family. You have no need for anyone else."

"I'll find them."

"No, you will not. You belong to me, and you'll do as I say."

She clenched her hands into tight fists. "Let me pass."

He reached out and stroked her cheek. "I think not. I rather enjoy being near you."

Alexandra's heart thudded against her rib cage. She took a step down the staircase. Bartholomew followed and caught her by the wrist. Rising fear threatened to choke her. "Let go of me."

Instead, he removed her ruffled cap. "Lovely, just lovely." He slid his fingers through the silken waves. "You must wear it down, but only for me. When we are alone."

"Never," she said. "I'll never be alone with you again."

Bartholomew's onyx eyes glittered. "Oh, but you will. I have such plans for us. Glorious plans."

Alexandra shook her head. "Polly won't let you."

"Polly?" His eyebrows curved upward. "Polly won't let me? She depends on the rent I pay. My brother doesn't earn enough to support a flea let alone the passel of mewling brats living here."

He tightened his hold on her wrist and jerked her forward until her body was flush against his. He lowered his mouth toward hers and goose bumps rose on her flesh. "Polly will hear naught of this, else..."

She arched away from him. "E-else what?"

"Do you really want to know, my dear?" He brushed his lips against hers. "Soon." Then he was gone.

Alexandra raced up the remaining stairs to the second floor. Once inside her chamber she ran to the washstand and scrubbed her lips and arms to rid herself of Bartholomew's touch.

What was she to do? She could not, she *would* not marry him. Yet, if she remained here, she would be powerless against his wishes. He *always* got what he wanted.

She could think of only one way to thwart his plans—she must run away. Uncertainty nagged at her. Where would she go? She could not ask Polly to help her. Not in the face of Bartholomew's veiled threats. How could she leave Polly and the young ones? For the past score of years the dear woman had opened her home to orphaned and abandoned children. So much needed to be done before winter— candles dipped, soap made, spinning, weaving. Thank goodness she could leave Mandy in the capable hands of Polly and kind Dr. Sebastian.

Memories flooded over her. For as long as she could remember, the undercurrent of tension in the house had made everyone—Polly, Henry, and the children alike—uncomfortable.

Though Polly despised the man, Alexandra knew she tolerated his presence for the sake of her husband. Disturbed by Bartholomew's unpredictable rages, Alexandra had learned early to avoid the upper floor. The atmosphere changed during his frequent sea ventures, becoming more relaxed, more carefree. Since his return from his most recent voyage, his unnerving vigilance had increased. She often felt his gaze upon her.

A burning anger fired deep within Alexandra. All these years he had refused to discuss her parents. He had allowed her to believe they had deserted her or had died. He never divulged how or where he had found her. Dare she hope to find her parents? She had to try. Before her resolve weakened, she made her decision. She would leave this night. She prayed Polly and the children would forgive her.

A glance out her window at the fading daylight told her she must hurry if she wished to leave before eventide settled like a mantle over the city. The streets were not safe after nightfall.

From the wardrobe she gathered two dresses, both well worn, and tossed them onto her bed. Next, she withdrew several undergarments from the walnut highboy. Her hairbrush joined the growing pile. She thrust her clothing into her valise and glanced about her small chamber. Her gaze stopped at the stack of medical books on her dressing table. If only she could take them with her.

With shaking hands, she picked up her diary and opened it to the entry she had recorded earlier, upon waking from a troubled sleep.

Again this morning I woke with a frightening sense of evil in my mind. But, there is no evil here—

She closed the small book and slipped it into her apron pocket. How naive she had been. Overwhelmed by the day's revelations, she walked to her window on unsteady legs and stared out over the silhouetted city. A shape moved away from the shadows below. Bartholomew! She raised her hand to her throat. His mocking grin sent terror scurrying through her.

She stiffened her spine and struggled to make her expression impassive. She would not show her fear. With a slight bow, Bartholomew departed into the half-light. But he would return. Would he accelerate his plans now that she knew of his intentions?

She fastened her cloak around her shoulders, then stilled her movements. The realization that she might never see Polly or the children, especially Mandy, again stabbed her heart. Unable to disappear into the night without saying good-bye, she penned a brief farewell note and propped it up on her dressing table.

Alexandra grabbed her bag and left her room. She hurried toward the third floor. "Bartholomew must have *something* to lead me to my parents."

She stole inside his office, closed the door behind her, and drew a deep breath to calm the uneasiness this room always roused within her. She dismissed the imposing tall-case clock and bookshelves as places to search, passed the richly upholstered wing chairs, and took care to avoid the table displaying a silver and porcelain tea set.

The black walnut secretary in front of the large multi-paned window seemed the logical place to begin. She searched its pigeonholes and pulled on the drawer handles, but found them locked. Aided by Bartholomew's pen-knife, she pried open the drawers and dumped their contents on the floor.

Still no clues about her parents.

After a few frustrating minutes of feeling around in the empty spaces, Alexandra discovered a secret compartment. She slid it open and pulled out a pile of documents. They listed names, dates, places, and profits. Why would he hide these, unless... She rose to her feet. They might be the means to rid Polly's home of the scoundrel.

Shuddering to think of Bartholomew's reaction should he discover her with them, Alexandra stuffed the papers into her valise. She would conceal them in the bag's lining later. A golden glint drew her attention to the floor. She took a closer look. A delicately carved cameo locket. Where had it come from?

The papers. Bartholomew must have hidden it in the secret compartment. A tremor of inexplicable fear passed through Alexandra and a vague memory tried to surface. Compelled by an unknown force, she picked up the locket and opened it. Inside, she found a painted miniature of herself as a small child. Her fingers trembled as she turned the cameo over and read the flowing script.

My Dearest Laurel,
Our love will withstand the test of time.
Eternally yours,
Jared
Williamsburg, 1730

She had found her clue. She was heading south. To Williamsburg, Virginia.

****

...I could not wait for your return. I'm sure I have located my granddaughter, but I must proceed with caution. She seems to have no memory of the event. I must not force her.

Do not tell Jared or Laurel of my findings. I must be certain it is really her.

Sebastian

Derek Tremaine folded the hated letter along the worn crease lines, frustrated by his inability to locate its author. Had Dr. Sebastian found Charlotte? There had been many false hopes in the past. Damn the man. Why did he have to stir up the past again, after Derek had finally put it to rest?

"We might as well return to the *Wind Spirit* and resume our search in the morning, Max."

Before Derek could turn the stallion in the direction of his schooner, Max, his Newfoundland dog, growled. A movement to Derek's left caught his eye. "Shhh, Max." They remained among the shadows, prepared for trouble.

A woman on horseback came into clear view. A small gust of wind blew back the hood of her dark cloak, revealing a wealth of black hair and the delicate features of the woman he had seen on the waterfront yesterday. Her sapphire eyes had seemed to make a silent appeal. He'd had the strange urge to ask her heart's desire and try to fulfill it, an urge he had suppressed.

His brow furrowed. She should not be on the streets at this time of night. Her wariness—or was it fear?—became apparent. She concealed herself within the large hood and cast furtive glances behind her before moving forward.

Perhaps she was meeting someone. A man? Why should he care if she was meeting a man? Puzzled by the queer lurch of his heart at the thought of the young beauty in someone else's arms, Derek decided to follow her, at least until she arrived at her destination. What sort of a gentleman would he be if he allowed a woman to ride without an escort through darkened streets?

What had driven her out after nightfall? She was no doxy. He could spot one of those at fifty paces. Mayhap she had visited an ailing friend. Perhaps she had just arrived in Philadelphia. She might be lost. He noted the way she peered down the shadowed streets and alleys and wondered if someone was pursuing her.

He continued to follow her down Chestnut Street. It went against his nature to stand by with careless disregard while a young woman plunged headlong into possible trouble, even if she did have dark hair and blue eyes. Each time the woman looked around, Derek and Max blended with the shadows so they would not spook her.

****

Alexandra pulled her heavy cloak closer against the cool autumn air, unable to shake the feeling that she was being watched. Had Bartholomew discovered her absence already? *Please, don't let it be so.*

She urged Old Betsy, the mare she had "borrowed" from Polly, to quicken her pace and turned south onto Third Street. She could not risk riding near the waterfront where Bartholomew's hirelings would surely see her. It was proving difficult enough just avoiding taverns. Each night Bartholomew visited the public houses, but she did not know which ones he favored.

Alexandra rode past row after row of three-story brick houses and found the quiet disconcerting. Throughout the day, clatter and clangor reverberated through the streets until sometimes one could not hear oneself think. But this evening she would have welcomed a crowd of people. Now, she started at every sound, jumped at every ghostly shape cast by the whale-oil lamps.

"Half past eight and a starry night!"

Alexandra's heart pounded in sudden fear and she muffled a startled gasp. *'Tis only a night watchman.* She waited until he continued his patrol down Cedar Street, then she resumed her flight.

Alexandra arrived at a wooded area and swallowed hard. It was so dark. Did she dare enter the wild tangle of trees? She glanced back toward Philadelphia. Bartholomew's leering, mocking gaze appeared before her mind's eye. She must face the mysteries of the forbidding forest.

Whispering words of encouragement to Old Betsy, Alexandra struggled to quell the quiver of fear in the pit of her stomach. How could she go? How could she not? Her fear of Bartholomew dwarfed her fear of this forest.

"It's just a lot of trees...and...small animals."

And bears and highwaymen and Indians. She leaned forward and patted the mare's neck. "Come on, girl. We can do it." Alexandra drew a steadying breath and ventured into the silence. Her heartbeat thundered in her ears.

She felt Old Betsy's uncertainty as the horse picked her way through the twisted, gnarled trees. Low branches pulled the hood off Alexandra's head and tangled in her hair. The mare pranced around. Alexandra winced at the sharp tugs on her scalp.

Snap! Crunch!

Old Betsy reared. Alexandra fought for control. "Easy, girl."

"Eee-aah!"

The screech of an owl overhead raised goose bumps on Alexandra's flesh. For a split second she forgot to breathe. Old Betsy reared again. The cinch loosened, and the saddle slid back. Alexandra grabbed for the horse's mane. Powerless to stop herself from being hurtled to the ground, she squeezed her eyes closed and hit the hard earth with a bone-jarring thud. Old Betsy raced away into the night, swallowed up by towering clusters of trees silhouetted by pale, silvery moonlight.

"Whoa, Betsy! Come back here!" Alexandra rose slowly to her feet. *Bloody hell.* The wretched horse had run off and left her. She shivered from the cold and the eeriness of the unfamiliar place. Her teeth clenched against a groan, she bent over and retrieved the valise and food hamper. Because of its weight, she'd have to leave the saddle behind.

Animal sounds echoing throughout the bushes hurried Alexandra on her way. She had not put enough distance between Philadelphia and herself. Following the Delaware River seemed wisest, else she risked losing her way in this maze of trees.

She continued on. *Ignore the damp, musty smell. Focus on each step. Refuse to hear the chittering sounds of an unseen nocturnal creature. Don't think of what could happen.*

A short distance behind her twigs snapped, leaves crunched. She choked back a startled cry and whirled around. Had he found her? She bit her lower lip and willed her racing heart to slow. She would not make it easy for him. She moved deeper into the forest and crouched down behind a black walnut tree.

She waited for what felt like an eternity. No one appeared. All seemed quiet. *Don't be a fool. He's out there. Waiting for you to show yourself.*

Alexandra wrapped herself in her heavy, woolen cloak and settled against the rough bark. She smothered a yawn and struggled to remain awake, alternately staring up at the heavens and peering deep into the frightening forest.

The scent of the Delaware River stirred thoughts of the intriguing sea captain on the waterfront. She remembered his tall form clad in a snowy white shirt and dark breeches. His dark brown hair had been secured at the nape of his neck. A flush warmed her cheeks. How would it feel to be in his arms?

Safe. It would feel safe.

An ache of longing pierced her heart.

****

Early morning light filtered through the burnished leaves. A small gust of wind ruffled the shimmering branches. The abrupt quieting of the chattering squirrels and twittering birds startled Alexandra from her dreams of the dashing sea captain.

She scanned the immediate area, prepared to see Bartholomew coming toward her. Birches and maples blazing crimson-orange greeted her wary eyes. He wasn't there! Lightheaded with relief, she frowned in puzzlement. What had she heard?

A moment later, she noticed two bear cubs frolicking a short distance away. Her mouth rounded in surprise. The smaller of the two climbed almost to the top of a young tree. The second cub watched its twin for a few minutes and then proceeded up. The sapling bent close to the ground. The first cub hopped off and the tree straightened. Its sibling sailed through the air. They repeated their game several times.

Delighted, Alexandra watched the antics of the two charming characters. A sudden crashing in the bushes brought her to her feet, despite the protest from her stiff, sore muscles.

An enormous black bear emerged with an angry snort.

Alexandra's first instinct was to flee, but she knew the bear could outrun her and her long skirts would impede her flight. She groped the tree behind her. Could the mother climb as well as her cubs?

The black beast drew nearer.

Keeping the bear in plain sight, Alexandra lifted her skirts and stepped onto the lowest branch. Ever watchful, she maneuvered her way up two more limbs.

Rrrip.

Startled, she lowered her gaze to discover her pocket had torn and her diary had tumbled to the ground. Troubled by the loss of her possession and her inability to go after it, she reached for the fourth branch and misstepped.

Her hands slipped free.

With a noiseless scream, she slid down the length of the tree, scraping her arms and legs on the rough bark. Alexandra ignored the stinging scratches and eased her way to the food hamper. She tossed tasty morsels toward the furry creature. The bear batted the food around with her paws.

Alexandra stepped back one pace and froze. The

mother bear had gulped the meager meal and advanced toward her again. Alexandra picked up a stout tree branch and waved it.

"Go on now. I didn't harm your babes." Her words went unheeded. She worked her way to the Delaware. Her arms grew weary from waving the branch.

Even her eyes were tiring. Now she saw two black beasts. Alexandra blinked and looked again. No, not a double image of the stalking animal. A snarling dog emerged from the tall trees and covered the distance between them with effortless power. It hurled itself at the bear the same moment the bear charged Alexandra.

She lost her balance and fell backward into the river. A blood-curdling scream escaped her lips.

Chapter Two

Her sapphire gaze beckoned him. He moved toward her, aching to caress her softness. Slipping his arm around the ebony-haired beauty's waist, he pulled her close, melding their bodies. Enveloped by the headiness of her scent, he lowered his mouth toward hers, eager to taste the promising sweetness of her tempting lips...

Slurp.

A rough, wet tongue dragged across Derek's cheek and dashed his dream. He opened one eye. Max stared back, wagging his tail, unable to stand still.

"What do you want?" Derek growled.

With his ears cocked, Max barked, then turned and raced through the crimson and gold-trimmed forest. Moments later a piercing scream of terror split the air.

Derek's heart sank in sudden dread. He scrambled to his feet and mounted his dark gray stallion. They sped through the woods.

He came upon Max engaged in a fierce battle with an enraged black bear. The great dog lunged at the bear, then drew back and circled her. As Derek neared the battleground, Max charged again. The infuriated bear roared and struck out at him with her claws, this time drawing blood. Max continued to circle, attack, and draw back.

At times, Derek found it difficult to tell where the dog ended and the bear began. Nature had endowed Max with a massive head, a strong neck, a broad chest, and powerful hindquarters. He hoped Max's heavy, jet-black coat was providing some protection from the bear's assault.

Derek withdrew his flintlock from the saddle and fired into the air, startling the bear. During the scuffle, two bawling cubs had worked their way close to their mother. She took them and fled into the forest.

Without a moment's hesitation, Max turned and plunged into the Delaware River. Derek dismounted and reached the river bank as Max paddled toward something pink bobbing in and out of the water.

Damn. It *was* the woman.

She grabbed hold of a nearby bough. "Help! Someone help me, please!" She disappeared under water for a few seconds and came up sputtering. "Help!"

The current dragged along several large branches. One of them struck her head, and she vanished beneath the surface. Max grabbed hold of her.

Stripped of his coat and boots, Derek dived into the cold river. A few powerful strokes later, he took her from Max. He swam against the current and brought her to the shore where he placed her on the soft soil and dropped down beside her. Max, who had followed close behind, shook himself dry.

Derek rolled the woman onto her stomach and pushed on her back to force out the water she had swallowed. She coughed and moaned, but did not awaken. Scanning the immediate area until he noticed a small clearing, Derek lifted her and covered the distance in several long strides.

After settling her upon the leaf-littered ground, he checked her face and scalp for lacerations. He winced at the nasty gash on her forehead and applied pressure to it with his kerchief until the bleeding subsided. His quick glance detected a valise behind a tree.

As he neared her bag, he stepped on a small object. He paused long enough to see it was a book, slipped it into his pocket, and collected her belongings. Inside her bag, he found warm, dry clothing.

Derek judged her age to be eighteen, possibly nineteen. He hesitated for but a moment before removing her clothing. Although he was not in the habit of disrobing unconscious women, especially the dark-haired, blue-eyed variety, it would take time to reach his schooner. Her condition would worsen if she became chilled, and he'd be damned if he would have that on his conscience, too.

He struggled a bit with the sodden bowknots of her pink dimity bodice, then eased it off her soft ivory shoulders and slid it down her smooth arms, past delicate wrists. He drew a harsh breath against an urge to caress the satiny smoothness of her skin, and removed her waterlogged skirt and petticoats. The saturated stays and chemise followed. The scrapes scattered along her legs and arms brought a frown to his forehead. Had her battle with the river produced all these abrasions?

He gritted his teeth against the self-reproach ripping through him. He should not have lost her in the woods the night before. When her horse ran past him riderless, he had searched for her, but he had not found a trace. Fearing the worst, yet unwilling to abandon her to the whims of the forest, he had made camp and waited for morning.

A golden glimmer caught his eye. Upon closer inspection, he realized a necklace was tangled in her hair. The chain had undoubtedly broken during her skirmish with the Delaware. He disentangled it and put it into his pocket.

He glanced at her tiny waist and the gentle curve of her hips, and chose not to replace the stays.

Disturbed by the wayward course of his thoughts, he slipped a faded calico gown on her, mindful of the angry scratches she had acquired. He retrieved his clothing from the riverbank and covered her with his coat, then donned his boots.

He tore a petticoat into strips, dampened several of them in the river and cleansed her wounds. He made a makeshift bandage from the remaining strips and placed it over the injury on her forehead, then combed his fingers through her hair so it would dry faster. A shiver shook the woman's slight form.

"Max, stay." Derek set off to find kindling so he could warm her.

After several minutes of scouring the forest floor for suitable bits of wood, his arms were nearly full. The sound of incensed barking reached him. Something must have happened to the woman. He raced back through the trees and stopped just outside the clearing.

Four men surrounded Max and the unconscious woman. The apparent leader was tall with dark hair, deep-set black eyes, and a small moustache. His haughty stance and his tailored coat and knee breeches marked him as one accustomed to having his way.

Derek picked up a stout branch and entered the campsite. "Move away from her."

At their surprised expressions, complete with open mouths and widened eyes, a humorless smile curved his lips. Two of the men retreated several steps.

"I'm only claiming what is mine," their leader said in a smooth voice. "The wench belongs to me."

Derek stood several feet away. He braced his legs in a seaman's stance and gripped the branch in his right hand. "In what way does she belong to you? Indentured servant? Show me the papers. Wife? I see no ring upon her finger."

"Why you—" The tall stranger lunged at Derek, but stopped at Max's menacing growl. "Alexandra is to be my wife. You've no right to keep her from me."

"If she is to be your wife, why was she wandering the woods last night?"

The intruder's face purpled. "'Tis none of your concern. I demand you return what is rightfully mine."

"You can't have her," Derek said. "Not until she tells me it is her wish." He could not prevent the corners of his mouth from turning up as he gestured toward the unconscious woman. "At this moment that is impossible."

The other man's eyes narrowed. "You dare to laugh at me?" His face taut, he signaled to his men.

One appeared to be a simple-minded sort with a wide gaze. He held back. A short, balding man and his lean, blond companion exchanged knowing, confident nods and closed in on Derek.

Damnation! Derek tightened his hold on the branch. Its sharp edges bit into his palm and he winced. He didn't have time for this, but he sure as hell wasn't about to turn a helpless woman over to the likes of the approaching men. One reminded him of a bull and the other of a viper. He wouldn't turn a *man* over to them.

"What are you waiting for?" Their leader shook his fist at them. "Take him!"

They sprang. Derek swung his weapon into the midsection of the bull. He doubled over and gasped out a curse in a rush of stale air. Before Derek could bring the tree limb between the downed man's shoulders, a glint of metal arced, then whirred with a flat sound. He ducked and rolled, aware of a sudden, blurred movement. A growling, black mass leaped through the air.

Derek turned his head to see his Newfoundland try to gain a throat hold on the viper beneath him who was shielding his neck with crossed wrists.

Iron bands crushed Derek's arms to his sides. The bull charged and hammered Derek with his fists. He spit out the coppery taste of blood and threw his weight back, trusting his captor to keep his hold and unwittingly aid his prisoner's assault. Kicking up and out, he knocked the bull back in a rush of exploding breath. Jarring pain shot up the length of him.

Derek glimpsed a swirl of fabric around the outer edges. He heard the dark one cursing his men. The bruising hold of the idiot eased just a hair. Derek drove his elbow into the man's stomach. The soft tissue yielded. He twisted free and delivered a blow to his foe's chin, followed by another and another.

Time ceased. Derek was aware of nothing but the give of muscle and flesh beneath his fists. The satisfying crunch of bone against bone. The wet, sticky feel of blood, his and theirs, and its sweet, nauseating odor.

When the dust settled, the bull and the idiot lay at his feet. Max held the viper pinned to the forest floor. The dark one's face was a distorted, grotesque mask of impotent fury.

"Take your *men* and leave," Derek ordered. "Or I'll allow Max to finish what he's started and move on to the rest of them."

The leader stiffened, his expression unreadable. "Very well."

"Let him up, Max."

After the Newfoundland obeyed, the viper rose to his feet and helped pull the other two upright.

Once they were all mounted on their horses, the dark stranger faced Derek. "This does not end it. Alexandra is mine and I shall have her back. Those foolhardy enough to interfere in my business suffer quick and painful consequences. So shall you rue this day." He turned and rode away.

Derek flexed his bruised knuckles and watched until the men disappeared from sight, not doubting the parting words. "Alexandra." His gaze slid over her lustrous black hair, her parted lips, and came to rest on her petite and softly rounded body. He scratched the Newfoundland behind his ears and tied Alexandra's valise to his saddle.

"If she were mine, Max, I would risk the hounds of hell to keep her." A remembrance of dark curls and pleading blue eyes brought a swift, unrelenting pang to his heart. He gave himself a mental shake. This woman was not his. She could never be his. Another woman expected to become his wife.

His forehead creased with concern. This woman had been in the arms of Morpheus too long. He must get her on board his schooner so her wounds could be properly tended and she could be delivered out of his hands and to her family.

She moaned. He laid his hand across her forehead. She was fevered. With some alarm, he noted she had begun to shiver.

He bundled her quickly and slipped his arms under her. The discovery that she fit as if she had been made for them disturbed him. He swung up onto the stallion and settled her before him, then set his horse to gallop toward Philadelphia where his vessel lay docked.

By the time they reached the *Wind Spirit,* violent tremors shook the ill woman, and the bandage had turned scarlet. Every step of the last few miles had wrung a moan or cry of pain from her. Dread washed over Derek. He had been caught in the grip of this gut-wrenching helplessness once before.

He motioned to Travis Greyson, his mate and closest friend, coming down the gangway. "Here. Take her." Travis's eyes widened. Derek dismounted and took Alexandra back into his arms. "Find Dr. Sebastian."

"What happened to you? And who is she?" Travis grinned. "Most women flock around you, wide-eyed and willing. 'Tis the first time you've brought one senseless to your bed. And a dark-haired one at that. Mayhap you have lost your charm?"

"'Tis not the time for whimsy. She's ill and requires a doctor."

"What about your search for Charlotte Montgomery?"

"I have not abandoned my search, but I must first see to this woman. She needs Dr. Sebastian. Have the crew cover the city."

"Aye, Capt'n." With a nod of his head, Travis gathered the crew and strode off to carry out his instructions.

The young captain carried Alexandra to his cabin and kicked open the door. He placed her on his bed and covered her with warm blankets from his sea chest. She moaned and pushed away the bedcovers. Perspiration bathed her flushed, trembling body and dampened her dress. She rolled her head from side to side and threw an arm over her head as if to ward off additional waves of pain.

Derek splashed water into a basin and carried it to his bed. He removed the blood-soaked bandage from the left side of her brow and replaced it with a fresh one. Next, he wet a cloth and covered her forehead to lower her raging fever.

Remembering a childhood story his grandmother had told him, he placed a whisper of a kiss on her parted lips and willed her to open her eyes. She stirred, but did not rouse.

He stroked her hot cheek. "Open your eyes, Alexandra. Tell me who you are." He slid his finger down to her chin. "I won't let you die. Do you hear me, beautiful lady? You are going to live. I won't have your death on my conscience."

Would the doctor never arrive? She moaned again. He could wait no longer; he had to break the fever. After pouring more water into the basin, he looked through her valise for another change of clothing. He found a bedgown, a hairbrush, and a bar of sweet-scented soap, and placed them on the sea chest near the bed.

After removing her dress, he found it difficult to keep a rein on his desire. Her alluring body played havoc with his self-control, despite his attempts to view her dispassionately. Mesmerized by the satiny sheen of her ivory skin, he watched her breasts rise and fall with every breath.

He applied the wet cloth to her stomach and explored the gentle curves of her waist, skimmed along her hips to her thighs. His body hardened with the touch. Yearning shot through him. Sweat beaded on his forehead. His hands strayed to the downy triangle concealing her womanhood. With a groan, he reached for the towel.

After dressing her, Derek toweled off as much moisture from her hair as possible and brushed the heavy mass until it was dry and glossy. With a will of their own, his fingers stroked the silken length.

He traced her jaw line and rested his thumb against her lower lip. Drawn by her enticing mouth, he lowered his head. *Nay!* He pulled back. He could not do this. What was he to do with her? After adjusting her blankets one final time, he tended to Max's wounds and removed his own clammy garments.

As he started to toss his wet clothes aside, a bulge in one of the garments caught his attention. He reached into the pocket of his coat and withdrew the small book he had found in the woods.

Perhaps it belonged to the woman sleeping in

his bed. He opened it to the first page. Most of it was gone, ripped from its binding, as were several pages. Many others looked as though they had been chewed upon. By the bear most likely.

Because he needed to know if it did belong to her, he scanned several sheets scarred by teeth marks.

1 September 1752
...came again today as promised and showed me how to...

16 September 1752
...can feel his eyes upon me at all hours of the day. Puts a shiver in my bones and a coldness in my blood...

30 September 1752
I visited the waterfront again, searching, waiting. For what? 'Tis strange, but I feel bound to go, led by a sureness that I must continue till the reason is made known...

An odd eeriness crept over Derek. Remembering his first glimpse of Alexandra at the waterfront, he glanced toward her, now certain the diary did indeed belong to her.

Who had visited her?

Anger flared. Who had been watching her and made her afraid?

Had she discovered the reason compelling her to go to the waterfront?

A strangled cry cut short his musings.

"Mama," Alexandra cried out in a little girl voice. "When will Papa be home? Where's Papa?"

Derek set the diary aside and rushed to her. She fought the imprisoning blankets, kicking and pushing them away. Her distress evoked feelings he

25

had thought were long dead and buried.

"Shhh. Papa's here," he said.

Alexandra's eyelids fluttered open and gave him a brief glimpse of glazed sapphire eyes fringed with long, sooty lashes. "I'm glad you've come home, Papa. I've missed you so."

He brushed his lips against her brow. She gave a contented sigh.

"I love you, Papa."

She dozed for a brief time, then screamed. Chills raced down Derek's spine.

"Mama, Papa, who is that man? Why is he looking at Papa like that? No! Get up!" She shook Derek's arm with surprising strength. "Please get up...I want to stay here. No, I don't want...*Please*, Mama..." Her voice trailed off in a pitiful wail.

Powerful tremors shook her petite frame. He lay down beside her and gathered her into his arms. "Papa's here. Everything will be all right. Shhh. Papa will stay right here. I'm not going to let anyone harm you."

She snuggled closer to Derek.

He spoke in a soft, comforting tone until little by little, she quieted and fell into a peaceful slumber. He continued to hold her, haunted by her pleading blue eyes. It was vitally important to him that she feel safe. He would not fail her.

Hours later, as the rainbow hues of the approaching morning streaked across the sky, her fever broke.

****

Seated in a secluded corner of the tavern, Bartholomew re-read then crumpled the note he had found lying outside his office the day before. The note informing him a Tremaine vessel had sailed into port. Familiar stirrings of anger swirled within him. He would *not* lose her again.

Not now. Not ever.

Especially to another Tremaine.

He looked up to see Harold and Myron emerge from the night-darkened streets. They searched the faces of the establishment's patrons. Freddie lumbered up behind them.

Irritation bubbled to the surface. "Sit down."

The balding man and his blond-haired partner exchanged uneasy glances.

"I said sit down."

The silent trio obeyed.

Bartholomew traced the rim of his tankard with his fingertip. "You failed me."

Myron stared down at his faded jacket and patched breeches. His stringy hair concealed his face. "It w-was that v-vicious cur."

A contemptuous smile curled Bartholomew's mouth. "Your wife would be none too happy if she learned about the comely wench you've been bedding, now would she? I've a feeling you'd prefer another brush with the dog."

Myron's head shot up. He blanched.

"And, Harold. What would your poor old mum do if Freddie were arrested for the mysterious deaths of young women, which seem to occur with the new moon? You and I know they were all innocent mishaps, but..." Bartholomew shrugged his shoulders and rolled his eyes toward the ceiling.

Harold's mouth gaped, but no sound came forth.

"I'm giving you an opportunity to redeem yourselves. Fail me again and this job will be your last."

Harold tugged on the red waistcoat which revealed his more than abundant middle. "We won't fail you."

"See that you don't. Go to the waterfront. I have reason to believe Alexandra is being held aboard the *Wind Spirit*, a schooner captained by Derek Tremaine. Find out if it's the truth. I want her back."

Following a flurry of nods, the three men made a hasty retreat.

Bartholomew stared into the dark contents of his tankard. Hot blood coursed through his veins. "I *will* have you again, Alexandra. And when I do, may God have mercy on Tremaine's interfering, black soul."

Chapter Three

Alexandra burrowed deeper into the warmth enveloping her. She felt safe and secure for the first time in a long while. A feather-light current of contentment flowed through her, refreshing her spirit and bringing a smile to her lips. A smile that began inside her soul and radiated outward.

With a sigh, she indulged in the inviting urge to stretch. Her feet met something warm, firm, and furry. A wet tongue flicked across her bare toes.

Alexandra froze, then cautiously opened one eye, not convinced she wanted to know what lay at her feet. A blurred black animal stared back. The sight of it released a rush of memories. The bear!

A scream lodged in her throat and emerged as a strangled whimper. Panicked, she shoved the bedcover aside and tried to jump off the bed, but could not. Her glance down revealed a strong, masculine arm wrapped around her waist. Tremors of despair convulsed her slight form until she could scarcely draw a breath. How had he found her?

She blinked back burning tears of frustration and struggled against the sick feeling in the pit of her stomach. Steeling herself for the forthcoming confrontation, she slowly turned to face Bartholomew.

Her eyes widened in disbelief. She blinked, then squeezed them shut and counted to five before daring to look again. The sea captain she had seen on the waterfront slumbered beside her.

The tall, dark, and oh-so-handsome sea captain.

She swallowed hard. Was she dreaming? She hoped not.

Her gaze dropped to his broad chest. The deep v-neck of his white shirt provided an intriguing glimpse of bronzed flesh sprinkled with dark hair. She warmed to the tips of her toes. The steady rise and fall of his breathing brought a measure of comfort to her frenzied nerves. She reached out and touched his tanned face.

He felt real.

His eyes fluttered open. His gaze pulled Alexandra into their honeyed brown depths and held her captive for the space of several heartbeats. Barely aware of her actions, she stroked the planes and angles of his sculpted cheek. Her fingertips lingered on a fresh abrasion.

"'Morning, Sleeping Beauty," he murmured.

Alexandra pulled her hand away. "Sleeping beauty?" Perhaps *he* was dreaming.

"You've not heard the tale of the fair maiden Sleeping Beauty?" A faint smile appeared on his drowsy face.

She shook her head, now aware of his arm around her waist.

"Would you like to?"

She nodded.

He smothered a yawn. "Once upon a time a king and a queen were finally blessed with a baby, a baby daughter. They gave her a fine christening. She had for her godmothers all the fairies they could find in the kingdom—seven, I believe. An old fairy, whom no one remembered, came into the hall, enraged by the unintended slight. She'd have none of their apologies."

Alexandra lay beside him, spellbound by the deep timbre of his voice. Her gaze wandered over his tanned face, memorizing the pleat of his furrowed brow and the shadows and mysteries hidden within his brown-gold eyes. With great strength of will, she concentrated on his words.

"The fairies began to give their gifts to the princess. I don't recall all the gifts, but among them were beauty, wit, and grace. Shaking with spite, the old fairy gave her gift." His voice lowered. A delicious shiver of expectation pulled Alexandra forward. "She declared the princess would pierce her hand with a spindle. And die."

Alexandra gasped at the image of the fallen princess and drew back. Once again she encountered the sea captain's arm. Gentle puffs of his breath glided along her cheek and stirred an unfamiliar longing. She caught her lower lip between her teeth.

A sudden, loud rapping on the door echoed around the room. "Capt'n?"

The man beside her jerked his arm away and sat up. The spell that had been woven around them shattered, and the warmth left his gaze. The transformation startled Alexandra.

"Capt'n," the person behind the door called again. "It's me. Travis."

The sea captain tossed the bedcovers aside, strode to the door, and opened it with such force that Alexandra flinched. "What?"

The tall man with light colored hair—Travis, the captain had said—frowned. "We haven't been able to find the doctor. How is the woman?"

Alexandra, seeing Travis's quick glance in her direction, slid farther down the bed and pulled the blanket over her head. She groaned. She had been seen in a man's bed. Now her reputation would be in tatters. Why couldn't she have been dreaming after all?

"She's conscious. Continue looking for him." Derek started to close the door.

"Capt'n?"

"Yes?"

Travis's voice dropped to little more than a murmur. She strained to hear what he said, but only caught snatches. "Someone...questions...could be..."

"You know what to do."

"Aye, Capt'n."

Alexandra heard the door close, followed by heavy footsteps across the floor and around the bed.

"He's gone. There's no need to hide."

She peered over the edge of the woolen blanket. The tall sea captain towered over her and impaled her with his glare. Her mouth went dry. "I wasn't hiding."

His dark eyebrow rose. "Weren't you?"

She felt herself flush beneath his heated gaze. She struggled to sit upright and hoped to diminish the unsettling effect he had upon her.

Unable to maintain eye contact, she quickly surveyed her surroundings and discovered she was aboard a ship. Her cheeks flamed. She must have taken leave of her senses not to have noticed the smell of the river, the slight rocking of the ship. The man before her *was* a sea captain after all. How long had she been here?

She met his hard gaze. "Who are you? Why am I here?"

His eyes narrowed. "On this vessel I ask the questions. You answer them."

Prickles of fear skittered along Alexandra's nerve endings. Perhaps she had misjudged him. She moistened her lips with the tip of her tongue. "Sir, if you would be so kind—"

A harsh chuckle escaped his well-defined mouth. "Kind? Me? I think not."

The room grew warm, and the man before her looked a little fuzzy around the edges. She shook her head to clear her vision, an action she instantly regretted. A swift, blinding pain brought a cry to her lips and her hand to her forehead.

Two arms slid around her and lowered her to the pillow. "Easy, now." The captain smoothed back wisps of hair.

Wave after dizzying wave crashed over her. She panicked and reached out. "Help me."

He caught her hand. "Shhh. I'm right here beside you. Take a deep breath and release it slowly." The roughness had left his voice.

She tried to do as he requested, but brilliant colors exploded behind her eyes. White-hot shards of agony pierced her. "I can't."

"I'll help you. Now, breathe with me. Inhale. Exhale. Inhale. Exhale. That's it. You can do it." The gentle warmth of his voice stilled her fear and eased her distress.

The last vestiges of pain ebbed. She opened her eyes and thought she caught a fleeting glimpse of concern cross his handsome features. Her fingers felt along the bandage on her brow. "What happened to me?"

"You fell into the river and hit your head. Max and I pulled you out."

"Max?"

"My dog. Come, Max."

The Newfoundland eased his large frame between his master and Alexandra. She gasped in surprise—he outweighed her by at least three stone! She tried to sit up.

The man assisted her. "Easy now, lest you cause yourself further injury. Mayhap you should lie still." Impatience crept into his voice again.

She winced at his mild rebuke and lowered her gaze, only to realize she was clad in her bedgown. "Sir, has a woman been caring for me?"

"Nay." Amusement glittered in his eyes. "Women are not allowed on vessels. They bring bad luck."

Heat flooded her cheeks, but she forced herself

to continue. "I'm—" She cleared her throat and tried again. "I'm not wearing my pink dress."

"Aye, that is true." He nodded, his expression unfathomable.

"Wh-why?" She could not keep the quiver from her voice.

"After Max and I plucked you out of the river I had to change your clothing."

Alexandra choked back a cry of horror and hid her face in the Newfoundland's thick fur. "*You* removed my clothes?"

"I did what any gentleman would have done. Would you have preferred to catch your death?"

"N-no, sir," she whispered, stung by his curtness. "But..."

"But, what?"

She refused to look at him. She could not look at him. "It wasn't proper—"

"Proper be damned. If it's your virtue you're concerned about, rest assured. 'Tis still intact."

He clenched his jaw so tight she could see a muscle jump. Mortification swept through her. Would her torment never end?

Max licked her face. She lifted a weak arm and stroked his dense, coarse coat, unsure of how to proceed in the face of his master's displeasure.

The sea captain's voice broke the lengthening silence. "Why were you running from a tall, dark-haired man, Alexandra? Are you to be his wife as he claimed?"

Her hands stilled. Coldness gripped her heart and settled in her soul. Panic seized her. Her heartbeat quickened. She squeezed her hands together to still their trembling. "H-how do you know my name?"

The man beside her clenched his jaw again, a habit she was growing to dislike immensely, and released a long stream of breath. "I believe we've already established that *I* ask the questions."

"So you've stated," she said. "But that doesn't mean I'll answer them. I appreciate all you've done for me, but I think I'll be going now."

Alexandra moved off the bed, away from the arrogant, disturbing stranger, but was unprepared for the spinning of the room and shifting of the floor beneath her feet. A loud roar filled her ears.

Unable to focus her eyes, she reached out, thankful for the solid wall which somehow materialized and prevented her from falling. In the distance she heard a masculine voice call her name. It grew fainter and fainter. A black mist swirled around her and beckoned her to relinquish herself to its peaceful, embracing darkness.

"Fight it, Lexi. Stay with me."

She heard the voice again, only now it was stronger and nearby. The frightening haziness receded. She drew a deep, steadying breath. Her vision cleared, revealing her hands braced against the all too broad chest of the sea captain.

Not a wall.

Her fingertips tingled. She chanced a downward glance and discovered her entire body was held flush against his. A strange languidness worked its way through her limbs.

"Promise me?" He gave her a slight shake.

"Promise." She frowned in puzzlement. "What?"

He bent down and scooped her up. Startled by the suddenness of his actions, Alexandra wrapped her arms around his neck. Tendrils of delicious pleasure ribboned through her and filled her with a curious inner excitement. It was nice being held in his arms. *Too nice.* "Put me down."

An unusual light flickered in his eyes, then disappeared so rapidly she wondered if she had imagined it. His mouth straightened into a grim line. "You are in no condition to leave. Promise me you'll stay in bed."

"No."

"No?" He tightened his hold. Her slight weight settled more firmly against him.

The intimate pressure of his arms against her legs brought a flush to her face. "I've no desire to further inconvenience you."

"You're not inconveniencing me."

"But you said women were bad luck on vessels."

"Never mind what I said." His voice sounded gritty with irritation. "Will you stay abed or not?"

She withdrew her arms from his neck and poked her finger against his chest. "I won't be bullied. Put me down."

His eyes narrowed. "I am not bullying you. When I pulled you out of the river I accepted responsibility for you. Give me your word that you'll rest."

"And if I don't?" Alexandra struggled to maintain a semblance of composure.

The corners of his mouth turned up. "Then you shall remain in my arms."

A current of longing traversed the length of her spine. She tamped it down. "I promise."

"Thought you might."

She shot him a mutinous glare. He placed her on the bed and tucked the woolen blanket around her. His fingers lingered near her cheek. He smoothed wisps of hair in place before he straightened abruptly and spoke in a rough voice. "Sleep. I'll check on you later." He started toward the door.

Sleep. She didn't want to sleep, for sleep brought the nightmare. "Sir?"

He halted and glanced back. A scowl marred his brow. "Yes?"

She refused to be intimidated by his daunting expression. "You've not told me your name."

He held her gaze for a moment. "Tremaine.

Derek Tremaine."

"You never finished the story, Captain Tremaine."

His eyebrow arched. "The story?"

She nodded, hoping he'd stay and hold the shadows and demons of her dreams at bay. "If you have the time."

"Very well." He sat beside her on the bed. "Where were we?"

"The old fairy said the princess would pierce her hand on a spindle and die."

"Ah, yes. I remember." He paused for a moment. "A young fairy who had not yet given her gift said the princess would pierce her hand, but she would not die. Instead, she would fall into a sleep which would last a hundred years, when a king's son would awaken her."

"What happened to the princess?"

"The king forbade everyone to have spindles in their homes. When the princess was fifteen or sixteen years of age, she visited a little room on top of the palace's great tower where an old woman was spinning with a spindle. The princess wanted to try. It ran into her hand and she fell down in a swoon."

"Tell me about the prince. Did he revive her?"

"Patience, Lexi." He tempered his scolding with a smile.

Alexandra caught her lower lip between her teeth. She resisted the impulse to tweak his nose for teasing her, then straightened. What had he called her? *Lexi.*

She mulled his name for her over in her mind and decided she liked it. *Lexi.* A small glow of pleasure supplanted his forwardness in shortening her name without asking permission. She folded her hands in her lap and waited for him to continue.

"One hundred years passed. Curious about the towers hidden by the woods, a young prince approached the castle. The impenetrable wall of bushes and brambles parted. In the palace he passed through several rooms of sleeping ladies and gentlemen. At last, he came to a chamber decorated in gold and silver. Upon the bed lay the beautiful princess."

Alexandra edged nearer to Derek. "Please don't stop now. Tell me more. What did he do?"

Derek reached out and stroked the curve of her cheek. His eyes turned molten. She held her breath. His finger traced her jaw line and stopped beneath her chin. "According to the story he fell down before her on his knees and she awoke, but—"

"But, what?" she whispered.

He cradled her face between his hands and lowered his head toward her. "But, I think he did this."

Her insides twisted into a jumble of knots. Alexandra watched Derek's mouth move closer to hers. She swallowed hard. Alarm bells collided with intense longing. As sure as she was breathing, she knew he was going to kiss her. She couldn't allow this stranger such an intimacy.

Could she?

She placed her hands against his broad chest, intent upon removing herself to a safer distance. Instead, her fingers splayed over the fine linen of his shirt. The rapid thump of his heart beneath her palms matched the swiftness of her own. Intrigued by her discovery, she lifted her startled gaze and encountered an unsettling glimmer in Derek's darkening eyes.

Ever so lightly, he brushed her lips with the barest of kisses. Once. Twice. Thrice. Her eyelids fluttered shut at the wondrous magic he evoked. A sweet sigh escaped from her parted lips.

Derek caressed her cheek with his thumb, then drew her against him and deepened the kiss.

Tasting, testing, exploring. The enkindled glow in her midsection expanded and encompassed her entire body. Her hands traveled upward and entwined around his neck. Alexandra paid little heed to the voice of caution whispering in the back of her mind.

"Lexi?" Derek murmured against her soft mouth while stroking her arms with slow, languid motions.

"Hmm?" She shivered at the exquisite touch of his lips upon the curve of her neck.

"Why were you in the forest?" His low voice slid over her like warmed molasses.

Confusion muddled her thoughts. She opened her eyes and peered up at him. "What?"

"Who are you running from?"

Chapter Four

Stunned by his questions, and by the moment he had chosen to ask them, Alexandra stared at Derek. Had his sole reason for kissing her been to lower her defenses and obtain information?

Burning with shame, she withdrew her arms from around his neck and pushed against his chest to free herself. He tightened his hold.

"Let go of me." She choked back a sob and summoned anger in its stead. She would not give him the satisfaction of seeing her cry.

"Why?"

"*Why?*" He had kissed her senseless, had resorted to trickery, and still pretended ignorance? Of all the insufferable, handsome, overbearing men.

Indignation fired her blood. Why, she had half a mind to...to...do whatever sea captains did to miscreants. Well, fine. Two could play at his game.

Though unskilled in coquetry, she fell back onto what little she knew. She drew a deep breath to calm her frenzied nerves, then placed her hand on Derek's forearm and sagged against him. "I need to lie down."

"You do?" One of his eyebrows arched in apparent skepticism, and a corner of his mouth twitched. "As you wish. We can lie down."

Before Alexandra could blink, Derek settled her against her pillow and stretched out beside her. "Th-this isn't quite what I had in mind."

"No?" He smoothed wisps of hair from her face and favored her with another of his unnerving gazes.

Intent upon ignoring the disturbing pressure of Derek's thighs against hers, she wet her lower lip with her tongue. "I meant I need to rest."

He nodded his head. "Hmm, I see."

"You do?"

"Aye." He covered an exaggerated yawn with his hand and pulled the woolen blanket over them. "Yesterday was a long one, at that." He closed his eyes and draped his arm about her waist.

Alexandra gasped and stared with mounting horror at the man beside her. "Sir, Captain Tremaine, you can't mean—"

"Can't mean what?" Derek's warm breath feathered across her cheek.

Her mouth went dry. "Surely you don't intend to sleep...*here*."

"'Tis my bed."

Scorching heat flooded her face. "But *I'm* here. I mean, we cannot, that is, it isn't proper."

"Would you prefer to sleep in the chair or upon the floor?"

"No, well, I...if I must." She attempted to scoot off the bed, but his arm kept her anchored beside him. She cast him a puzzled glance.

"You will stay in this bed. I'll not have you risk your health further."

She glared at him. "You've put me in an impossible position. You, sir, are no gentleman."

The remnants of his grin faded. "No, not always. But may I remind you that no matter how intriguing I find your current *position*—" He raked her slender form with his heated gaze. "—'twas not by my hand that you entered the woods and fell into the river."

Almost certain he could see through the thin fabric of her bedgown, then remembering with a start that he had already seen what lay beneath it, Alexandra yanked the blanket up to her chin. "Please don't misunderstand me. I am grateful for all you've done on my behalf, but I can't abide by these arrangements. There must be another way. Another cabin, perhaps?"

"Nay, I have no empty cabins, but I may have a solution."

"Which is?"

"We'll share the bed."

Alexandra bristled and edged away from him. "That is *not* acceptable."

He pressed his finger to her lips. "Let me finish. We'll use a divider of sorts. Perhaps rolled up blankets."

"You call that a solution?"

"You've never heard of bundling?"

She shook her head.

"It was my understanding that it is practiced in New England as well as the Middle Colonies."

"Bundling." She stared at him through narrowed eyes. "You're making this up."

"Nay, I am not. 'Tis a method employed to allow two people to court during cold weather."

"We are *not* courting." She drew a sharp breath to ward off the sudden onset of giddiness.

"I am aware of that, Lexi. Nothing will happen between us."

Alexandra continued to regard him with suspicion.

"Nothing will happen. You have two choices. Either agree to the divider, or tell me who you belong to and I'll return you to him."

Alexandra blanched and touched her hand to her throat. The locket! It was gone! Sadness washed over her in undulating waves at the loss of her only link to her parents.

"Well? What have you decided?"

"I agree to the divider. I'll be off your ship as soon as possible." She caught her lower lip between her teeth, then asked, "Captain Tremaine, after you pulled me out of the river, did you by chance see a piece of jewelry?"

"A cameo on a gold chain?"

She caught her breath and nodded.

"The chain had broken and was tangled in your hair. I put it in my pocket." He turned and glanced toward a corner of the cabin. "My cabin boy, Obadiah, must have taken my clothing to be laundered. I'll fetch your necklace."

The wait seemed interminable. Finally, he returned and held it out to her. She stared at it in fearful fascination. A mixture of dread and anticipation welled inside her.

"Is it yours?" He startled her out of her reverie.

"Yes." She closed her fingers around the locket and examined it. "You said the chain is broken?"

"Obadiah repaired it. He planned to return it to me tomorrow. I apologize if I caused you undue worry. Is it an heirloom?"

A familiar sense of unease seeped through every nerve, every bone. She tried to resist the frightening pressure constricting her internal organs, but gave in and fastened the necklace around her neck with trembling fingers.

"Lexi?"

She looked at him in silent appeal as the chain seared her flesh. She could not remove it. She could not withstand the force compelling her to wear it. Her breath came in short, quick gasps. She clutched the cameo against her breasts and rocked to and fro, blinking back stinging tears.

Derek pulled her close and swayed back and forth with her. He rode out the silent sobs ripping through her body and murmured soothing nonsense words until the tremors quieted. Neither of them said a word. She listened to the steady, lulling thump of Derek's heart. In the refuge of his embrace nothing frightened her, nothing stirred memories that hinted of darkness.

"How are you feeling?"

His chest vibrated pleasantly as he spoke. Aware of the intimate contact of their bodies, Alexandra straightened and eased away. "I've been a lot of trouble for you when I should be repaying you for helping me."

Derek flipped back the length of her hair and rested his hand on her shoulder. "You're no trouble. You owe me nothing."

She ached from the tenderness of his touch. "I don't want to be in your way or interfere with your business here in Philadelphia."

A strange light glittered in the depths of his eyes, then disappeared. He removed his hand from her shoulder. She bit back an involuntary protest. Why was he so inconstant? Every time she began to think she could trust him, he renewed her doubts.

"I insist you stay here." A gruffness had crept into his voice. "For your safety, stay below deck for the time being."

Her worst fears awakened, a chill slithered down her spine. "B-because of...because of..." She could not say Bartholomew's name aloud.

"After I pulled you from the river, I had an unpleasant encounter with several men, one of whom insisted you belong to him."

Fear lanced Alexandra. "You refused his request."

"Aye."

"Why?"

"I wasn't sure he spoke the truth. Did he?"

She fidgeted with the blanket. "I'd rather not say."

He shrugged. "As you wish."

The distance in his voice saddened her. He gathered two blankets from his sea chest, rolled them lengthwise, and placed them down the center of the bed. At the implication of his actions Alexandra's heart rose to her throat.

He walked toward his desk, but she couldn't see what he was doing. Moments later he stood beside her once again.

"I found this in the woods." He handed her a small book. "Is it yours?"

Her diary! A startled cry escaped her lips. She had thought it lost. She hugged it to her chest, grateful to have it back, and smiled at him. "Thank you for returning it to me."

"I'm afraid it will need to be replaced. Many of the pages have been ripped or torn out. You'll also discover a liberal sprinkling of teeth marks on most of the remaining pages."

Alexandra's smile froze. "You read my diary?"

The sea captain clenched his jaw. His expression hardened. "Parts of it. How else was I to know who it belonged to?"

"But it's my diary. My private thoughts. You had no right."

He loomed large and threatening as he towered over her. "I had no right? I didn't ask to spend the night in the woods or the morning in the river. I didn't ask to fight off four men or tend to an ill woman. And I certainly didn't ask to be saddled with a sassy, ungrateful bit of baggage!"

Derek stormed out of the cabin. The door slammed shut behind him.

Alexandra blinked at the closed door, dazed by the morning's confusing events. None of it seemed real.

She noticed Max curled up in a far corner, watching her. "Come here, Max." She patted the bed. The Newfoundland walked to her and placed the upper portion of his body beside her.

Alexandra scratched behind his dark ears. "What shall become of me? What if he has tired of me and plans to send me back to Bartholomew?"

Icy fingers of dread skipped along her spine. She pulled the dog closer, needing his warmth. "'Twould be truly unbearable." The dog nuzzled her shoulder.

She gave him a sad smile. "I shall miss you after I leave, but you do understand it's too risky for me to remain here, don't you?"

Alexandra eased Max away from her and tried to stand, but the cabin tipped sideways. She dropped back onto the bed. "Perhaps tomorrow will be soon enough."

****

Derek leaned against the door to his cabin and released a ragged breath. God save him from contrary females, especially those with ebony hair and sapphire eyes.

Recollections of a long ago autumn barbecue celebrating Charlotte's fifth birthday filtered through his thoughts and brought a slight smile to his lips. He had been a lad of sixteen years. Tossing her black curls and favoring him with her laughing blue eyes, she took him by the hand and led him to her special place. In her most serious manner she informed him he was to wait for her to grow up. *She* was to be his wife and no other. When they were back amongst the guests, she told everyone she and Derek would be wed one day. He had taken much jesting.

His smile faded at another memory. The memory of her abduction a day later.

All the old feelings flooded back. Anger. Emptiness. A profound sense of loss. A helplessness that had driven him to promise her mother he would find her—a vow he had failed to fulfill.

Raw guilt burned at Derek's insides. She had been in his care that day. She had been his responsibility. He clenched his hands into tight fists and tried to ignore the echo reverberating through his mind, the echo of her cries for help. He couldn't fail her again.

Damnation! He slammed his fist against the door frame. Where could Dr. Sebastian be?

Derek's mental image of Charlotte wavered, then assumed the form of Alexandra. Dark-haired, blue-eyed, picture-of-innocence Alexandra.

Rankled by the intrusion into his thoughts, he turned and leveled a glare at the door. How much longer before she was recovered and back where she belonged? Wherever that might be.

Resisting the unwelcome urge to poke his head back into the cabin and check on her, he headed toward the quarterdeck, determined to focus on his sole purpose for being in Philadelphia. Once he found Charlotte and returned her to her parents, he would be able to put the past to rest and look toward the future. He had a marriage to prepare for.

His own.

Derek rounded the corner and came face to face with the bull and the viper. *Bloody hell!* Fury blazed through him. He clenched his jaw and narrowed his eyes to slits. After landing a sharp blow to the viper's chin and dropping him to the floor, Derek drove his fist into the soft flesh of the bull's belly.

He grabbed the gasping men by the back of their necks and dragged them to the main deck. "Travis!"

His mate appeared and stopped short at the sight of the two strangers. "Want me to relieve you of them, Capt'n?"

"In a minute." Derek pushed the bull toward Travis, then caught the viper by the front of his shirt. He glared into his slightly yellowed eyes. "Who sent you?"

The blond-haired man opened his mouth.

"Don't tell him nothin', Myron," the bull warned, struggling against Travis's iron grip. "*He* won't like it."

The viper clamped his mouth shut.

Derek jerked him closer. "Perhaps a ducking from the yardarm will loosen your tongue?"

Myron's face drained of color, but he remained mute.

Derek signaled to Travis to follow him, then pulled his captive along the deck. "Step foot on my vessel again and I'll see the two of you keelhauled. Tell your master I'll be coming for him." He shoved the trespassers down the hard length of the gangway.

He watched them scurry away, then turned to Travis. "No one save the crew is to board the *Wind Spirit*."

"Aye, Capt'n."

"And, Travis? She is to hear naught of this."

"Aye, Capt'n."

****

Alexandra sat up, gasping and perspiring. A horrible sense of evil clawed at her insides. She blinked against the bright light streaming through the mullioned windows, grateful for the swiftness with which morning had arrived. She had slept much of the previous day and had written in her diary during the evening.

Her gaze flew to Derek's side of the bed, but she saw only an indentation on the pillow and a mussed blanket. Even after he had entered the cabin at the end of the day, she had lain awake into the small hours. She had drawn comfort from the deep steadiness of his breathing, and hoped to keep the terrors of the night at bay.

She had been unsuccessful. Now, she struggled again to gain control of the fear clogging her throat. She unfastened the necklace with trembling fingers.

Why did it stir such conflicting emotions within her? She traced the elegant scrolling whorls of goldwork and the delicate border of small pearls and stared at the carved image. *Who are you? What do you want from me?*

Distressed by the maelstrom swirling around her mind and dragging her toward the ominous black pit she knew awaited her, she swung her legs over the side of the bed and stood. She must not think. She must not remember.

Her vision grew fuzzy, and a loud roaring sounded in her ears. Sudden heat suffused her body. The planked floor rose to meet her as the cabin tilted sideways. She reached for something, anything, to break her fall, but grasped only air and collapsed onto the floor. Max barked and ran to her side. He nudged her with his nose.

She remained still and took deep breaths, resisting the pull of unconsciousness and the peacefulness it offered. She cleared her mind of all its troublesome thoughts, as she had done so often in the past. The Newfoundland barked again and again.

"Shhh, Max. I'm all right. I shouldn't have gotten up so fast." She rolled onto her side and pushed herself onto her knees, then closed her eyes against another wave of dizziness. When it subsided, she grabbed handfuls of the bed sheet. With supreme effort, she pulled herself onto the bed and rested against the pillow.

As her breathing slowed, Derek entered the cabin, carrying a large tray. The heat of a guilty flush stole across her cheeks.

"Lexi, have you been out of bed?"

"No. Well, that is... Mmm. What do you have? It smells wonderful."

"Don't try to change the subject."

She tried to look properly chastised for a full half-minute, then gave up. "You treat me as if I were a child. I'll have you know I'm nineteen years of age."

An inner fire warmed Derek's brown-gold eyes. "Nay, Lexi. A child you are not."

Her cheeks grew hot beneath his bold gaze. He cleared his throat and averted his eyes. "Forgive me if I seem to be a bit overbearing, or if my methods upset you, but I'm concerned about your health."

His unexpected apology surprised her. "I'll forgive you *if* you tell me what you brought."

"Breakfast." He settled the tray on the leather chair and removed its cover with a flourish, revealing an elaborate feast of pastries, cheese, fruit, eggs, and ham.

Alexandra's mouth watered at the enticing aroma wafting toward her. Derek heaped generous portions upon two pewter plates. He handed one to her and attacked the other.

His nearness sent tingles radiating through her. As the heat of a blush climbed from her neck to her cheeks, she chanced a sideways glance at him. He seemed unaffected by their close proximity. Why couldn't she be?

To cover her awkwardness, Alexandra lifted a pastry to her mouth, though she scarcely tasted it. The silence lengthened and her nervousness increased. His gaze bore through her. What if he began questioning her again?

Derek placed his empty plate on the tray and glanced toward her. His brow furrowed. "Lexi, where is the cameo?"

"It, uh—" She lifted her hand to her throat and searched for an explanation. "It fell off."

He held his hand out to her. "Let me help you put it back on."

She hesitated. "It's on the floor." She tried not to fidget while he retrieved it and fastened it around her neck.

"At least the clasp hasn't broken again. How did it end up over there?" The edges of his fingers grazed her neck.

Her pulse quickened. "I, uh, well, you see—"

A loud knock sounded on the door. Derek opened it to reveal Travis Greyson.

"I must speak to you, Capt'n. Privately."

Derek turned back toward Alexandra. "I've business to attend to. Finish your breakfast. And, Lexi, the nourishment is for *your* stomach alone. As you have probably surmised, Max does not miss too many meals."

Derek's footsteps faded, and Alexandra chuckled softly to herself. "Indeed. Did you hear your master, Max?"

The Newfoundland settled himself before her and sniffed her meal.

"Well, I won't tell if you won't." She rolled up a slice of ham and fed it to him. "Good, isn't it?" After she finished the last piece, she set her plate aside and rose. She refused to lie abed all day.

Once her legs adjusted to her slight weight, she took her first faltering footsteps. Pleased by how quickly the wobbliness faded, she searched the cabin for her valise. She had worn her bedgown far too long and it was in need of a good washing. Finding her bag in a built-in cupboard, she placed it on the bed and pulled out a simple chintz gown and necessary undergarments.

After she finished dressing, she sorted through her remaining belongings. She reached back into the valise and her hand brushed a bulge in the lining. The papers! She had forgotten about them. Apparently Derek hadn't discovered them yet, but what if he decided to go through her possessions to learn more about her?

What should she do with them? She glanced around the cabin. Remembering the secret compartment in Bartholomew's secretary, she searched Derek's desk where she found charts, bills

Penny Rader

of laden, and his log, but no hidden panels.

She ran her fingers over the walls and floor and felt for loose panels or planks. Nothing. Frustrated, she tapped her foot. There had to be a safe place.

The bed, perhaps? She could open a seam of the mattress and slip in the papers. No. They would crackle and then Derek would demand to see them. She wasn't ready to trust him with her secrets.

Her gaze alighted on Derek's chair. He would have no reason to look under the seat. She opened the door to see if anyone was in the corridor. It wouldn't do to have Derek walk in on her. "Excuse me. Obadiah?"

The cabin boy hurried toward her. "Yes'm?"

"I'm going to lie down. Please make sure I'm not disturbed. If your captain should come by, please tell him I'm resting."

"Yes'm." He nodded.

Alexandra rushed back into the cabin and removed the papers from her valise. To these she added needle, thread, and a petticoat.

She hastened to the large chair and tried to turn it on its side. Grunting aloud from the effort, she pushed and strained, but the stubborn, heavy chair wouldn't budge. There had to be a way. With a sheepish grin, she realized it was bolted down.

Determined to complete the task, she lowered herself to the floor and slid the upper part of her body beneath the chair. While adjusting the petticoat to fit the length and width of the seat, she heard panting. She tipped her chin and gained an upside-down view of a familiar face.

"Max, what are you doing?" In her urgency to conceal the documents, she had forgotten about him. He licked her cheek. She giggled and dropped the undergarment.

"Now, Max, behave. I must finish this." The dog settled his large body on the floor and lay so close his

52

breath tickled her ear. She bit back a smile.

Mindful that Derek would soon return, Alexandra deftly stitched up three sides of the petticoat, forming a pocket of sorts. She slipped the papers through the open end.

Her playful helpmate plopped himself down on her stomach.

"Ooof!" She gasped for air. "For heaven's sake, Max. What has gotten into you?"

The furry animal turned his head toward her. She could swear he was grinning at her.

"Move, Max." She struggled to wriggle out from beneath the chair and the dog.

The cabin door opened.

Chapter Five

Derek glared at Alexandra from the doorway. "Damn it, woman. Are you stupid or merely obstinate?"

She peered around a leg of his chair, revealing little more than her widening gaze. "There's no need to swear at me."

"And how do you suggest I deal with a recalcitrant chit such as yourself?"

"You could help me up."

"Help you up?" His irritation melted away as he tilted his head a little to the right and received a most intriguing view of her shapely calves amid a flurry of petticoats.

"If you had any decency—"

"Decency?" He arched his eyebrow. "Would that be yet another gentlemanly quality which I ofttimes lack?"

A scowl lined her forehead and she pushed against the furry creature atop her. "Get off, Max." The Newfoundland yawned. She grumbled beneath her breath. "Make him move. I can scarcely breathe."

He shrugged. "'Tis doubtful he'll do as I say. Disobedience runs rampant in this cabin."

She wrinkled her nose in response. "And how will you explain the suffocated woman beneath your dog to your crew?"

"They'll think I forgot to feed him so he made a meal of the tempting morsel in my cabin. But then, as you'll recall, I don't *have* to explain anything."

"Oh, yes. How foolish of me to have forgotten I'm in the presence of the high and mighty sea captain." Her sapphire gaze snapped with undisguised fury and fired his blood. "If you won't help me, I'll scream so loud the governor and his council will hear me all the way in the State House."

Derek crossed the short distance to her side. He trailed a finger along her jaw line and paused on her chin. "Scream away. My men will assume you're caught in the throes of passion and they won't think anything of it."

"Why, you...you...rogue!" She shoved his hand aside. "Max, *move!*"

Max glanced at his master and heaved his bulk to his favorite corner.

Alexandra scrambled to her feet and shook her finger at the Newfoundland. "Shame on you, Max."

The dog whimpered and laid his head on his paws. Alexandra whirled to face Derek and jabbed his chest with her finger. "I can understand Max's behavior because *you* trained him, but for you to just stand there, smirking and ogling me, exceeds ill manners. 'Tis disgraceful."

Amused by her display of temper, Derek suppressed a smile, lest she begin another tirade. Not that he minded watching her cheeks flush and her eyes flash, but he did have another matter to attend to. He held out a package. "Please accept these as apology for my appalling lack of manners."

She took his offering with obvious reluctance. "What is it?"

"Open it and find out."

Alexandra unwrapped her gift. "Books. And a new diary." A hint of a smile curved her mouth.

Her reaction pleased Derek. "They're to help you pass the time until you're recovered."

"Thank you." She stroked the leather cover of the diary, then seated herself at his desk and paged through the novel on top of the stack.

Somewhat disgruntled by her dismissal, Derek moved behind her and stared down at her ebony tresses. A sudden yearning to filter his fingers through the silken length seized him. He tightened his hands into fists. "What were you doing under the chair, Lexi?"

"Hmm?" She opened the second book.

He tipped her chin and forced her to meet his gaze. "Why were you under my chair?"

She blinked, then pulled away and leaned against the leather back of the chair. "Why do you ask?"

Her breathy response and lavender essence ignited an escalating desire to taste her again. "It isn't every day I find an exasperating woman lying beneath my furniture and my dog." He lifted a lock of her hair and wrapped it around his fingers.

Alexandra's pink tongue darted out of her mouth and moistened her lips. Derek was hard-pressed to focus on her answer. "We, uh, were playing a game—hide and seek—and Max misunderstood the rules. He was supposed to find me, not sit on me."

Derek's eyebrow rose a notch. "Game? Rules? Who insisted just this morn that she's not a child?"

"Me."

Derek placed his arms on the chair and trapped her between them. "And what sort of punishment do you suppose this misbehavior might warrant?"

Uncertainty flickered across her exquisite features. "Punishment? Because I played a game?"

"Aboard a ship, discipline is of utmost importance. A captain's commands must be obeyed without question, without hesitation, because someone's life may depend on them."

Alexandra leaned forward and searched his eyes. "Y-you can't mean to punish me."

He affected his most wicked leer. "Can't I?"

Her face drained of all color. She nimbly slipped out from beneath his arms and put the massive desk between them. "You have no right to punish me." Her voice wavered. "And I'm quite aware you're the captain here, but I will not be bullied by you or anyone else. Never again."

Derek advanced toward her. The utter terror in her eyes chilled him to the center of his soul. He took another step forward.

"Stay back!" She pelted him with navigational instruments from his desk, then bolted for the door where she fumbled with the latch.

Derek edged his way to her side, but resisted the urge to hold her, to shield her from her panic. He worried she might shatter into innumerable pieces if he touched her.

Pieces he might not be able to reassemble.

"You have naught to fear from me, Lexi. I was only jesting about punishing you. Forgive my foolishness?"

Alexandra's frantic attempt to open the door stilled. Confusion replaced the overwhelming distress he had witnessed, a sight he would never be able to drive from his memory.

A lone tear slid down her cheek. Compelled to ease her heartache, he reached out to smooth away the drop of moisture. She flinched. He dropped his arm to his side. Self-recrimination and loathing lanced through him. He hadn't considered how she might interpret his teasing and repeated reminders about her status aboard his vessel. She was different from the women he was accustomed to.

Her cloud of dark hair and her glistening sapphire eyes, her vulnerability and her fragility snared him and dragged him into the past. Into the dark abyss of utter and complete failure where guilt roiled low and deep, no less shadowy for the passage of years. Would he ever be able to look into blue eyes and not hear Charlotte crying for him to save her? Would blue eyes ever come to mean happiness?

Silence stretched between them. Neither of them spoke nor moved.

Finally, Alexandra straightened her shoulders and lifted her chin. "You were jesting? It wasn't your intention to hurt me?"

"I'll never hurt you." He held his hand out to her, palm up.

After the briefest of hesitations, she placed her trembling hand in his.

Heartened by her act of trust, he stroked the slender length of her fingers with his thumb.

"I believe you," she whispered, her gaze lowered.

"Who is he, Lexi?"

A frown furrowed her brow. "Who?"

"The man who taught you to be afraid."

She tried to remove her hand, but Derek urged her closer. "Let me help you." He mentally kicked himself. He needed her to recover and be on her way, not to become further entangled in his life. Yet it seemed she had always been with him. He refused to think of the gaping void her absence would leave.

"I'm not afraid." She eased free of his gentle hold. "You've already been quite generous with your assistance."

He knew he could not expect to gain her complete confidence right away, so he did not force the issue. "I'll take my leave. We'll talk again, after you feel stronger."

"I feel fine, Captain Tremaine. The cut on my forehead is nearly healed."

Relieved by the hint of rebellion in her eyes, though he knew he would see the consequences soon enough, Derek pressed his finger to her soft lips. "Perhaps we'll take a stroll above deck. After your health has been restored."

Aware of her stiffening stance, he left his cabin and entered the one next door where he dismissed Travis.

The occupant of the bed turned his head to look at Derek.

Derek forced back the lump rising in his throat. "Good day, Dr. Sebastian."

****

The afternoon crept by. Alexandra laid the novel *Pamela* aside, disturbed by Mr. B's abduction of his young maidservant, Pamela Andrews. "Men should not have the right to impose their will on women." Rankled by Derek's insistence that she rest, she rose to her feet and paced the confines of the cabin. A few minutes later, she picked up her diary and seated herself at his desk.

Who does the aggravating sea captain think he is? He is not my father. Nor is he my husband.

Alexandra paused mid-stroke. Husband? Her stomach lurched, evoking a low groan of frustration. She moved the quill pen rapidly across the page.

Why does the bothersome man rouse such maddening reactions within me? Why does it ofttimes feel as though I've known him for always and forever, that I've been waiting for him, knowing he would come?

Yet, I cannot allow him to keep me a virtual prisoner or return me to Bartholomew. I must leave this vessel and continue on to Williamsburg.

Unsettled by the realization that her time with Derek was growing short, she yanked her cloak from its peg and fastened it about her shoulders. "Come, Max."

The Newfoundland moved to her side. She eased the door open and listened for voices. *His* voice. Greeted by silence, she slipped out of the cabin and tiptoed down the corridor.

As she neared the next cabin, a strange

sensation washed over her. She slowed her footsteps and bent her head toward the door. A low murmuring voice raised goose bumps along her arms. She placed her trembling hand on the latch, tempted, almost compelled, to look inside.

She scolded herself for considering invading someone's private quarters and hurried toward the stairs, then proceeded to the main deck. Blinded by the glare of the afternoon sun, Alexandra stepped into a coil of rope and lost her balance.

"Steady as you go, miss." Strong arms caught her and maintained their hold until she regained her footing.

"How clumsy of me." She straightened her cloak.

"Think nothing of it, Miss Alexandra."

A small shiver of alarm traveled down her spine and her head shot up. The bright light concealed his face. "You know my name?"

"I was here when Derek brought you aboard. I'm Travis Greyson."

Alexandra's face grew hot. He had seen her in Derek's bed. What assumptions had he made?

"Are you all right, Miss Alexandra?" He placed a steadying hand on her. "You shouldn't be up here."

She shielded her eyes from the sun and studied the man before her. As tall as Derek, he had kind blue eyes with nary a flicker of censure in their depths. His light brown hair fell past his shoulders in waves many women would envy, though there was nothing feminine about this broad-shouldered, square-jawed man.

"Are you all right?"

"I'm fine, Mr. Greyson. Thank you for assisting me."

"'Twas my pleasure." He released his hold on her. "Does Derek know you're up here?"

"He promised I could walk about a bit after I rested."

His expression showed his doubt. "Perhaps you should wait for him in your cabin."

"I've been there for days. Please let me stay. I won't be a bother." She met his concerned gaze with quiet determination.

"If anything happens, Derek will have my head. You wouldn't want to see me keelhauled, would you?"

"Max is with me. I'll be careful." She took her leave.

"But, Miss Alexandra..."

Alexandra continued on her way, but she saw him throw his hands in the air and signal Obadiah. Probably to send for their captain. Resolved to make the most of her stolen time above deck, she hurried past the curious sailors mending sail canvas and overhauling the rigging.

Upon reaching the ship's rail, she took a deep breath. Exhilarated by the crisp autumn air, she allowed her gaze to roam over the busy Philadelphia harbor.

Wharfs servicing ships covered the waterfront. In the midst of the bustle and confusion, windlass pawls clacked, hoisting cargo up out of ships' holds and lowering it to waiting draymen and wagoners. Men with boxes and bales on their shoulders pushed their way toward nearby warehouses while a group of fishermen in a tiny sloop heaved the day's catch onto the wharf's planks.

Images of a certain sea captain drifted through her mind. The man didn't even have to touch her to make her pulse quicken. She had only to think about him. As she remembered the feel of Bartholomew's hands on her, her musings turned dark. Chilled by the recollection, she hugged her arms around her midsection.

She whirled away from the waterfront scene and came face to face with a towering thundercloud.

A muscle worked in his jaw. "Woman." He caught her by the wrist and pulled her away from the rail. "Is there no end to your rash behavior?"

"You're angry." She had hoped he wouldn't be difficult. His wrathful glare rid her of that notion.

"How observant you are. What are you doing up here?"

She moistened her lower lip. "I wanted some air."

"What about our agreement?"

"Agreement?"

"Did we not agree you could come above deck in a day or two?"

"You did. I didn't."

He tightened his hold on her wrist. "Why do you insist on flouting me?"

"I couldn't stay cooped up another minute."

"If one of my crew disobeyed—"

"I'm not one of your crew, for which I am eternally grateful." She tried to pull free. "And you're hurting me."

Derek dropped her arm and raked his fingers through his hair. "Is a breath of fresh air worth the risk of being found by this unidentified man you are fleeing?"

Her heart thudded against her ribcage. "What do you mean?"

"Look beyond my left shoulder."

She complied.

"Do you see the two men partially concealed behind the cargo being unloaded from the *Beatrice*?"

"Is one portly and balding and the other thin with blond hair?"

"Aye."

A horrible sinking feeling enveloped her. "Who are they?"

"You don't recognize them?"

"No." Her answer was barely audible.

"They were among the men surrounding you in the woods shortly after I pulled you from the river. And they've already boarded this vessel once. Looking for you."

Chapter Six

Panic fluttered, then welled within Alexandra. But she steeled herself against it, refusing to spend every moment fearing discovery by Bartholomew. She peered around Derek's shoulder again. "They're gone."

"No doubt reporting to their boss."

"Y-you said they've been here. On this ship?" She scanned the waterfront for another glimpse of them.

"Aye."

"When?"

"Yesterday."

"Yesterday!" She gasped, then turned her gaze toward Derek. "Why didn't you tell me of this?"

"You've been unwell—"

"You should've told me. 'Tis *me* they're after."

"I am aware of that. Perhaps now you'll reveal the name of their leader?"

Alexandra swallowed hard and ignored his question. Her stomach tightened into a knot. "They saw me?"

"They'd have to have been blind *not* to see you leaning against the rail. 'Twas careless of you, Lexi."

She winced at his rebuke. "Please spare me your lecture."

"Have it your way." He grasped her by the elbow and forced her to walk with him. "You shall have your fill of fresh air and non-confinement. By remaining by my side for the rest of the day."

"But—"

"No buts. Come along."

Frustrated by his high-handed manner, Alexandra dug in her heels and tried to pull free of his iron grip. "Did it even occur to you to ask me? Must you always issue commands?"

Derek halted and glowered down at her. "You have but two choices—keep up with me or be hoisted over my shoulder."

"You wouldn't dare."

His mouth curved at her challenge. In the space of a heartbeat, she found herself lifted several feet from the floor and clutching his shoulders for balance.

"Put. Me. Down."

"I think not. This way I know you'll stay put."

She bristled at his comment. "You can't hold me up here forever."

"I'm quite strong, I assure you." He tightened his hold on her and molded his fingers against the curve of her waist.

Liquid warmth unfurled through her veins. She trembled beneath his touch. Unwilling to admit she rather liked it, she brought her knee up hard, square against his chest. Derek shifted her weight and trapped her leg against him. He caressed her calf beneath the cover of her gown, which drew sly glances from his crew.

Her face burned with embarrassment. "I demand...I *request* that you release me."

"Will you come without complaint?" His fingertips reached the sensitive underside of her thigh.

"Yes," she said through clenched teeth.

He lowered her down the hard length of his body. Intense longing ribboned through her. Her knees weakened. She cursed her body's traitorous response and took a step back. But he wrapped his arm around her waist and prevented her departure.

"Changed your mind so soon?" His fingers traced the small of her back in unhurried strokes while his breath fanned across her cheek, his mouth inches from hers.

Her mind clouded from the tendrils of pleasure he wrought within her. "Nay, I'll accompany you."

Derek offered his arm, and she accepted it. He pointed out various duties being performed by his crew. Two sailors overhauled the rigging. Two others repaired and oiled gear while a fifth man mended sail canvas.

Travis Greyson stood near the main hatch. Reminded of his earlier concern about his captain's reaction to her presence above deck, she glanced up at Derek. "Have you ever had anyone keelhauled?"

He frowned. "This is not an appropriate topic of conversation for a young woman."

"Have you?"

"I do not choose to discuss it with you."

She lifted her shoulder in a shrug. "Then I'll ask someone else."

Derek's hand shot out and yanked her against him. "This is *my* vessel. If you ask any of my men, you'll receive first-hand experience of keelhauling."

She stared at him, skeptical of his threat, though so very aware of his masculinity. "You would have me dragged under the length of this ship, scraped across the barnacles, and possibly drowned because I asked a simple question?"

He nodded, but she saw the corner of his mouth twitch.

"You're lying." She searched his gaze for the truth. "Why do you want me to fear you?"

A muscle jumped in his clenched jaw. "Did no one ever teach you obedience?"

"To my elders. Are you my elder, *Captain* Tremaine?"

He rolled his eyes heavenward and shook his

head. "Come along, Lexi. And call me Derek."

The remainder of the day passed in a flurry of activity. Derek combined his duties with her tour of the schooner. His crew's respect and admiration made her grudgingly admit to herself he wasn't the tyrant she had thought him to be.

Even his earlier irritation with her seemed to fade, tempered perhaps by his obvious affection for the *Wind Spirit*. A strange yearning built within her, a yearning for more than his gentle assistance down the stairs and around the array of tackle, ropes, and gear. At odd moments she'd remember sliding down the length of his body, and the intimate pressure of his hands around her waist.

She followed Derek down to the hold to check the provisions and stores. Her mind whirled from all she had seen and heard during the preceding hours. The foremast. The mainmast. Standard rigging. Running rigging.

She stepped around the spare sails and ropes and recalled more confusing details. Hitches and knots. Reefing and furling.

A sharp tug on her skirt drew her attention down. One of the wooden spars had somehow become entangled in her hem. She pulled on the faded chintz fabric, only to be rewarded by a slight tearing sound. She groaned. Hadn't Derek told her coins were placed under the mast for luck? Perhaps she should have tried it.

Thrumming began in her head and soon developed into a persistent, nagging ache. She brought her fingers to her brow. A cask of salt meat greeted her weary eyes. Telling herself she would rest for but a moment, she settled her tired body onto it.

****

Derek smiled at the young woman slumped on the cask. "Contrary female." He slipped his arms

67

around her and lifted her slight weight.

"I'm not—" She yawned. "—contrary." With a drowsy sigh, she burrowed against his broad chest.

Derek carried the sleeping beauty up two sets of stairs, conscious all the while of her warm, soft curves. Upon reaching his cabin, he placed her on his bed, removed her cloak, and tucked the blanket around her still form.

Drawn by her tempting mouth, he bent and brushed his lips against hers. She turned in her sleep and murmured his name. Damnation! He straightened and stepped away from the bed.

What was he thinking? He couldn't permit her to dream about him any more than he could dream of her. He had saved her life, to be sure, but she was nearly recovered. Soon his responsibility toward her would end.

He had a mission to accomplish and she had a… Hell, he didn't know what she had, but it didn't involve him. He could not allow it to involve him.

Forcing his thoughts to his other responsibility, he paced the floor, frustrated by Dr. Sebastian's inability to aid him and by the lack of clues to lead him to Charlotte.

There had to be a way.

****

Alexandra sat upright, gasping in fear, bathed in perspiration. She turned and reached for Derek, but her fingers clutched air. Her hand sought the cameo locket. "Derek, are you here?"

Deafening silence answered her.

Unnerved by the hints of darkness whispering to her through the slivers of moonlight, she slid off the bed and rushed from the room. As she neared the next cabin, her footsteps faltered, then stopped.

Low murmuring reached through the door and drew her closer until she placed her hand on it. She paused a moment, then knocked on the smooth surface. The door opened.

"Derek?"

"Lexi?"

"What are you doing here?" they asked in unison.

"You first," Derek said.

"I woke up and it was dark. You were gone and—"

"You had another nightmare," he said, concern evident in his voice.

"Yes. No. I don't know." A penetrating chill passed through her. She shivered and hugged her arms around her midsection.

Derek removed his coat and placed it around her shoulders. "Come inside, lest you further harm your health."

She entered the small cabin. Her gaze alighted on the bed and she came to a surprised standstill. "Dr. Sebastian?"

With a small cry of joy, she ran to his side and threw her arms around him. "I'm so happy to see you. Have you seen Polly and the children?"

At a low, guttural sound, Alexandra drew back. The right side of Dr. Sebastian's face sagged. His eyelid, his cheek, even his mouth. She blinked back the sudden sting of tears and wiped away a bit of moisture along his chin. The silent pleading in his eyes saddened her.

"He cannot speak or move," Derek said.

"Why not?"

"Apoplexy."

Shaken to her core, Alexandra took one of Dr. Sebastian's hands between her own. She attempted a smile, determined to hold her emotions in check. His dark blue eyes never left hers. "How long has he been ill?"

"Several days. I didn't realize you knew him."

"He takes care of the children when they're sick

and teaches me about healing when he can. We met at the market by chance a time or two before then and became friends." Warmed by the pleasant memories of their time together, she patted the older man's hand and hoped she had succeeded in concealing her distress at his condition.

A sharp frown pleated Derek's forehead. "You have children?"

"Don't be absurd. I've never been married." An icy hand closed around her heart and froze her in place.

His expression softened. "You've told me little of yourself."

"The same might be said of you."

"True. Perhaps 'tis time that changed."

Alexandra waged an internal battle. She weighed the risks and the rewards of revealing more of her past, but she could not bring herself to tell him the whole truth. Not yet. The basic instinct of self-protection overruled all else. "Several children lived in the same house I did. Why is Dr. Sebastian here?"

Sadness lurked in Derek's eyes, caused, she guessed, by her inability to share herself with him. She had hurt him.

He glanced at the ill man. "I discovered him in the Pennsylvania Hospital and brought him here. His family and mine have known each other for many years."

Dr. Sebastian opened his mouth, but nothing intelligible came forth. His struggle to communicate tugged at her heart and filled her with the urge to lay her head on his chest and weep at the injustice he had suffered.

She balled her hands into fists and turned toward Derek. "Why didn't you tell me he was here? I should have been with him."

"I didn't know you knew each other. And as

you'll recall, you've been recovering yourself."

Unable to sit still a moment longer, she rose from the bed. "What kind of care is he receiving?"

"Dr. Sebastian has never been left alone. I've taken great pains to ensure he is looked after."

"How? What are you doing for him?"

Derek's eyes narrowed. "I'm following the hospital's instructions to the letter."

Alexandra ignored his clenched jaw. "What were the instructions?"

He grabbed her by the elbow and pulled her away from the sick man's earshot. "Are you questioning my competence? I can captain this vessel. I can manage a plantation. I can follow a doctor's instructions. If you feel qualified to take over his care, by all means do so."

She stared at the angry lines of the sculptured mouth so close to hers and cleared her throat. "I will."

"Fine. You shall have everything you need."

She jumped at the resounding slam of the door. She had really made a mess of things this time.

She pasted on a bright smile and resumed her place by Dr. Sebastian's side. She strove to hide the worry tormenting her and chose instead to ease his obvious confusion. "Did you hear Derek? I'm going to stay here and take care of you. You'll be well in no time, you'll see."

She spoke past a lump in her throat. "I want you to close your eyes and rest while I prepare a tonic."

Alexandra pressed her trembling lips against his wrinkled brow and hurried from the room. She choked back her concern, her fear. Blinded by tears, she used the wall as a guide and ran several feet until her legs collapsed beneath her. Relinquishing herself to the soul-deep pain, she buried her face in her palms, muffling the sound of her weeping.

****

Still reeling from the irrational reaction he had experienced at the thought of Alexandra having a child by another man, Derek rounded the corner and placed his hand on the door of the cabin occupied by Dr. Sebastian. An incoherent whimper down the corridor caught his attention.

Lexi?

He crossed the distance in long, quick strides, and he reached down and pulled her up from the floor. He held her against him while great sobs shook her slender frame. All remnants of anger dissipated in the face of her distress. He stroked the length of her hair. "Shhh, 'twill be all right. You needn't worry about him."

A fresh flow of tears dampened his shirtfront. He lifted and carried her into his cabin, away from prying eyes. After he settled her upon his chair and knelt before her, he patiently waited for her grief to subside. When it did, interrupted by an occasional hiccough, he pulled a handkerchief from his pocket and dried her eyes. She kept her gaze averted.

"Dr. Sebastian's illness upsets you. Perhaps caring for him is more than you can handle."

"No." Alexandra turned her glistening eyes to Derek. "I am capable of doing it. I *must* do it."

"You can visit him all you want, but—"

"No." Her chin quivered. She stilled the slight movement and continued. "I am skilled in the art of healing. When I attend a patient, I keep my emotions under control."

She rose from the chair the same moment he stood. Their bodies touched. He slipped his arm around her waist to steady her. Desire snared him in its silken web.

His loins tightened. Derek drew her into the circle of his arms, brought his mouth down on hers, and feasted on her unique sweetness. Teasing, tasting, exploring. Accepting all she gave in return.

Their breath mingled, their tongues met, his boldly, hers shyly, and inflamed him with bone-melting need, scorched his soul with its intensity.

A loud, unmistakable thud from the next cabin rent the silence and shattered the moment.

Chapter Seven

Her insides knotted in apprehension, Alexandra broke free from Derek and raced to the next cabin. To her dismay, Dr. Sebastian lay unmoving on the floor.

"Oh, no!" She rushed to his side and checked for injuries. Derek knelt beside her. "Please help me get him on the bed."

He did as she requested. She leaned over the elderly man and studied his eyes. Aside from looking fatigued, he seemed more frustrated than frightened.

"It's my fault." She stroked his wrinkled hand. "I shouldn't have left you alone."

"It wasn't your fault, Lexi."

She shook her head. "I left him alone. I should have waited for you to return before leaving to prepare a tonic."

"You were trying to help him. If you'll remember, *I* told you he couldn't move. How were you to know he would fall out of bed?"

"Still, I shouldn't have—" She paused mid-sentence and glanced from Derek to Dr. Sebastian and back again. "How *did* he fall from the bed?"

Derek lifted his broad shoulders in a shrug.

The flickering spark of hope within Alexandra kindled into bubbling excitement. "That's it!" She jumped to her feet and peered down into Derek's eyes. "Don't you see?"

"See what?"

"He moved. Dr. Sebastian moved." She threw

her arms around Derek's neck and kissed him, nearly toppling him over. "Isn't this wonderful?"

"Aye, 'tis wonderful." He drew her closer. "'Tis wonderful indeed." He brushed his mouth against hers.

"Derek." She pressed trembling fingers against his chest and slipped out from beneath his heady embrace. "This is not the appropriate time or place."

He caught her before she could turn back toward the doctor. His darkening gaze smoldered and robbed her of breath. "Tell me, Lexi," he said in a silken, sensual undertone. "When and where."

A delicious shiver spiraled through her. She allowed herself a small grin. "Anywhere you say...when Max sprouts wings. Until then, I have a patient to attend to. Please have port wine, water, and rags brought to me. I shall also require enough Peruvian bark to dose him three or four times a day until he's recovered."

"It's late. You should rest."

"I can't rest now."

He placed a finger to her lips. "Shhh, he's asleep."

"He is?" She whirled and smiled down at his slumbering form. "So he is."

"Tomorrow will be soon enough to begin your medical regimen, don't you think?"

"So it would seem." She smothered a yawn and settled herself in the chair beside the bed.

"What do you think you are doing?"

"I'm keeping watch over my patient."

"You will *not* spend the night in that chair."

Alexandra lifted her chin a notch and ignored the muffled thunder of his voice. "I have to be close by in case he needs me. And, if you continue to speak so loudly, *you'll* awaken him."

"If you neglect your health, you'll be of no help to him."

75

"I'll make a pallet on the floor."

"Travis has already given up his bed to Dr. Sebastian. Without reservation, I might add. Would you also put him out of his cabin?"

"No. I didn't realize—" She drew a deep, steadying breath. "I'm staying."

"Then so am I."

"You can't!"

Derek arched one of his eyebrows.

Alexandra flushed beneath his mocking gaze. "Well, you *can*, but you can't."

A wicked gleam twinkled in his eyes and he stretched out on the floor beside her. "Travis shall use my cabin."

"I couldn't do that."

"'Tis done."

Alexandra knew it was pointless to argue the matter further. As the silence between them lengthened and grew awkward, she searched for another topic of conversation. "You mentioned your family and Dr. Sebastian's are well acquainted. Where do you live?"

"Virginia. Near Williamsburg."

She froze. "Williamsburg? How long before you return home?" She nibbled her lower lip.

"As soon as I complete my business. Within a week or so, I hope. I'd rather not be trapped here should the Delaware River freeze as it is wont to do."

Alexandra pondered his words. Perhaps she could convince him to take her with him. She cast a sidelong glance at Derek. "You'll be taking on new cargo soon?"

"In a matter of speaking."

Her curiosity aroused, she longed to ask for an explanation, but held her tongue, certain he would interpret her question as interference and refuse to answer. *He* was the captain, after all. "Do you plan to take Dr. Sebastian to Virginia?"

His brows drew together. "Of course."

"And me? What are your plans for me?"

"Ah." He smiled. "You've no need to fear. I'll see you recovered and settled before I set sail."

So he meant to leave her behind. She fought against the emptiness gnawing at her insides, and scolded herself for even daring to expect more of him. Fatigued to the depths of her soul, she pulled her feet up onto the chair and wrapped her arms around her calves. She rested her chin on her knees, unable to even look at him lest she give in to the overwhelming sense of abandonment by yet another person and burst into tears.

That wouldn't do at all.

****

"'Tis time for your next tonic, Dr. Sebastian." Alexandra unfolded the slip of paper containing Peruvian bark and poured it into port wine to help mask its bitter taste. She ignored the nagging ache in the small of her back and placed the mug on the chair, then slipped her arm behind her patient to ease him upright.

The door opened. "I told you this morning to send for me when you needed assistance."

She glanced over her shoulder at Derek and bit back a caustic reply. She had depended on his assistance far too often as it was. "I'm quite capable of administering a tonic on my own."

That infernal muscle in his jaw jumped. She returned her attention to Dr. Sebastian and held the wine to his lips. She wiped away the bit that dribbled down his chin.

"There." She smiled. "All finished." She set the empty mug aside and reached around him. Her hands brushed against Derek's. Liquid heat sped through her and traveled to her center.

With great strength of will, she lifted her gaze to his. The intensity of his brown-gold eyes held her immobile. Her breath caught high in her throat. Scarcely aware of her actions, she allowed him to help her settle the doctor against the pillows.

"What time will you dose him again?"

The deep timbre of his voice washed over Alexandra. Her mouth went dry from his thorough perusal. Heat flooded her face. "Four o'clock."

He nodded. "I'll be here."

"Won't that interfere with your captainly duties or the mysterious cargo you're awaiting?"

An indefinable emotion flickered across his face. His expression hardened. "I'm allowing you to care for him, but not at the expense of your health."

The reminder that he planned to leave her behind cut to the quick. "As you wish." She steeled herself against the tears pricking the back of her eyes and concentrated on removing the damp cloths from Dr. Sebastian's legs.

Derek placed his hand upon hers, stilling her movements. "You haven't left the cabin yet this day."

"No, I haven't." Alexandra's heart pounded. She pulled her hand out from beneath his.

"You are to go above deck for fresh air at least once a day."

"What happened to 'You will stay below deck'?"

"The damage has been done. They've seen you and know you're here."

She inwardly flinched at his displeasure. Her face grew hot. "I can't go now. These cloths must be changed."

"I can do it."

She lifted one eyebrow, skeptical of his sincerity and unsure of his motive for helping her.

"If I convince you, will you go for a daily stroll while Dr. Sebastian convalesces?"

"Yes."

"Very well. You will also take Max with you since he seldom seems to leave you unattended."

After rolling up the sleeves of his white linen shirt, he plunged a cloth into the basin of cold water, wrung it out, and placed it on Dr. Sebastian's leg. He repeated the process until all of the cloths had been used. "Satisfied?" He folded his arms against his chest.

"Hmmph. Obadiah could have done just as well." She motioned for Max and left the cabin.

Derek's roar of laughter pursued her through the corridor. Striving to shrug off his effect on her, she rounded a corner and collided with Travis Greyson. She took an instinctive step back and nearly fell over the large dog behind her.

"Excuse me, Miss Alexandra." Travis reached out to steady her. "Did I hurt you?"

She clutched his shirtsleeves and waited for her head to clear, grateful for the support he offered.

"Miss Alexandra? Should I fetch the captain?"

"Nay," she murmured, struck by a discovery. Aside from Derek and Bartholomew, no other man had ever laid hands on her. Although Travis had kind eyes and was quite attractive, he did not affect her like Derek, whose presence stirred her senses and quickened her pulse, or like Bartholomew, who made her flesh crawl. Curious.

She studied Travis's eyes, but saw only concern reflected there. Not so much as a flicker of desire or lasciviousness.

"Miss Alexandra?"

Aware of his growing discomfort and the sleeves she still clutched between her fingers, she released her hold. "Thank you for your assistance. Come, Max." With a nod to Travis, she proceeded to the ship's rail where she would be able to ponder this new revelation.

****

27 October 1752
For the past few weeks I have been caring for Dr.

79

Sebastian. Less and less do his eyes remind me of a caged, imprisoned soul. Ofttimes I've been aware of his watchful gaze upon me. Other times I've felt he has desperately been trying to tell me something of great importance. Much improved, he can now lift his arms and legs and sit upright. However, his right side remains weak and he is still unable to speak.

Except for his continued presence during Dr. Sebastian's treatments, I've seen little of Derek. Even then he is distant and preoccupied, almost driven. 'Tis as if he's slipping away from me, even though he never has been mine and never can be. He spends a great deal of time off the Wind Spirit. *Why is he here? What is the cargo he's awaiting? How will I find the strength to tell him farewell once it arrives?*

I long to beg Derek to take me to Williamsburg. Alas, I cannot. Though I no longer fear he'll return me to Bartholomew, I do fear Bartholomew's retribution should he discover Derek has aided my flight and my search for my parents. If only circumstances were different.

Her heart heavy, Alexandra placed her diary in her apron pocket. She tried to summon anger toward Derek, but failed. He had saved her life, true, but that one act did not obligate him to be responsible for her for the rest of her life.

A knock on the door drew her to her feet. She opened it to reveal Travis.

"'Afternoon, Miss Alexandra. The capt'n had to leave the *Wind Spirit* and asked me to sit with Dr. Sebastian while you take your daily stroll."

"You wouldn't mind?" She glanced at the slumbering doctor.

"Not at all."

"Thank you. I'll return soon." Alexandra fetched her cloak, took Max and left the cabin. Mayhap a walk and fresh air would clear her mind of the troubling thoughts plaguing her about Derek's mysterious trips into town. She ambled over to the ship's rail and studied the busy wharf.

The image of Derek's face rose before her mind's eye. She sighed at the unbidden memory of caressing his sharply defined features, of entangling her fingers in his dark hair, of returning his kisses.

"Ally! Ally!"

The insistent cry startled her. She scanned the bustling crowd of people, and her gaze came to a rest on a boy jumping and waving his arms about.

He cupped his hands around his mouth. "Ally!"

"Who are you?" she called.

"Devan. You gotta come. 'Tis Polly. She needs you."

Chilled by his words, Alexandra picked up her skirts and raced down the gangway. Max ran along beside her. "What happened to her?"

"She's been hurt. Bad!"

The lad's unkempt appearance raised her suspicions. "I've never seen you before."

A fat tear rolled down his cheek and left a muddy rivulet. "She took me in a couple weeks ago after my mama died." He sniffed. "Please come. She calls your name over and over."

The realization that Polly would never permit a child to look as Devan did unless she was seriously injured hurtled Alexandra into the throes of panic. Tentacles of fear squeezed her heart. Bartholomew must have thought Polly had aided her escape and followed through on his threat. "Is she home?"

"Yes."

"Let's go." She pulled him along with her as she dashed along the wharf to High Street beside tumbrils, carts, and great wagons. The street teemed with horsemen and gentlemen's chaises and chariots. Countless porters carrying parcels crossed their path. Max followed at her heels.

Propelled by increasing urgency, Alexandra threaded her way to Chestnut Street. She steered Devan clear of piles of smelly refuse and the roaming dogs feeding on the garbage. Young men raced their horses at breakneck speed and narrowly missed them.

Her heart thumped from their near brush with disaster. She clutched Devan's hand and led him through a throng of people. Suddenly he pulled his hand from hers and vanished from sight.

"Devan!" She stood on tiptoe and strained to see over the people milling about.

The crowd thinned and a niggling worry worked its way to the fore of her thoughts. Polly hadn't known where she had fled. How had Devan known where to find her? She shivered from an impending sense of danger and reached for Max.

The Newfoundland emitted a menacing growl.

"Max? What—"

Before she could utter another word, a large hand covered her mouth.

Chapter Eight

A fleshy arm fastened around Alexandra's waist and lifted her from the ground. She struggled against her assailant, pleased by his pained grunts each time her foot connected with his shin.

Max's snarls and growls echoed in the alley. His furry body brushed Alexandra's leg.

"Ouch, you misbegotten whelp," her captor said.

Max launched another attack and received an answering blow. At the dog's wounded whimper, Alexandra increased her resistance with unleashed fury. The sound of tearing fabric rent the air and instilled within her the full impact of her precarious situation.

"Settle down, missy, or I'm gonna have to hurt you. When I take my hand from your mouth, tell this cur to leave. And *no* screaming, understand?"

She wrinkled her nose at his rancid breath and gave a curt nod, but the moment he removed his foul-tasting hand she dragged a gulp of oxygen into her lungs. "Run, Max! Run! Find Derek!"

The stranger cuffed her. Her wound reopened. A warm stickiness trickled down her temple. "Damn troublesome female." He swiped at the blood.

A fog descended upon Alexandra. Her vision blurred. Max's growl grew more and more distant. She desperately tried to claw her way through the gray mist enveloping her and resisted the pull of unconsciousness.

"Myron, take her!"

Startled by the reference to another person, she

strained against the first man's iron grip.

"Take this blasted woman."

"I-I can't, Harold. It's th-that dog."

Cursing, Harold withdrew his flintlock from his saddle. Alexandra was powerless to stop him from striking Max's head and throwing her over his horse. Through a veil of tears, she watched the still form of the loyal Newfoundland until he disappeared from sight.

The three of them tore through the streets. Myron whined excuses, scarcely taking a moment to draw a breath.

The flintlock pressed against her back kept her quiet and frozen in place. She had realized right away that she was being taken to Bartholomew, but then they entered Society Hill. Why were they riding among the homes of the city's principal merchants?

Harold and Myron dismounted before an elegant two-story brick house. Harold dragged her from the horse and pushed her through a side entrance where they encountered an enraged Bartholomew.

"You fools. You were to bring her to me unharmed." He grasped her by the elbow and pulled her by his side. Alexandra flinched at his touch.

"We couldn't help it, sir," Harold said. "What with all her screaming and the cursed dog who near took off my leg. I thought—"

"You thought? I don't pay you to think."

"He didn't hit her very hard, sir," Myron said.

"Neither of you were to lay a hand on her except to escort her here, yet you managed to tear her gown and make her bleed. You will suffer the consequences of your actions. Stand guard outside the house. If that damned Tremaine reclaims her, I'll see you dead."

Alexandra swayed on her feet. Her head ached with a fury. The world trembled and faded in and out of focus. A loud roar obscured her hearing. For several moments she thought she was floating through the air before settling into a cushioned surface.

A cool, wet softness moved across her forehead, followed by a low murmur. "There, it's not as bad as I first thought."

Icy fingers of terror encircled her heart. Her vision cleared and revealed Bartholomew leaning over her. She shoved him away, scrambled off the bed, and flew toward the door. But he reached it before she did and advanced toward her.

"Stay away from me." She backed away. "You've no right to keep me here."

A slow, evil smile spread across his face. "Ah, Alexandra. You are mistaken. You're mine."

"You have no claim on me." She bumped into the wardrobe and searched for the words to stop him. "I'm...married."

"No. You speak falsely." He dragged her against him and covered her mouth with a bruising kiss.

Nearly gagging from the taste and feel of him, she bit down on his lower lip. He grabbed a fistful of her hair and jerked her head back.

She twisted in his grasp. "I speak the truth."

"Then I shall soon make you a widow."

Fear for Derek leapt into her heart. "Nay. I'll not let you."

Bartholomew's penetrating eyes held an evil glint. "You will never again be with Tremaine. *Never.* You will not speak of him. You will not think of him. In two days you will become *my* bride. *Mine.*"

"I'll never wed you. Neither will you decree my thoughts, whether they be of my...my husband or aught else."

He gripped her jaw with his hand. "You'll do well to mind your tongue or I'll do it for you."

She shuddered beneath the force of his wrathful glare. He was mad. She needed time. Time to think.

Time to plan. She feigned calmness and pulled the tattered edges of her torn bodice together. "Please allow me to rest. I do not feel well. My head hurts."

Concern softened the anger in his dark eyes. He reached out to touch her forehead. She winced and pulled away. His jaw tightened. He charged out of the chamber and bellowed for Harold and Myron.

Alexandra peeked into the hall in time to see him disappear into a nearby room. Seizing the opportunity, she tiptoed down the hall in the opposite direction and descended the stairs. She hurried down the empty central hall and opened the door a hair's breadth. A tall, thin man passed before her.

She eased the door shut and crept into the closest room where she leaned against the wall to still her racing heart. She scanned the parlor and smothered a gasp of disbelief, then moved closer to the fireplace.

Closer to the portrait.

She lifted trembling fingers toward the painted figure clad in a gown a generation out of fashion, disconcerted by their shared likeness, by their uncanny resemblance.

The locket.

The other woman wore a locket matching the one Alexandra had discovered among Bartholomew's papers. She touched her throat.

The locket was gone! Her only link to her parents must have loosened during her struggle with Bartholomew's men.

Dark, fuzzy thoughts tugged at the outer fringes of her memory. Not again. Not now. Derek. She would think about Derek and plan her way back to him.

Footsteps sounded outside the parlor. She grabbed a silver candlestick from the tea table and hid behind the heavy blue velvet curtains.

The hair on the nape of her neck stood on end. Her breath caught. Bartholomew had entered the room and was moving nearer.

The nauseating odor of his pipe permeated the curtains. Tendrils of smoke weaved back and forth before her eyes, taunting her and strengthening her resolve. She raised the candlestick above her head.

Bartholomew's fingers appeared on the edging of the curtains. She watched, horror-stricken, as he flung the curtain aside. She brought her weapon down toward his head.

Twin bands of steel closed around her wrists until her hands grew numb and the candlestick dropped to the Persian rug with a dull thud.

Bartholomew held her against him. "Your spiritedness excites me. The challenge of taming you will enliven many a winter day and night."

Alexandra refused to meet his gaze. She did not want to witness the leer she knew glimmered there.

"Where are the papers?" he asked.

His question startled her. "Papers?"

He gripped her shoulders. "I know you took them. Where are they?"

"You'll never find them. I'm going to see you punished." She tried to shrug out from beneath his hands. "Let go of me!"

He bent forward, flung her over his shoulder, and headed toward the staircase. She pummeled his back with her fists, scratching, clawing, and kicking with every ounce of her strength. Her skirts and petticoats billowed over his head, forcing him to blindly make his way up the stairs.

At the top of the landing, he set her on her feet and pushed her into her bedchamber. She shook free, indignant and angry.

"Stay back." She held out her hand to ward him off. "You're not going to bully me."

"I'm a gentleman, not a bully."

"Not a bully? I beg to differ. This day I've been abducted, roughly handled, struck. My gown is torn."

She lifted her hand to her aching forehead. Images of Derek and his tender, gentle touches flashed through her thoughts until she nearly cried out from a stab of longing. Would she ever see him again?

Alexandra returned her attention to the man before her. "Unless the definition of 'gentleman' has changed since this morning, you are anything *but* a gentle man."

Bartholomew had the grace to flush. "I...uh... never intended for you to be harmed. Rest here while I do something about your gown."

She watched him leave, then sank onto the bed, determined to think of a way out.

****

The morning's search had proved fruitless. Derek worked his way through the throng of housewives and servants crowded around the market stalls and crossed over to Chestnut Street. Frustrated by his inability to find Charlotte or even a clue to her whereabouts, he quickened his steps. He dismissed the lump of black he saw from the corner of his eye.

Until he heard the whimper.

A sick sense of dread swirled around the pit of his stomach and he turned back to confirm his fears. "Max." He knelt beside the Newfoundland and discovered his bloody wounds. "Who did this to you?"

The dog lifted his head and tried to rise, but fell back weakly.

"Easy, boy. Easy." Derek spied a glimmer beside his pet. He reached over and picked it up.

Alexandra's locket.

"No." He clenched the cameo in his palm, bombarded by wave after wave of renewed guilt and raw pain. "Not again." He bowed his head against the self-recrimination clawing at his insides.

He had failed once more. Remembrances of Charlotte skipping along, her black braids flying, her whole being an appealing wreath of happiness and sunshine, mingled with images of Alexandra smiling at him, playing with Max, nursing Dr. Sebastian back to health. The entwined memories burned themselves into his soul, branded him, condemned him.

This time he should have prevented it. No longer a callow youth, he had seen for himself the danger awaiting Alexandra, the fear in her eyes, her nightmares.

He gently gathered the Newfoundland into his arms. Anger at himself and the man who had dared take her and injure Max drove him to his feet.

The bastard would rue this day.

****

"Travis, disperse the men among the city. I want the blackguard found and Alexandra returned."

"Aye, Capt'n."

"You can depend on us, Capt'n," Zeke, the balding cook, promised. "Ain't nothin' gonna happen to the lovely miss."

For a moment Derek's mood lightened. Alexandra had touched their hearts, reminding them of their wives, sweethearts, and daughters back home. As the men filtered off the schooner, he said, "Obadiah, you'll remain here."

The cabin boy's expression fell, and he dragged himself to Derek's side. "Ah, Capt'n. I want to help."

"You will be helping, but in a different way."

"Yes, sir." He followed Derek to Travis's cabin.

Dr. Sebastian looked up as they entered.

Derek walked over to the older man's chair. "How are you feeling?"

Dr. Sebastian nodded his head.

"Good. Obadiah is going to sit with you while I

attend to an important matter."

The doctor placed his left hand on Derek's arm. Derek could see the question in his eyes.

"I am going to look for her. 'Tis why Obadiah is here. My crew and I will find the man who has taken her."

Dr. Sebastian stiffened in his chair. "B-Bar-th-tholo-m-mew T-Tay-l-lor." He slumped back into his chair.

Derek forced himself to speak in a lighthearted manner. "'Tis good to hear you speak. Lexi will be pleased." He turned toward the young man beside him. "Obadiah?"

"Capt'n?"

"See that no harm comes to him."

"Aye, Capt'n."

****

Alexandra had paced back and forth across the bedchamber for hours. Every few minutes she would stop, consider an option, then discard it. She dropped onto the bed and stared up at the curtain embroidered in fanciful patterns of blues, greens, reds, and yellows.

A short while later, she pulled her diary from her pocket and wrote:

There must be a better way, but I don't know what it is. Bartholomew has guards stationed outside every door. Derek doesn't know where I am. For that matter, I have been such a bother to him, he might very well wash his hands of me. If I'm to be rescued, I shall have to do it myself.

Alexandra wrinkled her nose at the most plausible of the plans she had considered.

Will I be convincing? I must or else it will all have been for naught. Though the idea sickens me, I must make Bartholomew believe I care for him until I can gain his trust and free myself.

Sudden rapping on the door brought her

upright. She willed her heartbeat to return to normal and slipped her diary into her pocket. "Come in."

A woman entered the chamber to Alexandra's relief. The tall brunette must have been quite beautiful in her youth, though she now seemed a sad, faded shadow.

"I'm Evelyn. Mr. Taylor asked me to bring these to you." She deposited several gowns on the bed beside Alexandra and left the room.

Alexandra stared at the rainbow of satin, silk, brocade, and taffeta. Her first instinct was to refuse, but then she looked down at the torn fabric of her garment. With a sigh of reluctance, she chose the simplest of them, a gown of dark blue satin.

Several minutes later, Alexandra turned toward the looking glass. Her eyes widened in surprise. The low cut décolletage bared her throat and exposed so much of her bosom that even the ruffled edge of her chemise failed to provide adequate coverage.

She began an earnest search of the highboy, hoping to find a fichu or a modesty piece, even a kerchief to conceal the abundance of flesh. The drawers contained chemises, stays, and stockings.

She hoped one of the other gowns would be more suitable and picked them up, one by one. The gray taffeta laced up the front over a stomacher and had a low rounded neckline, as did the rose silk gown with ribbon fasteners. She considered the sacque dress of biscuit-colored taffeta scattered with colorful butterflies and flowers. Surely the flowing overdress worn over the matching petticoat would be a more modest choice.

As she began loosening the lacings, someone knocked on the door. Her hands stilled. "Yes?"

"It's Bartholomew. I've come to escort you to supper."

"Just a moment." Alexandra re-laced the gown

and hurried to the door. She opened it so only her head was visible.

"Is something amiss, Alexandra?"

"Uh...no."

"Did Evelyn bring the gowns I ordered for you?"

"Yes."

"Then come, let me see."

She reluctantly stepped out from behind the door.

Bartholomew's eyes darkened. "Perfection. I knew this gown would match your eyes."

He wasn't looking at her eyes. Repulsed by the obvious direction of his thoughts, she once again took refuge behind the door.

"Is something wrong with the gown?"

She couldn't meet his gaze. "There isn't enough of it. Does Evelyn have a kerchief I might borrow?"

He summoned the housekeeper. She followed his instructions and soon returned with the requested item and a brooch to secure it. He placed the muslin kerchief around Alexandra's shoulders and brought the ends together in front. His fingers grazed her skin.

Alexandra choked back a cry of revulsion and stepped back. "I-I can finish it." She clutched the ruffled covering against herself. She held her hand out for the brooch.

He placed it in her hand. His fingers lingered there for a moment. "We have time for a brief tour of our new home before we dine," he said, while she completed the task. "I think we shall begin with the first floor."

Inwardly flinching, Alexandra placed her hand upon the arm he offered. He led her down the stairs and toward the parlor. It required all of Alexandra's courage to enter the room. The same prickles of fear she had endured earlier while hiding behind the blue velvet curtains assaulted her anew. She glanced sideways at Bartholomew. Did he believe her abrupt turnaround? What would he do if he suspected it required every ounce of control she could muster to abide his company?

How long could she keep up this pretense?

She glided toward the cheery fire in the fireplace on the pretext of warming her hands, and stared once again at her likeness. The resemblance unsettled her. "Where did this portrait come from?"

Bartholomew took his place beside her. When he slipped his arm around her waist and drew her against him, she stiffened but forced herself to relax lest he become angry and mistrustful. She concentrated on his answers rather than the feel of his arm.

"Don't you remember? I commissioned this portrait many years ago. While awaiting the day when you and I would share our lives, I kept this image of you on the wall beside my bed. It helped ease the long, lonely nights, but now the need to make you mine becomes more difficult to endure." He spun her around and assaulted her tender mouth.

Alexandra, who had listened to his passionate declarations with growing unease, tried to escape his grasp, but the more she struggled, the tighter he held her. In desperation, she rammed her knee into his groin.

He howled in pain and doubled over. The look he directed at her drove away all hope for escape. What had she done?

Harold burst through the parlor door. When he saw Bartholomew's fierce scowl, he hesitated. Alexandra remained frozen in place.

"Leave us, Harold."

"But I have to talk to ya, sir. 'Tis urgent."

After throwing a quelling look at her, Bartholomew waved his hireling out to the hall and closed the door. Alexandra caught only snatches of their heated conversation.

"...blazing fire...warehouse..."

"...authorities...contraband..."

Bartholomew re-entered the parlor, accompanied by his housekeeper. "Evelyn will escort you to your room, Alexandra. You *will* answer for your actions upon my return." He limped away from the house with Harold close on his heels.

Alexandra followed the other woman up the stairs and formulated a plan for escape. Upon entering the bedchamber, she crossed the room and doubled over as though in pain.

"Are you ill, miss?" Evelyn touched her on the shoulder.

Alexandra shoved the housekeeper inside the wardrobe and latched it. "Forgive me." Retrieving her diary, she scurried from the room and down the wide staircase. She tiptoed to the back door and opened it just a crack. A big hulk of a man walked past. She stole down the entrance hall to the main doorway. Peering through one of the side lights, she found another guard stationed there.

She ran into the parlor, grabbed a silver candlestick from the tea table, and rushed back out to the hall. She opened the front door a tiny bit, then situated herself at the foot of the stairs and concealed her weapon in the folds of her skirts.

"Ohhh." She glanced at the door. When her guard failed to appear, she tried again, a little louder. "Oh, I think it's broken."

The tall, blond guard entered the hall. His eyes narrowed at the sight of Alexandra lying on the floor.

"Please help me." She contorted her features into a grimace. "I've hurt my ankle."

Uncertainty flickered across his face. "Where's the housekeeper?"

"Upstairs. Ouch!" She fell back in a pretend swoon.

"Miss?" He leaned over her. "Are ya all right?"

Sickened by the odor of his unwashed body, Alexandra held her breath. She prayed for strength, knowing she mustn't miss. She would not get another chance.

She drew a slow, deep breath to calm her jittery nerves, lifted the candlestick, and clubbed his head.

He slumped over her, unconscious. She dropped the weapon, then pushed and prodded until the heavy man finally rolled off her lap. She ran out the front entrance without a backward glance and disappeared into the night.

Chapter Nine

Derek searched the darkened streets of Philadelphia, driven by frustration, fear, and guilt. He must find her. He *would* find her, even if he had to take every house in the city apart, brick by red brick.

The face of every woman he encountered became a beacon of hope all too soon dimmed as he desperately sought his Lexi.

His Lexi?

Derek stopped short, and a slow smile spread across his face.

Yes, *his* Lexi. He could no longer deny it. The woman had struck a chord deep within him.

He closed his eyes and summoned the image of her leaning against the ship's rail, her ebony tresses whipping about her sun-kissed cheeks, her eyes dancing with laughter and merriment.

He had known many women, but none had gained access to his heart. His heart, such as it was, had been encased in an impenetrable fortress of guilt and pain for fourteen years. He had allowed himself to believe he could marry someone he felt only affection for, someone suited to the role of a planter's wife.

Until Lexi.

He ached from the bleak emptiness created by her absence. How he missed her shy smiles, her warm embraces. Aye, even her saucy tongue.

The town bell tolled.

"Fire! Fire!"

"Grab your buckets!"

In the distance, a red glow illuminated the horizon. The crowd swept Derek toward Southwark, where he soon discovered the source of the blaze— several warehouses engulfed in flames. Thick smoke poured from the buildings.

Firemen pulled down burning timbers and parts of menacing walls. Black soot and ashes rained from the heavens. The townspeople quickly formed two lines. He could hear them yell instructions over the popping and crackling of the fire. Derek joined the men passing leather buckets of water and returning the emptied ones through the line of women.

He ignored the acrid smoke burning his eyes and stinging his nostrils. His entire concentration centered on receiving, emptying, and passing pail after pail of water. Finally, the last flame was extinguished, the last ember doused. He stretched against the knot in his back and glanced around the surrounding sea of unfamiliar smoke-blackened faces. Wet and weary, he turned to leave. A conversation behind him bade him stay.

"Wonder who owned those warehouses, Ben."

"One of 'em belongs to a merchant by the name of Taylor."

The first man pursed his lips in a low whistle. "Would that be Bartholomew Taylor?"

"Ya know 'im?"

Derek heard no more of their exchange. Bartholomew Taylor. Here in Philadelphia. Derek's fatigue vanished, replaced by the certainty his quest was nearing its end. If this man was indeed Bartholomew Taylor, he'd soon discover Charlotte's whereabouts.

He forced his way through the throng of interested onlookers. He needed a closer look at the warehouse. As soon as this Taylor fellow learned his profits had gone up in smoke, he would come see for himself.

Derek would be waiting.

A short while later, a coach pulled up in front of the charred building. Derek recognized the man entering the warehouse as the one who had claimed Alexandra in the woods several weeks past. Could *he* be Bartholomew Taylor? Had he made a habit of abducting females with dark hair and blue eyes?

While searching his memory for remembrances of Taylor's appearance fourteen years earlier, he covered the distance between them in several long strides. He grabbed Bartholomew by the front of his shirt and dragged him into a dark corner. "What have you done with them, Taylor?"

"Who?"

"Charlotte and Alexandra, you fool." With each word he uttered, Derek tightened his hold on the stranger's clothing.

"Don't know anyone named Charlotte." Bartholomew gasped for air and squinted into the darkness. "Who are you?"

"Tremaine. Derek Tremaine."

"Tremaine." The word came out as a strangled, choked sound. "You can't have her."

"'Tis not your decision to make." Derek slammed him into the one wall still standing. "Where are they?"

Bartholomew brought up his knee and caught Derek in the midsection. He doubled over and Bartholomew came at him. Derek blocked one blow with his left forearm and delivered an answering shot with his right fist. His opponent fell to the ground.

"Tell me what you've done with them." He closed his hands around his adversary's throat.

"Never!" Bartholomew grasped Derek's wrists. "Do something, Harold!"

Alerted by a sound behind him, Derek turned

his head and met the loose piece of timber being swung by the bull. Stars exploded before his eyes. He dropped to his knees and dragged Taylor down with him. Bartholomew shoved him aside. From the outer edge of consciousness, Derek listened to the two men talk.

"What'll we do with him?" Harold asked.

"Finish him off." Gasping and wheezing, Bartholomew stumbled toward his carriage.

Harold stood over Derek's still form and rolled him onto his back. Unable to move, Derek ignored the blood trickling from his mouth and braced himself for what was to follow. His thoughts alternated between silent pleas for Alexandra's and Charlotte's forgiveness and cursing Taylor's black soul to eternal damnation.

"He ain't breathin'," Harold said.

"Leave him."

"Who do ya think this Charlotte chit is?"

"Don't know. Don't care."

****

Alexandra stopped to catch her breath. Trembling from the cool air, she drew her arms around her body and studied the streets. She was unfamiliar with this part of the city. Which way led to the waterfront? To the *Wind Spirit*? To Derek?

Footsteps echoed nearby. A chill of foreboding slithered up her spine. She had heard tales about foolhardy young women out alone at night.

As the footsteps continued to advance, tremors of cold and alarm penetrated her bones. She summoned every ounce of courage she possessed, picked up her skirts, and ran. Her shoes clicked against the cobblestones. She ducked into an alley and slowed her breathing, lest he hear her.

Alexandra listened to the deafening silence with growing unease. The hair on the nape of her neck stood on end. She could feel his presence.

A hand shot out and grabbed her around her waist. She screamed in pure terror. Fleshy fingers covered her mouth.

"Settle down, missy. I ain't gonna hurt ya." Alexandra drove her heel against his shin and jabbed her elbow into his paunchy middle. He howled in pain and loosened his hold. She shoved him against a brick wall and fled down the dark alley.

She ran and ran, unmindful of the stares she received from the few people on the streets. Derek. She must find Derek. Her entire being focused on reaching his ship. Her feet carried her down Pine Street, past lavish homes.

Lexi.

Her footsteps slowed.

Come to me.

She turned around, searching. "Derek?"

I need you, Lexi.

Sudden, blinding fear welled within her. Fear for Derek. Her hand moved to her throat. Something had happened. She knew with unshakable, unexplainable certainty that he needed her.

"I'm coming, Derek!" Alexandra followed her heart. She knew it would lead her to him.

****

Derek pushed himself into an upright position and leaned against the wall. He gingerly touched the back of his head. His fingers discovered a bump the size of a goose egg oozing a warm, moist stickiness.

Blood.

He clenched his teeth and pulled himself to his feet. A sudden wave of dizziness washed over him. He had to find Alexandra and Charlotte, and when he did, Taylor would beg for mercy. A mercy Derek would not give. He swayed in the entrance of the warehouse. Several minutes passed before he realized someone was calling his name.

"Derek? Derek?"

He turned toward the voice. Damn, his head ached. Wincing, he peered into the darkness. Was he hallucinating? "Lexi?"

"Derek?" Within moments she reached his side.

He pulled her into his embrace, molding her against him, his injury forgotten. She felt so good. He cradled her face between his hands and pressed his lips to hers, feasting on her sweetness. She returned his kiss with equal fervor. He traced her delicate features with his fingertips to assure himself that, yes, she was real. Very, very real.

"Are you all right? Did he harm you?" He frowned at her brief shudder. "Lexi?"

She placed her finger on his mouth and gave him a watery smile. "Shhh. You're here. I'm here. I'm fine, but—" She tilted her head to one side. "You're not."

"'Tis nothing. How did you—"

"Move your hand. Let me see." She shook her head and clucked her tongue. "I must tend to this right away, but 'tis too dark here. Let me help you to your ship."

Derek shook his head and grimaced at the stab of pain. "It can wait."

"Your injury must be attended to or it shall become infected. Surely you know the dangers of infection, Captain Tremaine."

"Doesn't matter...tell me...what...happened." His words slurred. A maddening unsteadiness once again took hold of his legs. He opened his mouth to speak, then frowned in bewilderment. "Lexi?"

****

Alexandra struggled to cushion his descent to the hard ground. "Easy, Derek. Easy. Here, rest against this wall."

"No, I—"

"Sit still." She softened her voice. "At least until

the cobwebs clear." She worried her lower lip. An array of emotions warred within her. Her initial burst of joy at seeing him alive was now overshadowed by dismay that he had been hurt and indignation at his assailant, but she pushed these feelings aside. His wound needed attention.

Several moments passed, each seeming to last an hour. "Do you think you can walk now?"

"Aye."

Alexandra wasn't so sure. "Let's try one step at a time. Stand up. Slowly now. Don't rush."

With her assistance, Derek pulled himself up. She saw determination in his handsome, though pale, features. Perspiration beaded on his forehead. The muscles of his jaw tightened. She could only imagine the effort required to remain upright.

"Very good, Derek. Now, lean on me."

The two shuffled out of the warehouse. Alexandra refused to falter beneath his weight. "One foot, now the other. One foot, now the other. Just a little farther, Derek."

Concerned about his sluggish steps and labored breathing, she guided him down Front Street. When the *Wind Spirit* finally came into view, relief flowed through her.

"Capt'n? Miss Alexandra?"

Alexandra glanced up to see Travis Greyson race toward them.

"What happened, Capt'n?"

"Taylor," Derek mumbled.

"Help me get him to his cabin," Alexandra said. "His injuries must be tended to."

With Derek between them, Travis and Alexandra half-walked, half-dragged him up the gangway amidst a swarm of crew members.

"'Tis the capt'n!"

"What scurvy bilge rat dared t' lay a hand on 'im?"

"I say the slumgullion gets a taste of the cat-o-nine-tails, then hung from the yardarm!"

"Let the knave run the gauntlet!"

"Put 'im in irons!"

Alexandra inwardly echoed the sentiments of the loyal men. "Please step aside. We must get him to his cabin." She scanned the group before her. Her gaze rested on the cook. "Zeke, bring fresh water and bandages."

"Yes'm."

After he eased Derek onto the bed, Travis moved the sea chest next to Alexandra. Zeke entered with a basin of water and fresh linens and placed them on the sea chest. Max moved out from beneath Derek's chair and placed his head beside his master.

"Max!" Alexandra knelt beside the dog and gathered him into a gentle embrace. "I was so worried about you." He nuzzled her neck. She giggled.

She ran practiced hands over his furry body to assure herself of his well-being before shooing everyone from the cabin. She then removed her needle and thread from her valise. Seated beside Derek, she moistened a cloth and wiped away all traces of blood, thankful he slept. Her mouth twitched at the notion that should he be alert, he would most likely tell her how to proceed, step by step.

After she cleansed the wound she sighed, relieved it wasn't serious. She couldn't bear it if more harm befell him because of her. Because of Bartholomew. She knew Bartholomew was responsible for Derek's injuries.

I need him, she thought, as she stitched Derek's wound and covered it with a bandage.

I love him.

She sat up straight. Wonderment flooded through her.

103

I love him.

Her trembling fingers filtered through his dark hair.

"I love him." A pang of regret at her impulsive declaration stilled her tongue.

Could it really be love? Perhaps 'twas merely gratitude warming her each time she thought of him, making her eagerly anticipate any and all moments he might share with her. Mayhap she'd have reacted in this manner to anyone who saved her life.

Nay. 'Twas more than gratitude. Much more. How much more and what, though, she wasn't certain.

She rested her hand upon his back and drew strength from the steady rise and fall of every breath he took. She pondered the bond they shared, and the feeling she had known him all her life. What if he didn't feel the same way? Oh, she knew he cared about her well-being, and she sensed he was fond of her, but what if he felt responsible for her and nothing more?

Dark whispers of dread crept over her. Bartholomew had tried to destroy Derek because of her. She must leave the *Wind Spirit* as soon as she saw Derek recovered. She couldn't ask him to risk any more for her.

Derek groaned, reinforcing Alexandra's anxiety. He rolled onto his back and tried to sit up.

She placed her hands on his chest. "Lie still, Derek. 'Tis too soon."

He waved her away. "I'm not a babe." By the time he finally succeeded in propping himself up against his pillow, his face had turned a few shades paler. Beads of sweat appeared on his forehead.

"You must rest."

"I'm fine. It takes more than a blow to the head to keep me abed."

104

"Bartholomew did this to you, didn't he?"

"You have questions of your own to answer, Lexi."

"Me?"

"Where have you been?"

Alexandra frowned. "Why, I've been here, with you." She placed her hand on his forehead. Perhaps he had a touch of delirium.

Derek's hand closed around her wrist. "I well-nigh turned Philadelphia upside down this day looking for you."

Her heartbeat quickened. "I-I..."

"You were with Taylor."

She nodded. "How did you know?"

"I'm asking the questions. Did he abduct you from this vessel?"

"No."

"Did you leave of your own accord?"

She squirmed beneath his penetrating stare. "Yes."

Derek pulled her closer until the upper half of her body lay across his chest. "Even after all of our discussions, you deemed it necessary to take such a risk?"

She couldn't fathom his expression. Was it anger? Hurt? Disappointment? Perhaps all three? She moistened her lips with the tip of her tongue. "When Devan told me that Polly was hurt—"

"Who is Devan and who is Polly?" He tightened his arm around her. "Your disappearance took ten years from my life. Promise me you won't take such chances in the future. Promise me, Lexi."

"I promise." She listened to the steady rhythm of his heartbeat. Very much aware of how the day could have ended, she soaked up his warmth. A quiet serenity crept over her and lulled her into a drowsy state. Her eyelids lowered. Disturbing images soon displaced the tranquility.

Shadows. Apprehension.
Trepidation. Haunting spectres.
Bartholomew.

Alexandra's eyes snapped open. She smothered a gasp and glanced at Derek. Unwilling to awaken him, she eased out from beneath his arms and off the bed and tiptoed to the mullioned windows to gaze upon the rippling water. Mayhap she could find peace in the moon's reflection. She had escaped Bartholomew again, but for how long?

A light touch upon the small of her back startled her. A scream gathered force.

"Shhh." Derek slipped his arms about her waist and molded her against him. "'Tis me."

She leaned back against his chest and pulled his arms tight about her. She needed the warmth only he could give. He dropped a kiss upon the curve of her shoulder. It would be so easy to turn in his arms, to lose herself in his embrace, his touch, and let him banish the horrors of the day from her mind.

"We must talk, Lexi." His low voice rumbled deep within his chest.

She sighed and searched for the right words.

He spoke first. "I think you and I should be wed."

Chapter Ten

Alexandra's heart skipped one beat, then two, followed by a surge of elation. She turned to face Derek. "You wish to marry me?"

"'Twould be your best protection from Taylor. Once you're my wife, he cannot force you into marriage."

Her hopes deflated. Love had not prompted his offer of marriage. Disappointment, sharp and acute, sliced through her. She forced it to the back of her mind and told herself she should be grateful for his help. She balled her hands into fists until her fingernails bit into her palms. "You know about Bartholomew?"

"Aye." A muscle worked in his clenched jaw. "He's the one who laid claim to you in the forest."

His reminder of her flight of terror chilled her. Her chest constricted and her nails dug deeper. "H-how long have you known his name?"

"Since today." Derek placed his finger beneath her chin. "Your reasons for fleeing him and your involvement with this Polly you mentioned, I can only surmise. Until you trust me enough to share the truth. Either way, my offer stands."

His not-so-subtle chiding shamed her. "Polly opens her home to children with nowhere else to go. I've lived with her for as long as I can remember."

"And her connection to Taylor?"

"Her husband, Henry, is Bartholomew's brother."

"I see." Derek's gaze darkened. "Did a girl

107

named Charlotte ever live with you?"

Alexandra searched her memory, then frowned. "No, not that I recall."

Silence stretched between them. She considered his proposal. How could she bind him to her for life simply because of the ingrained sense of responsibility he sported? He deserved better.

He broke into her thoughts. "Is the notion of being my wife so repugnant?"

"Oh, no. I-I'm...surprised. You've never mentioned marriage before."

A strange shadow flickered behind his eyes and vanished. "Taylor doesn't seem to be easily swayed from his purpose. He will pursue you until he gets you, and that I cannot allow."

She arched her eyebrow. "What do you mean you can't allow it?"

"Taylor has already stolen one person from my life." He clenched his jaw and stared at a point in the distance. "I won't let him take another one."

She turned her troubled gaze upon the moonlit river and hugged her arms around her midsection. An eerie vision rose before her and shimmered in the dark depths of the Delaware:

A woman with lifeless eyes and an empty heart drifted through a cold, somber house. A pervasive sense of hopelessness permeated the many rooms. She wandered into the parlor and stopped before an aged, faded portrait. A man entered the room. Taking the woman by the arm, he pulled her up a wide staircase toward a darkened bedchamber where he pushed her onto the bed. She remained there, passive, her eyes vacant, as he removed her gown and lowered his body toward hers.

Alexandra choked back a gasp and willed away the horrific glimpse of her future. A bleak future of despair...if Bartholomew had his way.

Aware she was a pawn in a contest of wills

between Derek and Bartholomew, she faced Derek. "How soon can we be married?"

"On the morrow."

Tomorrow! "But what about the posting of the banns? And if Bartholomew finds out—"

"I'll take care of the legalities. By the time Taylor learns of it, the deed will be done and we'll be halfway home."

The deed will be done. He made it sound impersonal, businesslike. Yet she was the one benefiting, not him. He offered protection, thereby placing himself at even greater risk from Bartholomew.

"I will become your wife, but..."

"But?"

She hesitated. Her love for this man warmed her, but did she love him enough to set him free? One day he would find the woman destined to share his life, destined to unveil the love Alexandra knew existed within him.

She drew a deep breath and plunged forward. "I will marry you, but there is a condition."

A frown pleated his forehead. "A condition?"

"Yes."

"What sort of condition?"

Alexandra stiffened beneath the pain rending her heart in two. "It must be a marriage in name only."

Derek's indecipherable gaze settled upon her. "Why?"

Uncomfortable discussing matters of such an intimate nature, she tried to ignore the hot blush she knew colored her cheeks. "Well, er, once we reach Williamsburg and the danger from Bartholomew has passed, our marriage will be annulled, freeing you to pursue other...interests."

Her face flamed anew. As she pictured him in the arms of another woman, agony shot through her.

"Annulled. Free." A flicker of confusion replaced by a hard, icy gaze held her immobile long after he lowered his arms and stepped away from her. "As you wish." He left the cabin.

Alexandra remained near the mullioned window, bewildered by his reaction. She had thought he would be grateful, not angered by her stipulation. Had she made another error in judgment? Perhaps she should have revealed her motives for agreeing to wed him and hoped he would understand her need to travel to Williamsburg.

A wet tongue flicked across her fingertips. She knelt beside Max and stroked his thick, dark fur. "What will happen when I tell Derek about my parents? Will he help or hinder my search?"

The Newfoundland tilted his head and cocked his ears. He regarded her with soulful brown eyes.

She sighed and lowered her shoulders in dejection. "You're a dog. What do you know?"

****

Derek paced the narrow confines of Travis's cabin. "One would think the chit would be grateful for my offer of marriage, but no, she had to set forth conditions."

"M-marriage?" Dr. Sebastian glanced up from his seated position.

"Aye."

"And J-Jillian?"

"She deserves better. She deserves a man who can love her as a husband should. I am not him."

"Wh-why...A-Ally?"

"To protect her from Taylor." Derek shook his head. "Not only did he steal Charlotte from her family, but he is now trying to force Lexi to wed him. I can't allow it."

"Wh-why?"

"Because—" Derek refused to acknowledge any tender feelings he might harbor toward Alexandra.

"Because I saved her life and I won't allow her to squander it on the likes of him."

"I s-see," the older man said.

"Wish I understood her reasoning, but I've yet to understand much about her. I've witnessed her nightmares, nightmares she never seems to remember nor wishes to face. She evades my questions and withdraws from me at every mention of her past." He ran his fingers through his hair in frustration. "Why this condition? No woman is ever willing to give a man his freedom."

"Hmm."

"The unanswered mysteries will have to wait. I've a marriage to arrange. Have a good night's rest, Dr. Sebastian."

"W-wait." The doctor fumbled in his pocket and fished out a small object. "H-here." He offered it to Derek. "F-for...w-wedding."

Touched by the other man's generosity, Derek stared at the sapphire studded band of gold. "'Twas Daphne's?"

Dr. Sebastian's expression softened and he nodded.

"But it belonged to your wife."

The doctor set his chin. "I w-want her t-to h-have it."

"Very well. Alexandra will be honored."

His eyes misty and his face wreathed with a smile, the older man gave a nod of apparent contentment.

****

"Ally. Wake up, Ally."

Visions of nine-year-old Mandy drifted into Alexandra's dreams. How she missed her young friend who had always occupied a special place in her heart.

Gentle hands shook Alexandra. "Time to wake up, Ally. It's me...Amanda."

"Mandy's here. How nice." Alexandra yawned. "Mandy?" Her eyes snapped open. Small, dark-haired Amanda Rourke stood before her, beaming from ear to ear.

Alexandra scrambled to sit up and blinked against the morning light streaming through the windows. "It *is* you. Come here."

Amanda slipped into her happy, bone-crushing hug.

"I...can't...breathe, Ally."

Alexandra released her and patted the place beside her. "Sit with me."

The young girl took the offered seat and Alexandra engulfed her in another exuberant hug.

"Let me look at you." Alexandra stroked the child's cheek. She drank in the familiar features of her petite friend whose wavy hair had grown a shade darker. The smattering of freckles across her pixie nose had faded some, but her eyes remained the same—a warm chocolate brown that revealed her every thought and feeling.

Mandy's lower lip quivered.

Alexandra smoothed wisps of hair from the little girl's forehead. "What is it, sweet?"

Mandy threw herself against Alexandra. "I thought I would never see you again."

A pang of guilt stabbed Alexandra. "I'm sorry I had to leave without telling you good-bye." She pulled back and met Amanda's troubled expression. "How did you find me?"

The young girl's face lit up. "Mr. Tremaine brought us. For your wedding. He's quite nice and so handsome. May I come with you to Williamsburg?"

"Mandy, I think you've been misled."

"Why? Aren't you going to marry him?"

Derek stepped into the cabin and silenced Alexandra's next words. "Of course she is. It's been decided and arranged."

Alexandra and Amanda turned toward Derek. Alexandra rose from the bed and walked over to the window. She forced herself to study the Delaware River glistening in the bright morning sunlight.

Amanda frowned at Derek. "Aren't you going to marry Ally?"

"Yes, I am." Derek lowered himself to her level. "Do you remember Mr. Greyson?"

"Yes."

"He's waiting in the corridor to give you a tour of the *Wind Spirit*."

Amanda clasped her hands together. "Oh, Mr. Tremaine, do you mean it? I've always wanted to see the inside of a ship." She bounded off the bed and out of the cabin.

Alexandra averted her eyes. She hoped Derek hadn't caught her watching him. Her heartbeat quickened as he approached her.

"The minister will arrive within two hours to perform the ceremony."

A quiet thrill ribboned through her. Two hours. "You arranged it quickly." She studied her fingers, then peered sideways at him. "If you so desire, I will release you from our agreement. I realize it was decided upon in haste."

"Which agreement? The marriage or the annulment?"

"The marriage."

"I asked you to be my wife. I'll not go back on it."

Giddy with relief, she fought the silly urge to grin. "But—"

"No buts. Close your eyes."

"Why?"

Derek groaned. "Must you question everything I say? I have a surprise for you."

"A surprise?"

Derek shook his finger at her. "Close your eyes or I shall give your present to another beautiful bride-to-be."

Alexandra clamped her eyes shut. Her cheeks grew warm. He had called her beautiful. "All right. They're closed."

"Don't you dare look, Lexi." The door opened and shut, followed by a rustling sound.

Alexandra bit her lower lip. He knew her well. Perhaps too well.

"You may look now."

She opened her eyes. Her breath caught high in her throat. Derek held the most exquisite gown she had ever seen. Her hand hovered above the shimmering fabric before she pulled it away, hesitant to touch the ivory silk shot through with silver threads. Ivory silk ribbon bows held the lace stomacher in place. The skirt opened over a satin quilted petticoat. Lace ruffles trimmed the elbow-length sleeves.

Derek carefully placed the dress on the bed and turned toward her. "Do you like it?"

The shadows of uncertainty flickering in the depths of his gaze drew her. She rose on the tips of her toes and placed a shy kiss on his cheek. "'Tis glorious. I've never worn anything as fine as this, but you shouldn't have bought it. It must have cost a king's ransom. How did you get it so quickly? Does it belong to another woman?" She bit her lip, dismayed by the jealousy she heard in her voice.

Derek swept her up in his arms, his eyes now shuttered. "My wife shall have the best of everything. It isn't important how I obtained it."

A bittersweet smile curved her mouth. *All I need is you.* Touched by his gentleness, his thoughtfulness, she reached up to stroke his cheek. Her lips twitched and she stifled a giggle.

His eyebrow rose a notch. "Do I amuse you?"

She shook her head. "'Tis your face. It's prickly."

"'Tis your doing."

114

She drew back and blinked at him in surprise. "My doing?"

He pulled her closer and spoke in a husky voice. "I've searched for you, turned Philadelphia inside-out, confronted Taylor, and arranged our wedding. Shaving has been the last thing on my mind."

Ever aware of the heat from his body, she shifted her weight in his arms. "I've been much trouble for you."

"You doubt my ability to care for you? To keep you from harm?"

A knock on the cabin door interrupted her reply. "Enter," Derek called.

Polly Taylor came into the cabin. Her eyes widened at the sight of Alexandra in Derek's arms.

"Put me down."

With a broad grin, he did as she requested. She ran to the woman who had been like a mother to her and clutched her in a tearful embrace. "I can't believe you're here."

"Stand back and let me look at you, child."

"Polly, I'm no longer a child."

The older woman's soft green eyes misted. "That is true. Your ordeal of the past weeks would have tested the mettle of even the strongest man." Polly pulled her into her plump arms and stroked her dark hair. "When Old Betsy returned without you—" Her voice broke. "I nearly went out of my mind with worry."

Alexandra straightened and dabbed at her own eyes with the handkerchief offered by Derek. "Have you met Captain Tremaine?"

"Yes, and I'm much beholden to you, sir. Thank you for bringing us here. The news of your wedding surprised me, but I'm pleased nonetheless." She turned toward Alexandra. "We shall miss you, but knowing you're safe will make it easier to bear."

"Did Henry come with you?"

"I didn't tell him for fear he'd let something slip to that brother of his."

Derek walked past the two women. "I shall take my leave so you can prepare for the ceremony."

The door closed without a sound. A sudden chill shook Alexandra's slight frame and she hugged her arms around her midsection. Polly placed a hand upon her shoulder. Alexandra pasted on a smile.

The older woman's forehead creased in concern. "You aren't fooling me. What's worrying you? Is it the wedding?"

Alexandra lowered her eyes.

Polly bristled. "I'll not have you forced into a marriage with a man you do not love."

"I do love him, but—" She bit her lower lip and turned away.

"But what?"

"I don't think he returns my feelings."

"He's marrying you, isn't he?"

"Yes, but only to save me from Bartholomew. He feels responsible for me. He doesn't love me."

Polly scoffed. "Nonsense. If the man doesn't have feelings for you, what were you doing in his arms when I first arrived?"

Alexandra whirled to face her. "Polly!"

"Forgive my blunt words, but I'm sure his mother raised him to be a decent, honorable man. If he's taking you as his wife, it means something, even if he hasn't realized it himself. Now, I do believe we have a wedding to prepare for." With quick, efficient movements, Polly began unhooking the fasteners of Alexandra's gown.

Two hours later, Alexandra stared at her reflection in the small looking glass. Could that really be her? She lifted trembling fingers to her coifed hair. Her ebony tresses had been swept up. Two long curls cascaded over a bared shoulder.

Her glistening eyes seemed overly large in her

pale face. Polly had pinched her cheeks to give them color. Her lips had taken on a rosy hue from the nearly constant pressure of her teeth. Her gaze wandered over her gown. Her skin glowed beneath the caressing silky fabric. She turned this way, then that, trying to get a glimpse of herself in the looking glass.

Polly approached her with a string of pearls and began to arrange them in the younger woman's hair.

"You brought your pearls?"

"Yes. They're my gift to you."

"Oh, but Polly, I can't accept them. They belonged to your grandmother."

Polly smoothed back a stray, wispy curl. "You're the nearest thing to a daughter I shall ever have. I want you to have them."

Alexandra swallowed hard past the thick lump in her throat. "I'm so very honored by your precious gift."

"My only wish is that you be happy." Polly sniffed. "Your Derek is a fortunate man to have you as his bride."

If only he could truly be hers. Alexandra traced the quilted pattern of the satin petticoat.

The door opened, admitting Derek. "'Tis time. Are you ready?"

She gave a numb nod. A feeling of unreality took hold of her. She placed her hand upon Derek's arm and girded herself for the moment to come.

Chapter Eleven

Derek, clad in a coat and breeches of uncut black velvet and a richly embroidered waistcoat of corded silk, took Alexandra's breath away. His unpowdered hair queued in the back revealed the strong features of his now clean-shaven face.

"...let him now speak, or else hereafter forever hold his peace."

Pulled from her reverie, Alexandra blinked and tried to focus on the minister's words. "I require and charge you both, as ye will answer at the dreadful day of judgment when the secrets of all hearts shall be disclosed, that if either of you know any impediment, why ye may not be lawfully joined together in matrimony, ye do now confess it. For be ye assured, that if any persons are joined together otherwise than as God's Word doth allow, their marriage is not lawful."

Alexandra held her breath, certain Bartholomew had discovered their plans.

"Derek, wilt thou have this woman to be thy wedded wife, to live together after God's ordinance in the holy estate of matrimony? Wilt thou love her, comfort her, honor, and keep her in sickness and in health, and forsaking all others, keep thee only unto her, so long as ye both shall live?"

Her heart fluttered and she cast a sidelong glance at Derek.

He met her gaze. "I will."

"Alexandra, wilt thou have this man to be thy wedded husband, to live together after God's ordinances in the holy estate of matrimony? Wilt thou obey—"

Derek coughed.

Alexandra glanced in his direction and saw his mouth twitch at the corners. He doubted her ability to obey him as much as she did, but then when had she given him reason to think otherwise?

"...keep thee only unto him, so long as ye both shall live?"

She opened her mouth to respond, but nothing came out. *So long as ye both shall live.* She had made Derek agree to a marriage in name only. She peered up at him. His reassuring smile dissolved her trepidation. "I will."

"Who giveth this woman to be married to this man?"

Dr. Sebastian took a faltering step forward. "I-I do."

"Join your right hands."

Derek held her cold hand in his warmer one and repeated the minister's words. "I, Derek, take thee, Alexandra, to have and to hold from this day forward, for better or worse, for richer for poorer, in sickness and in health, to love and to cherish, 'til death us do part, according to God's holy ordinance, and thereto I plight thee my troth."

Held captive by the liquid warmth of his gaze, Alexandra echoed the same words to Derek. For one instant, she allowed herself to believe every word they spoke and dreamed of a life with the man she loved.

He placed a band of gold glistening with sapphires upon her finger. "With this ring I thee wed, and with all my worldly goods I thee endow, in the name of the Father, and of the Son, and of the Holy Ghost. Amen."

The minister droned on. Renewed doubt swept through Alexandra. What was she doing to Derek?

How could she have allowed him to proceed with this foolish notion? She should stop the ceremony now.

The minister joined their right hands. "Those whom God hath joined together let no man put asunder. Forasmuch as Derek and Alexandra have consented together in holy wedlock, and have witnessed the same before God and this company, and thereto have given and pledged their troth, each to the other, and have declared the same by giving and receiving a ring, and by joining hands, I pronounce that they are man and wife together, in the name of the Father, and of the Son, and of the Holy Ghost. Amen."

Derek lowered his head and captured her lips in a slow kiss. Aching from the sweet sensation wrought by his touch, she closed her eyes and leaned into him. The pressure from his hand at the small of her back sent tingles to the tips of her toes.

"Harrumph!"

From a distant place in her mind, Alexandra heard someone clear his throat. She ignored it and slid her hands up Derek's shirtfront.

"Pardon me." The clergyman tapped Derek's shoulder. "Might you continue this—" He coughed. "—later?"

Alexandra tried to push away from Derek, but he circled his arm about her waist. "Not so fast, Mrs. Tremaine," he murmured into her ear. "Your husband requires your presence."

Her husband.

The words sounded foreign to her mind. If only he could one day return her love without hesitation and truly be her husband.

Polly and the children gathered around them, but no one spoke until five-year-old Christopher stepped forward. "We missed you, Ally. Why did you leave us?"

Tears stung Alexandra's eyes, and her heart

lurched. She gathered the boy into her arms and smoothed his fine blond hair. "Oh, my precious, I didn't want to leave you, but sometimes adults have to make difficult decisions."

She leaned back and cupped the child's winsome face. "I love you. All of you. You're my family." Her gaze rose to meet Polly's, then rested on the seven children before her. "My heart nearly burst from the ache I felt when I had to go away."

At the touch upon her shoulder, she rose to her full height. "I must speak to my...my husband. Katie, Liam, please help Polly with the children." She smiled her gratitude at their nods and turned to face Derek.

"Are you all right?" His forehead creased with concern.

Her eyes filled again. She moved over to the ship's rail and stared down at the Delaware River. Derek draped an arm around her waist. She leaned against him and drew comfort from his warmth, his strength.

"I left them without considering how they might be affected. My selfishness disrupted their lives."

"You had to protect yourself. What do you think would have happened if you had remained in that house?"

An involuntary shudder shook Alexandra.

"Correct. You'd be wedded and bedded and living in the home he built for you, away from those children, provided you lived through the experience."

She gasped and whirled to face him. Stunned by his crude comment, by the harsh glimpse of another side of him, she struggled to regain her composure. "Don't you understand? How can I just sail away and leave them behind again? They need me and I need them."

Derek placed his finger beneath her chin and tilted her face. "Once we are settled in Williamsburg, they shall visit us. Enjoy your remaining time with them because we'll set sail as soon as we have the appropriate winds."

She frowned. "But what about the cargo you've been waiting for?"

The light in his eyes dimmed. "'Tis not yet within my grasp, but you are, and I intend to do all within my power to keep you from harm."

Before she could blink, Alexandra found herself in his arms. She stared at him in wide-eyed surprise. Her breath quickened. His mouth moved toward hers, teasing her, tempting her, before capturing her lips in a searing kiss. Dizzying pleasure spiraled through her. Would that it never had to end.

Derek set her firmly back on the ship's deck. "Forgive me, Lexi. I seem to have forgotten about your condition. Alas, if you can abide by it, then so shall I." He strode off toward his crew.

Alexandra touched her mouth with trembling fingers and followed him with her gaze, torn by his reminder of the terms of their marriage. Why did it have to hurt so much?

"Ally! Ally!" The children surrounded her once again. "Wanna see our presents?"

Alexandra smiled down at the children's eager faces. "You brought me presents?"

The afternoon passed quickly as the children showed her the sketches, samplers, and carvings they had made for her. Mandy never left her side.

Every so often, Alexandra glanced up to find Derek watching her. His sharp, hungry gaze and knowing grin burned through her. What had she done? She had signed her life into his hands without offering anything in return. She suddenly realized how precarious her position was. She couldn't stop Derek from taking his husbandly rights, if he chose to. But she had to.

For his sake.

****

Bartholomew Taylor settled back against the pillows with a sigh of self-satisfaction. His doubts about his manhood had been resolved. Alexandra hadn't intentionally harmed him or tried to cause permanent damage, he told himself.

His smirk faded.

Tremaine had taken Alexandra from him again and had much to answer for. This time he would not escape retribution.

The sultry redhead beside him trailed a lazy path down his chest.

"Be gone, woman."

Her bold fingers continued their quest. "But, Bartholomew. We've only just begun."

He caught her hands in a harsh grip. "Leave me." He ignored her pained squeal and hurled her to the floor. She grabbed her clothing and scurried from the room without a backward glance.

He rose from the bed and began to dress. A conversation between two doxies drifted through the open door.

"Won't have 'nother night as profitable as last night for a spell."

"What's so special 'bout last night?"

"Derek Tremaine, that handsome sea capt'n, is shippin' out this evening. His crew came here for one last bout of wenching."

The second woman sighed. "Wish I could've been here. They're a generous bunch, to be sure."

Bartholomew's arm froze midway into his sleeve. Burning rage simmered and bubbled. He flew from the room. The two scantily clad prostitutes shrank away from him.

He ran the entire distance to the waterfront. Her name reverberated through his mind. *Alexandra. Alexandra.* On and on he ran, oblivious to his surroundings. Sheer instinct led him through the streets. An old man stumbled into his path. Bartholomew shoved him out of his way.

Alexandra. Alexandra.

He couldn't escape the echo.

Crazed with fury and jealousy, he made his way to the waterfront. Ship upon ship lined the harbor. He grabbed the nearest sailor. "Which one's the *Wind Spirit?*"

"There."

Bartholomew raced to the indicated wharf. He could see her. Alexandra stood near the ship's rail, restrained by Tremaine.

"I'm coming, my dear!"

Then, to his horror, the sails of the *Wind Spirit* filled, and she took flight down the Delaware River.

No. This couldn't be happening. He was so close. The ship drifted farther and farther down the river, carrying his beloved away. He raised clenched fists into the night sky.

"Alexandra-a-a!"

****

"I'm coming, my dear!"

Alexandra recognized that voice. Her stomach knotted with dread. She clutched Derek's arm and forced herself to turn toward the waterfront. Bartholomew ran toward them.

"No," she moaned.

Keeping her firmly by his side, Derek commanded his crew to hoist the sails and raise the anchor. They hastened to carry out his orders and completed the preparations necessary to set sail in record time.

Alexandra held her breath. Would they leave before he caught up with them?

Bartholomew grew nearer.

She looked up at Derek. He pulled her closer. "Fear not, Lexi. I gave you my word. He'll not harm you."

A strong north wind blew up and filled the sails. Within minutes the *Wind Spirit* cleared the docks.

Joy born of relief welled inside her. She turned in Derek's arm and gave him a mighty hug. "We made it!"

He grinned down at her. "Did you truly doubt it?"

In answer, she wrapped her arms around his neck and kissed him long and hard. Her heart beat a staccato rhythm. Partly from the exhilaration of escaping Bartholomew. Mostly from being in Derek's arms.

His hands began a slow journey down her back and roamed along her curves. Their bodies melded together until she couldn't tell where he began and she ended.

"Alexandra-a-a!"

The harsh cry of despair chilled Alexandra to the bone. She removed herself from Derek's embrace and turned toward the receding Philadelphia waterfront. There stood Bartholomew, his fists raised. Her hand moved to her throat. She stepped back in retreat.

"It isn't over." Another step brought her against Derek. "It isn't over."

His hands came out to her. "No. And it probably won't be until one or the other of us is dead."

Cold. She was so cold.

Derek led her to their cabin. She followed, scarcely aware of her surroundings.

It was only a matter of time.

Derek splashed brandy into a mug and pressed it to her lips. She gulped it down. It burned a fiery path to her stomach. He found her bedgown and helped her into it. Her stiff, wooden movements hampered his progress. After tucking her into bed, he turned to leave.

"Stay with me," she said. "Please."

Without a word, he slid beneath the woolen blanket. Alexandra pulled his arm about her and nestled against him, soaking up his heat.

"Do you have faith in me, Lexi?" Derek's warm breath fanned against her ear.

"Yes."

"We'll soon reach Williamsburg. You *will* be safe. My family and I will see to it."

Family. If she located her family, how might they react? Would they accept her or reject her?

She listened to the comforting rhythm of Derek's heartbeat. If only the rest of the world would go away and leave them in peace. She longed to feel Derek's mouth upon hers again. She chastised herself for her selfishness and wondered if she would be able to release him from their wedding vows.

Could she face life without him?

Chapter Twelve

The dark, haunting shadows frightened the child. Whirling voices and a thick gray fog wrapped around her, confusing her thoughts, holding her captive.

She looked to her left. "Mama? Papa?" Her voice shook. Why didn't they answer her?

The misty fog parted. A tall man moved toward her parents. A tall, bad man. She sensed danger.

"Mama! Papa! Make him go away!"

No one listened to her.

The man lifted his arm and pointed something toward her parents. First her mother, then her father fell to the floor.

"No-o-o!"

The man turned toward her. Why, oh, why wouldn't her pony run? She must get away.

His hand fastened around her wrist.

****

"No, no, no! Don't touch me!"

Derek woke with a start. She was dreaming again. He gathered Alexandra into his arms. "Wake up, Lexi. 'Tis only a dream."

She pummeled his chest with her fists. "I don't want to go! I don't want to go! Mama-a-a..."

Derek held her close, rocking back and forth, riding out her heartrending sobs. "Shhh, Lexi. It's me, Derek. You're safe. I promise. Shhh, shhh."

Little by little the tremors quieted. Alexandra opened her eyes and gazed up at Derek. With trembling fingers, she traced the planes and angles of his face.

He closed his hand over hers. "That's it. Touch me. Know that I am real. I shan't harm you."

"Hold me, please. Never let me go." She wrapped her arms around his neck and pulled his head toward her. She brushed his lips with hers. "Make me forget."

Derek tightened his arms around the woman clinging to him. She pressed against him and ignited flames of desire with her tempting, teasing mouth.

He wanted her. She needed him.

In the morning she would regret it.

He forced himself to remove her arms from his neck. With greater reluctance, he broke off the kiss.

"No." She reached for him. "Don't leave me."

He cupped her chin with his hand and stroked her smooth cheek with his thumb. "We cannot do this."

She traced his mouth with her fingertips. "Yes, we can."

"No." But he wanted to.

"Why?" She opened his shirt and pressed her lips to his bare chest.

He took a deep breath and steeled himself against the heat spiraling in his belly. "We must stop, Lexi, or soon there will be no going back." Her fingers trailed a path down his taut stomach. He stifled a groan.

"I know what I'm doing."

"Nay, I think not. Have you forgotten the condition you placed on our marriage? 'Twas your insistence our marriage be in name only."

"You don't want me?" A frown marred her forehead.

"That isn't the point."

"Do you?"

"Aye, I do."

"Then cease your protests and kiss me."

"You'll regret this come morning."

"Fie on the morning. I need you this night. If you want me to beg, I will." Her fingers continued down his stomach and dropped to his thighs. "Please, Derek, make me yours." She leaned forward and held her mouth a scant, tantalizing quarter-inch from his. "Now."

Derek stared at her soft, beguiling mouth. Her breath fluttered against his lips in gentle puffs. Her lavender scent fanned his desire to fever-pitch intensity. "Are you sure, Lexi?"

"Mmm-hmm." Her hands slid up the full length of his torso, along his flat stomach, up past his broad, muscular chest, until they entwined around his neck. Her fingers delved in his hair.

Unable to resist her bewitching invitation a moment longer, he familiarized himself with her every curve. He began with her shoulders, skimmed down the soft fabric of her bedgown, and searched the dip of her tiny waist and the gentle flare of her hips.

Their lips met in a searing kiss. His hands resumed their charted course while he tasted of her sweetness.

Alexandra tugged on his shirt until it came free from his breeches. "I want to feel you, Derek."

****

He eased away from her just long enough to pull his shirt over his head and dispense with his breeches. Her breath caught at his overwhelming masculinity.

Derek untied the ribbon closure of her bedgown and exposed one shoulder. She pulled her arms from the full sleeves and shrugged free of the gown before returning her attention to the man beside her.

He caressed the undersides of her breasts. She gasped and arched into his hands, wanting... Wanting what?

He nuzzled the hollow of her throat, then blazed a fiery path to her breasts. He suckled a rosy nipple, driving her mad with need.

"I want to please you," she whispered. "Tell me what to do."

He cupped her face and kissed the tip of her nose. "You already please me." He threaded his fingers through her ebony locks.

Her hands wandered over his warm flesh and rested on his trim hips. She lifted her head from the pillow and placed kisses along his strong jaw line. Her nipples grazed the dark, crisp hair on his chest.

Derek groaned aloud.

Delighting in her power over him, she gave herself free rein and traversed the contours and planes of his magnificent body.

Then she found his arousal.

Her startled gaze flew up and met the raw desire burning in his brown-gold eyes, a desire almost frightening in its intensity.

With infinite patience, he guided her hand to him and closed it around the hard evidence of his need. She moved her hand in tentative, unsure strokes.

Derek caught her mouth in another drugging kiss and caressed her soft inner thighs, coaxing them apart. He explored her moist femininity.

"Oh, Derek. Please..." Her body trembled. A sudden wave of pleasure crashed over her and carried her to a higher level of sweet torment. Floating in a haze of exquisite sensation, she looked at the man above her cast in the silver glow of the moon.

Their eyes locked.

Derek eased her thighs farther apart. "This will hurt, Lexi, but never again. I'll be as gentle as I can."

She nodded. Her heart thudded against her ribs.

He slid his hands beneath her hips and lifted her. With one quick movement, he thrust through her maidenhead.

Tears sprang to her eyes at the force threatening to rip her asunder. "Help me, Derek!"

Derek absorbed her outcry with a kiss and remained motionless within her until her rigid body adjusted to him. Her breasts rose and fell with her rapid breathing. He pressed tender kisses to the corners of her mouth, to her eyelids, to her forehead. "The pain will subside, Lexi. I promise."

He moved within her, slowly at first. Soon pleasant warmth replaced the burning.

"Come with me, Lexi." He quickened his movements.

She clung to him, moved with him and gasped in sheer wonderment as she soared higher and higher. Heaven must be like this. She matched him thrust for thrust, mindless with ecstasy, until she reached the pinnacle.

Her body stiffened, and calling his name, she clutched his shoulders and plummeted over the edge. Down, down, down, she tumbled. Every nerve ending pulsed *I love him, I love him, I love him* until her descent slowed and she drifted back down to earth.

Derek rolled onto his side and took her with him, molding her against him, stroking her hair.

Neither of them spoke a word.

****

Alexandra opened her eyes and blinked against the early morning sunlight streaming through the window. Disoriented, she lifted her hand to shield her eyes, only to discover Derek's arm wrapped around her waist. She glanced beneath the blanket and gasped at her nakedness.

She frowned in confusion and moved ever so slightly. Her buttocks brushed against Derek's bare hip. She froze.

He pulled her flush against him. His hand caught the fullness of her right breast. "Morning, Lexi." He nuzzled her shoulder.

Alexandra wriggled out from beneath his embrace and yanked the blanket to her chin. "Don't you 'morning' me, Derek Tremaine." She hugged her arms around her middle. "I demand to know why we are in bed together. Without the barrier. Without clothes!"

Frowning, Derek slowly sat up and slipped on his breeches. "What do you remember about last night?"

Her cheeks burned at the sight of his bared chest. She averted her eyes. "N-nothing."

"Nothing?" He rose from the bed and stood over her.

She turned away, confused by her body's traitorous reaction to his nearness.

"What *is* the last thing you recall?"

"I-I remember seeing Bartholomew on the waterfront. Then you brought me here."

"Anything else?"

She shook her head, unable to reveal her dream about him. He would surely think her brazen then.

"You had another nightmare."

She shook her head in denial.

"Aye, you did. I was there, beside you, comforting you, just as I have during one nightmare after another since I pulled you from the river. Sooner or later, you'll have to come to terms with them."

"I-I don't want to talk about them. Why were we...were we...?"

"Unclothed and in each other's arms?"

She nodded, her face flaming with warmth.

"We consummated our wedding vows."

"You did what?"

He met her glare without flinching. "*We* did, not me."

"But you promised."

"Aye, I did, against my better judgment. At the time your safety came first."

"And once we set sail you conveniently tossed aside our agreement."

"No. You did."

"Me?" Her mouth dropped open at his temerity.

"You begged me to make you mine, to make you forget your nightmares."

"You lie! You're making this up."

Anger glinted in his gaze. He flipped back the blanket. "Your maiden's blood."

"No. It can't be true. It mustn't be true." She scrambled off the bed. She found her bedgown on the floor and yanked it over her head to shield her nakedness.

A startled look froze Derek's features. He walked over to her, lifted her gown, and looked at the back of her knee. His face pale, he finished dressing and walked past her to the door. "You must stop denying the unpleasantness in your life, whether it's your nightmares or something else."

He clenched his jaw, then directed a burning glare toward her. "Rest assured, Lexi, next time you will remember every detail of our lovemaking. *If* I decide there will be a next time."

Then he was gone.

Alexandra stared at the closed door, numbed by his revelation. She walked back to her bed in a daze and ran her fingers over the stained sheet.

Images flashed through her mind. She saw herself pressed against Derek. Kissing him, touching him, responding to him.

It had not been a dream.

She sat down hard on the edge of the bed. What had she done?

Their marriage could no longer be annulled. She had shackled Derek to her for the rest of his life.

She rose to her feet and paced the confines of the cabin. What had she been thinking last night? And this morning she had called him a liar. Small wonder he had stormed out.

What a fool she had been.

****

Derek leaned against the cabin door, shaken by his discovery. It couldn't be true, yet when Alexandra had reached for her bedgown he had seen with his own eyes the heart-shaped birthmark on the back of her knee.

The past fourteen years fell away, hurtling him back to the day after Charlotte's fifth birthday. It had begun as many others had with his young neighbor dogging his every step.

"Please take me riding. Please," Charlotte *begged.*

"Not today." Derek had waited all week to go fishing, and he wasn't about to take her. She'd nearly drowned them both last time.

Tears pooled in her large blue eyes. She sniffed. "Mama says I can't go if you won't take me."

Why did her mama always say that? He knew full well his mother would concur with her mother.

"All right." He relented. "But you better stay close to me lest a bear decides to make a meal out of you."

She wrinkled her nose, then grinned at him. They walked to the stables and saddled a horse for her. Not five minutes into the woods the little imp raced away. "Help me, Derek! Help me!"

Her excited giggles spilled through the air. He knew she expected him to rescue her, expected him to play her favorite game.

This time he would not.

To teach her a lesson, he waited for her to come back. Five minutes crept by, then ten. His irritation and impatience grew. This was the last time he was taking her along.

No matter what their mothers said.

Gunshots splintered the air. From the Montgomery place.

Charlotte screamed.

He spurred his horse. His heart pounded. His mind reeled with thoughts of Charlotte in a pool of blood.

Through the woods he raced, finally reaching the edge of her family's plantation. How could she have gone so far? He pulled back on the reins and stopped cold. Mr. and Mrs. Montgomery lay on the ground. He had never seen so much blood.

Charlotte was bent over her parents' still forms, crying. A man grabbed her and forced her onto his horse.

"No!" Panic squeezed Derek's insides. They were so far away. He couldn't see the man's face. Who would do such a thing?

"Mama-a-a." Charlotte's wail pierced the air as the man rode away with her. "Help me, Derek! Save me!"

Her terror lanced through him. His stomach clenched. His fault, his mind accused. Should've played her stupid game. His responsibility.

His horse stumbled and pitched Derek onto the hard ground. He scrambled to his feet, raced toward the stables, and grabbed a fresh mount.

He couldn't see Charlotte. His throat tight, he searched the ground for clues, knowing they were already too far ahead.

Desperation clawed at him. He had to find her. He mustn't fail.

He had ridden south, beginning what had proven to be a futile search.

A search that had now ended.

He found it difficult to accept Alexandra as

Charlotte. She wasn't the little girl he had somehow expected to find.

But she had black hair and blue eyes.

She had the Whittaker birthmark.

She had horrible nightmares about a frightening event.

And she was fleeing from Taylor.

He reached into his pocket and withdrew the broken necklace he had kept with him since her disappearance. Perhaps it could tell him something. He turned the well-crafted cameo over and read the inscription on the back, the sentiment expressed by Jared Montgomery to his wife.

Derek opened the locket and stared at the pixie face of the child for whom he had spent many a year searching. The painted miniature dispelled his remaining doubts, but how could he prove that Alexandra and Charlotte were one and the same?

Dr. Sebastian! He must have been referring to Alexandra when he wrote the letter stating he had found Charlotte.

Derek hurried to the next cabin and entered without knocking. Dr. Sebastian was sitting in a chair. Beside him stood Obadiah. "You're needed above deck," Derek said to the cabin boy. He waited for the door to close, then asked Dr. Sebastian, "Do you believe Alexandra is Charlotte?"

The older man nodded his head.

"Why?"

"Sh-she l-looks l-like...L-Laurel used to," he stammered while pushing up his shirtsleeve to reveal a birthmark matching the one on Alexandra's leg.

"Why didn't you tell me?"

"I t-tried to."

"'Tis unbelievable." Derek paced the narrow expanse of the room. "All this time she has been right under my nose."

He had found her. An insane longing to gather her in his arms and smother her with kisses of sheer relief, sheer joy, surged through him.

He stopped dead in his tracks. "How am I going to tell her?"

****

Her somber gaze rested upon the wedding gown draped over Derek's chair. Alexandra picked it up and held it in front of her. Her fingers smoothed the ivory satin overskirt while her mind wandered back to the vows they had exchanged.

The cabin door opened, admitting Derek and Max. A guilty flush warmed her cheeks. The Newfoundland batted a rounded bone across the floor until it came to a rest under Derek's chair.

"Derek—"

"Lexi—"

Derek covered the distance between them. "Earlier my temper overruled my brain. I should have found a better way to discuss last night with you."

"You're not at fault. I am. I do remember parts of last night." She glanced away and lowered her voice. "I thought it was a dream."

He placed a finger under her chin and searched her eyes. "Any regrets?"

She moistened her lips with the tip of her tongue. "I've ruined your chance for an annulment."

"I didn't ask for an annulment."

"You entered into this marriage to protect me. You should no longer be bound to me once this trouble with Bartholomew is over."

He brushed ebony wisps from her face. "Do *you* want the annulment?"

She shook her head, confused. "I want what is best for you."

"Taylor or no Taylor, I want you for my wife."

She stared at him in astonishment. A thrill of

delight ran through her. "You do?"

"I feel a certain fondness for you and I find your company pleasurable. Successful marriages have been built on less."

Alexandra's delight died a sudden death. Her heart shattered into a million little pieces. She forced herself to breathe.

"I see." Though she didn't see at all. "A successful marriage. What about children?"

His eyes glinted with a flash of pain. "The last thing this marriage needs is children."

Alexandra reeled back as though he had struck her. "No children?"

"'Tisn't possible for me at this time."

She frowned. "Do you mean physically, because we have been...intimate."

"'Twas only once, and in the future, I will take precautions to prevent conception."

"But how do you know—"

"Please sit down. There is something else we must discuss."

His serious expression frightened her. "What is it?"

"Grrrr."

****

Derek looked down at the dog's growl. He had somehow squeezed his bulk beneath Derek's chair but now appeared to be stuck, despite his efforts to free himself.

"Max, stop!" Alexandra dropped down to the floor and tried to pull him out from under the chair.

"Lexi, what are you doing?"

"Be still, Max." Panic edged Alexandra's voice.

R-r-rip-p-p. The fabric pulled free, spilling papers and documents to the floor. Alexandra scrambled to pick them up.

Derek knelt beside her. "Let me help you."

"No! I can do it."

He frowned at her, puzzled by her sharp tone. A letter with familiar handwriting caught his attention. He plucked it from the pile and opened it:

22 September 1738

Dearest Polly,

It has been six heartbreaking months since Charlotte was taken from the Montgomery family. There has been no news since I wrote you last.

I fear for Laurel and for the babe she carries. She does not eat. She does not sleep. She just sits in her rocking chair, clutching Charlotte's doll to her chest.

What sort of monster separates a child from her mama? Why did Bartholomew Taylor avenge himself in this manner?

My son continues to search for Charlotte. For reasons known only to him, he has taken it upon himself to find her. I pray he is successful so we might all find a bit of peace.

Your letters have been few and far between. I hope all is well with you and the wee ones. Take care, Polly.

Your everlasting friend,

Elizabeth Tremaine

Chapter Thirteen

Alexandra stood several feet away, clutching the papers she had retrieved, and watched Derek read the letter a second time.

He glanced up. "How did a letter written by my mother fourteen years ago find its way aboard my vessel, into my cabin, and under my chair?"

Anger sparked within his eyes. "Have you been less than honest with me concerning your relationship with Bartholomew? Where did these come from and why did you find it necessary to conceal them?" With each question, his ire seemed to grow and drive him forward.

Alexandra lifted her chin and met his gaze without retreating or flinching. "I took them from Bartholomew's office."

"Have you been playing me for a fool? Are you in league with Taylor?"

Crack! The sound of Alexandra's palm against Derek's cheek resounded throughout the cabin.

She rose on the tips of her toes and punctuated each statement with a sharp poke to his chest. "You dare to make such accusations to me? After all I have endured because of him?"

Derek held his hand to his cheek. "What conclusions would you reach if you read a letter from your mother to Polly filled with references about Taylor?"

Alexandra clutched his chair for support. "You have a letter from my mother?" The possible implications of his answer stayed her breathing.

Tension mounted within her as she awaited his answer.

"No. I have a letter from *my* mother. What were you doing with it?"

The remaining hint of suspicion in his eyes sharpened her anxiety. The time to tell him the truth had come. She took a deep breath and tried to keep her voice steady. "I overheard a conversation between Bartholomew and his brother during which Henry asked Bartholomew if he had stolen me from my parents, but Bartholomew wouldn't answer him. He talked instead of our upcoming marriage and how it wouldn't be stopped a second time. I didn't understand what he was talking about, but when he stopped me on the staircase and made his plans for me painfully clear, I fled that evening."

"What do these papers have to do with Taylor?"

"After Bartholomew refused to answer my questions about my parents, I hoped to find something in his office."

Derek lifted his eyebrow.

"I found these documents listing names, dates, places, and profits of what appeared to be illegal activities. I didn't have time to read through them, so I gathered them up and planned to turn them over to the appropriate authorities. Then the locket fell out of the papers."

Derek reached into his pocket. He took her hand in his and placed the locket in her open palm.

A curious mixture of hope and anxiety enveloped her, warming and chilling her at the same time. "Where did you find it?" She lowered herself into his chair.

"At the site of your abduction, beside Max. But I have not yet repaired the broken chain."

She traced its delicate pearl border and tried to resist the disquieting pull of uneasiness the slight motion roused. "Why didn't you give it to me before now?"

"I've seen the effect this necklace has on you. Considering the events of the past days, I planned to wait a while before returning it."

"But I need it to find my parents." She opened the locket and pointed to the painted miniature. "This is me. Once we arrive in Williamsburg I can begin my search for the Laurel and Jared mentioned in the inscription." She turned the piece of jewelry over. "See this? They must be my parents." Her voice trailed off. "They have to be."

"Lexi. 'Tis time I told you the reason I went to Philadelphia."

Alexandra's stomach fluttered at his serious tone. She nodded and waited for him to begin.

"I came in search of a young woman named Charlotte Montgomery who was stolen from her parents when she was but a child." Derek paused. "Several weeks ago I received word that she could be found in Philadelphia."

She heard the hesitation in his voice. "Did you find her?"

"Aye." He took her right hand between his and stroked her fingers with his thumb while holding her gaze. "I believe *you* are Charlotte."

The silence weighted the air Alexandra tried to draw into her lungs. "Are you daft?" She squeezed her left hand around the locket, but frightened by the apprehension it stirred within her, she dropped it into her lap. She pulled her other hand free from Derek and twisted the suddenly heavy ring upon her finger. An inner peace calmed her. "'Tis impossible. My name isn't Charlotte."

The expression on his face halted further denial. He believed his words to be true. She trembled from the realization that her future hinged upon his belief. "And your theory is based on what?"

"I saw your birthmark."

Her hand moved to her knee. "Many people have birthmarks."

"Aye, but yours is distinctive. And it matches your grandfather's." A frown pleated his brow. "What is your surname?"

He had indeed gone daft. "You know my name."

"Nay, only your first name."

"'Tis Whittaker."

He pursed his lips and nodded. "As I suspected."

"Then why, pray tell, did you ask?"

"Laurel's maiden name is Whittaker. The man responsible for your disappearance was obsessed with your mother many years ago. 'Tis my understanding he wanted to marry her, but she refused. A matter he did not take lightly."

Alexandra's heart thudded. Fearing she already knew the answer, she forced the question past her lips. "Wh-who is this man?"

"Bartholomew Taylor."

She hugged her arms around her midriff and rocked to and fro. Would she ever be warm again?

Derek pulled her close. She burrowed deep against his broad chest and pushed away the confusion, the despair, the uncertainty. Instead, she listened to the steady beat of his heart and drew comfort from his quiet strength.

When she was once again warm and calm, she tried to absorb this newfound knowledge. Questions tumbled through her thoughts. "What are my parents like? Do I have brothers or sisters? Do you think they will like me? Why did my parents let Bartholomew take me? What if they don't want me back?"

The rumble of Derek's laughter flooded the room, reverberating about and within her.

She stiffened and pushed away. "You dare to laugh at me? I find nothing humorous about this situation."

"I'm not laughing at you, Lexi, but I can answer only one inquiry at a time."

Still a little miffed, she studied his face for sincerity. "Very well. But I'm giving you fair warning. If you make sport of me again, I'll tell Max to attack you."

The Newfoundland looked up from his place of repose, then moved from his favorite corner and placed his head on her lap. She scratched the dog between the ears and placed a silent challenge at Derek's feet.

"I'm quaking. What would you like to know first?"

"What are my parents like?"

"Your father, Jared Montgomery, runs a successful tobacco plantation near Williamsburg. He also commands the local militia and is a member of the House of Burgesses."

"And my mother?"

"She's beautiful. Kind. Devoted to her family." Derek touched a long curl that had fallen over her shoulder. "I've been told you bear a striking resemblance to her as a young woman."

The portrait above Bartholomew's fireplace flashed through Alexandra's mind. It was her mother.

She suppressed a shiver and forced Bartholomew from her thoughts. "Do I have brothers or sisters?"

"One of each. Jillian is seventeen and Marc is fourteen."

Alexandra searched her memory for bits and snatches, anything of her family, but found nothing. "Did my parents search for me?"

"Of course they did. They were heartbroken when you were taken." He showed her the letter written by his mother. "Bartholomew must have intercepted it somehow. Your mother and father began their search for you as soon as they were able. You must remember they were both injured."

"But I don't remember!" Alexandra's head began to ache and the smothering panic resurfaced. She rose from the chair and massaged her temples. "Please go. I no longer wish to think about this."

Derek picked up the locket which had fallen from her lap and turned her toward him. "You must face what happened all those years ago. Let me help you."

Every time she had allowed herself to wonder about her parents panic had set in. After a time, she had forced herself not to think, not to wonder. "I'm afraid."

He closed his arms around her. "I'll be with you."

Alexandra tried to focus on Derek's embrace. The gentle strength of his arms. The steadiness of his breathing. His soothing words and touch. But a disturbing question wriggled into her thoughts.

"How long have you known I'm Charlotte?" The name felt strange upon her tongue. "Why didn't you tell me earlier? Before we were wed?"

"The letter I received stated you had no memories of your first five years. I've been by your side several times while you relived the nightmare of your abduction, though you choose not to remember them. Look at how you reacted a moment ago."

"How long have you known?"

"Since this morning when you reached for your bedgown. 'Twas then I saw your birthmark."

She clenched and unclenched her hands. "Who wrote the letter that brought you here?"

"Your grandfather."

"When will I meet him?"

"You already have."

Alexandra stiffened and mentally reviewed the few men she knew. "Who is he?"

"M-me."

At the familiar voice, she whirled toward the cabin door in disbelief. "Dr. Sebastian?" She glanced between the two men.

Aided by his cane, the older man shuffled toward her. "'T-tis...t-true."

She stared at him and choked back the scream of frustration gathering force. Still reeling from the impact of the day's revelations, she turned her confused gaze to Derek.

He placed a gentle hand upon her shoulder. "He's Dr. Sebastian Whittaker. Your mother's father."

She shrugged away from his touch. A shudder of sadness rippled through her and threatened to swallow her whole. She looked at Dr. Sebastian. "You knew my last name is Whittaker. Why didn't you tell me who you are, who I am?"

"C-couldn't. N-no m-memory...b-best for y-you."

"How could it have the best for me?"

"Would you have believed him?" Derek's low murmur drifted over her shoulder.

She hugged her arms around her midriff and hardened her heart against the velvet softness of his voice. That very softness worked its way through her defenses and left her empty and bereft. She summoned anger to fill the hollowness, but it refused to come. "I want to be alone."

"Lexi—" Derek began.

"Either you leave or I will."

Dr. Sebastian placed a hand on Derek's shoulder.

"T-time...g-give her t-time."

Irritation evident in his every movement, Derek left the room. Alexandra wanted to grind her own teeth. What reason did he have to be angry? She was the one who had been deceived. Her whole world had been upended. Everything had grown more confusing, more complicated.

Dr. Sebastian closed the door behind them. Max lapped at her fingertips. She sank down beside the Newfoundland and stroked his dark, soft fur. "You would never lie to me, would you?"

He gave a short bark and licked her face.

****

2 November 1752

The past few days have crept by at a veritable snail's pace. Derek and I exist side by side, but it is the existence of strangers.

Polite strangers.

At night we lie back to back, separated by a now invisible, yet very real, barrier. I ache with the need to touch him, to overcome this estrangement between us, to be a true wife to him. But I cannot.

For his sake.

I must find a way to protect him from Bartholomew, for I know he is out there, waiting. I couldn't bear it if anything happened to my beloved.

Derek spends the largest portion of his time above deck, navigating our journey to Williamsburg. Mr. Greyson informed me we should reach the Chesapeake Bay on the morrow. This depends on the north wind, which has been undependable of late, thus delaying our progress.

I must confess to feelings of great trepidation about meeting my parents, my family. My greatest fear is that Bartholomew shall attempt to harm them again. He must be stopped.

****

A deep shuddering followed by a ghastly wail woke Alexandra from an uneasy sleep. She bolted upright and turned to Derek's side of the bed.

Empty.

The cabin pitched and rolled, flinging her to the hard floor. She gripped the sheets and pulled herself up. Again the ship lurched and upset her footing.

Derek's sea chest shifted and slammed against her. Pain exploded inside her shoulder and shot down her arm. She bit her lip against the stinging, throbbing nettles beneath her skin.

She had to find Derek. She had to make sure he was all right. He would not be caught up in the midst of this raging storm if not for her.

When she finally made it onto the wet main deck, her feet slipped on the slick surface. She dropped to her knees. With grim determination, she picked herself back up.

Lightning split the sky, followed by a resounding crash of thunder. Alexandra's muffled scream blew away with the wind.

Cold rain beat down upon her, plastering her bedgown against her slender form. Her long wet hair whipped around her face, temporarily blinding her. She lost her footing. The rolling of the ship bade her stay as she was. Bolts of lightning illuminated the deck. Alexandra scanned the area. Where could Derek be? Thunder boomed overhead while below deck the cargo thumped and banged against the sides of the ship.

Winds shrieked in the shrouds. Cables screeched in the pulley and tackles. Frightened by the chaos, she covered her ears and glanced up the masts in time to see a man scramble along the footropes and try to cut a sail free.

Suddenly, he was dangling in mid-air, holding on with one hand. Below him the sea swelled and raged. Waves slapped the bobbing vessel.

Scarcely breathing, Alexandra watched the man suspended between life and certain death. How long could he hang on? Could the others help him before he plunged into the foaming sea?

Another round of lightning set the dark, stormy sky ablaze. Alexandra gasped aloud.

It was Derek!

Chapter Fourteen

Alexandra's heart lodged in her throat. She held her breath, terrified by the sight of Derek being tossed about as though he were no more than a scrap of paper. Her thoughts turned to her first glimpse of the striking sea captain, the perfect rescuer she remembered thinking, never realizing how much he would come to mean to her.

More memories washed over her—the tale of the sleeping beauty, their first kiss, their wedding. A darker image pressed forward, that of Derek scarcely able to stand in the charred remains of the warehouse. He would not be facing this danger if not for her, if not for Bartholomew. If he lost his grip...

Suddenly, the tension of the past days seemed so petty, so minor. He had explained his reasons for concealing her identity from her. She should have accepted them. If he wanted a marriage not based on love, she could learn to accept that also. Couldn't she? Now it might be too late.

Nudged none too gently by the wind, Derek grabbed hold of the footropes and made his way down. The moment his feet touched the planked deck, she launched herself toward him. His arms closed around her shivering form for but a moment before he moved his hand to her shoulders and held her away from him. She started to object, but the fury on his face stopped her.

His lips moved, but the howling wind prevented his words from reaching her. She shook her head, trying to signal her inability to hear him.

The next moment, Alexandra found herself yanked along the deck by Derek. His bruising grip brought words of protest to her lips. Unheard, mayhap unheeded, words. It was either keep up or be dragged.

She resented his beastly manner and tried to dig in her heels. He turned, his eyes alight with anger, and tossed her over his shoulders. He did not slow his pace until they reached the cabin.

He kicked the door shut behind them and dropped her to her feet. "What the hell were you doing out there, on a slick deck in the midst of a raging storm? Haven't you the sense God gave a goose?"

Alexandra bristled. "A goose! You dare compare me to a goose?"

"If the slipper fits."

"I am not wearing slippers and I will *not* tolerate such abuse from the likes of you. To think I have spent these weeks fleeing marriage to one ogre, only to wed another."

A flash of lightning revealed the muscle working furiously in his jaw. "Are you comparing me to Taylor?" His growl bounced off the cabin's walls, matching the fury of the storm.

"If the boot fits."

The ship lurched and Alexandra fell against Derek with a sharp cry. She tried to shrug away from him, but his hands held her fast, though no longer harshly. She resisted the need to melt against him and glanced up, cautious about his abrupt change.

She trembled. Whether from her cold, clammy bedgown or from his touch, she knew not. She cared not. A warming glow in her middle radiated outward.

Derek caressed the length of her back. His fingers skimmed along her sides until they reached the curve of her shoulders. He cradled her face with an aching tenderness, then brushed her lips with his, teasing, promising.

He lifted a handful of her wet, curling tresses and nuzzled his way along the silken line of her throat. Alexandra tilted her head to one side. His breath fanned against her ear. Her knees grew weak. She clutched his sodden shirtfront, lest she dissolve into a puddle at his feet.

As though he sensed her unsteadiness, Derek lifted her from the floor and molded her against him. Her hands slid up his well-muscled chest and entwined around his neck. Tiny thrills shot through her. Her fingers delved into the thick softness of his dark hair, and she gloried in the feel of him.

Derek took her lips in a full, thorough, exploring kiss. Their breath mingled.

A volley of thunder rumbled across the sky. The walls of the cabin trembled in response. Derek and Alexandra jumped apart.

"I'm needed above deck." He gripped her by the shoulders and gave her a slight shake. "Stay in this cabin. If you defy me on this, I shall take a switch to your backside. And for heaven's sake, put on something dry. You'll catch your death and these past weeks will have been for naught. Come, Max."

Then he was gone.

Alexandra rubbed her hand against the shoulder bruised by Derek's sea chest and stared at the closed door in bewilderment. What had happened to stir his anger again?

Another ear-piercing thunderclap combined with shrieking winds rent the air. She nearly jumped out of her skin. Immediate chattering and shivering set in.

"Oh, bother. H-how 'm I s'posed t-to find my v-valise in the d-dark?" Common sense warned her of the perils of lighting a lamp in these conditions.

The ship rolled and pitched again. "D-drat it all."

Alexandra clamped her jaws together before every tooth shook loose. She peeled off her sodden bedgown with trembling fingers and slid beneath the blankets.

The numbing cold had seeped into the marrow of her bones. She clutched the covers tighter. Would she ever be warm again? How long would the storm rage? Through the mullioned window, fingers of lightning stretched from the cloud-laden skies to the seas. She tried to forget she was on a wooden vessel sailing in an angry ocean. She tried instead to conjure more pleasant musings.

A startling thought occurred to her. She frowned. Nay, it was too horrible to consider. Yet it continued to niggle at her. If the storm spared the ship and its inhabitants, might they be blown off course and her reunion with her parents delayed?

Perhaps that would not be so bad. Alexandra twisted her wedding ring around her finger. Soothing warmth enveloped her and eased her anxiety. She felt a comforting presence beside her, but when she peered around the cabin she saw nothing. Quiet certitude that they would survive this storm crept through her.

But would *she* survive Williamsburg?

Would her family welcome her? It had been such a long time, and coupled with her lack of memory, it seemed too much to ask.

Thoughts about Derek's family brought new worries. He had left on a mission spurred by friendship toward her family and by a youth's misguided sense of responsibility, and now returned to them with a wife.

She had heard several of the crew discussing Derek's romantic encounters. To hear the men tell it, women fell at his feet. Alexandra grimly added herself to that list. A short while ago she herself had craved his touch, but in the space of a heartbeat he had withdrawn from her and placed distance between them.

Would she ever understand him?

Would he ever love her?

****

The storm abated. The winds had died down. The sea had calmed. Thunder rumbled in the distance.

Now in the hours preceding dawn, Derek surveyed the *Wind Spirit*, pleased to note surprisingly light damages. A few sails and ropes required mending and the deck needed to be swept clean of debris. Down below, the cargo would no doubt need to be re-secured.

All in all they had fared well. Even the winds had not blown them too far off course. He still expected to reach Williamsburg on the morrow, or rather, later this day.

He motioned to Travis, who hastened over. "Put the crew on half watches for the time being. Notify me once we reach the York River."

"Aye, Capt'n."

Derek turned and trudged toward his cabin. Every bone in his body ached. He rubbed a rueful hand over his brow and recalled the moment the night before when he had hung upside down over the churning, black seas and stared death in the face. Then Alexandra's image had appeared beneath the surface of the water and he had redoubled his efforts to save himself.

When she had hurtled into his arms he had clasped her against him, grateful for the opportunity to hold her once again. At the same moment he had realized how easily she could have been swept overboard, and he gave free rein to his anger, infuriated that she had endangered herself.

Now he was on his way back to his cabin. To face Lexi. He shouldn't have left her on such a harsh note. Truth be told, his irritation had been directed toward himself. His desire for her had erased the storm and his vessel from his mind. The lives of his crew and the *Wind Spirit* had been at risk, while he had indulged his need to hold Lexi in his arms.

He eased the door to his cabin open. Unwilling to disturb her if she slept, he crossed the room on tiptoe and sat on his side of the bed. His boots hit the floor with a dull thud. He shrugged out of his clothes and slipped beneath the bedcovers. He faced Alexandra, his head propped up on one hand.

She had drawn the blankets up to her chin. Her ebony hair shimmered in the silvery moonlight streaming through the window. He stroked the luxuriant length of her wavy tresses. So soft. So silky. The thick curls imprisoned his fingers. He lifted them to his cheek.

His gaze wandered over her still form and followed the curves and contours of her body beneath her woolen shield. He released his hold on her hair and placed his hand on her shoulder.

****

Alexandra caught her breath. She had heard him approach the cabin, and unwilling to renew the occurrence of a few hours past, had squeezed her eyes closed.

Until he entered the cabin.

Until she heard him undress.

Until he slid beneath the covers and rolled toward her.

Until he touched her.

Now his hand continued its silent quest along her draped form. Her heart raced and her mouth went dry. She bit her lower lip to refrain from moaning and clutched the bedding to stop from turning toward him and returning the sweet torment, little by little. His hand settled on her hip. He traced the curve with his thumb before sliding up her back.

'Twas her undoing.

She inched closer to the edge of the bed and wrapped the blanket more securely about her.

"Lexi?" He bent over her. His breath tickled her ear.

She shrugged away from him, unable to meet his gaze.

"Are you awake?" He pushed her hair aside and pressed his lips to her neck.

"Go away."

"Lexi." Derek's low voice vibrated down her spine. He moved closer to her shrouded body. "Talk to me."

Ever aware of her lack of clothing, she damned her foolishness and wondered how long it would take for him to discover this fact for himself.

Deciding she might as well get it over with, she rolled over and faced him. She did her best to remain covered from chin to toe. "We have nothing to say. Please keep your hands to yourself so I can sleep."

The corners of his mouth quirked. She glared at him.

"I find nothing amusing about this situation." She set her chin. "If there is nothing more..."

She started to roll away, but somehow found herself flush against Derek.

"Let go." She pushed against his broad, bare chest, but couldn't escape his iron grip. She lowered her gaze, but when she realized the blanket barely covered his hips and left the rest of his body open to her shy perusal, she glanced away. To her mortification, she felt her own portion slipping.

Derek's gaze dropped to the expanse of flesh swelling over the bedding she clasped against her body. Fiery warmth flooded her face.

One of his eyebrows shot up. "What have we here?"

Alexandra tugged the blanket up. "'Tisn't what you think."

Derek explored her back. Upon finding the edge of the bedcover, he slipped his fingers inside. "And what might I be thinking?"

Longing clouded her mind. She moistened her lips with her tongue. "You might think I was waiting for you."

"And were you?" His hand grazed her hip then flattened on her stomach and crept up, seeking the fullness shielded from his view.

"No." Shivers of desire ribboned through her. "No. I was cold and wet and..." She couldn't think. "And..."

His lips discovered the pulse fluttering at the base of her throat. "Cold and wet, hmm? A likely story." He cupped the weight of her breasts with the lightest, gentlest of motions.

Liquid heat erupted within her. She choked back a gasp. "'Tis the truth. I couldn't find my valise."

Derek swept the blanket aside. "I think I shall conceal your valise on a daily basis." He bent his head and suckled a nipple until it hardened.

Alexandra bit her lip against a moan. "We must stop. This isn't right."

"We're married, Lexi, and this is most definitely right." His lips found hers and drew the breath from her very soul.

All rational thought, all further protests faded away, forgotten. White-hot need unfurled in her veins. She wanted more, needed more. Her hands trailed down his sides before sliding inward and lower until her fingers closed around him.

Derek groaned low in his throat, and thrilling Alexandra by the sound of his surrender, he deepened the kiss. He moved from her mouth to her throat and back down to her breasts. She arched against him as exquisite sensations shot through her.

Then his lips journeyed farther, to the juncture of her thighs, to the very essence of her femininity, where he brought her to one frenzied peak after another.

Just when she doubted her ability to withstand another moment of this exquisite torture, he lifted and united them. She cried his name and moved with him. He withdrew from her body and spilled his seed upon her belly. Before she could ask why, he continued to pleasure her with his hands and his mouth.

The world tilted sideways. She held tight to him, lest she shatter into a million pieces and drift through endless time without him. Her release rocked her to her innermost core. He sheltered her within his embrace.

Ever so slowly she drifted back down and snuggled against Derek. She couldn't help but marvel at the wondrous experience they had just shared.

Content, she rested a hand on his chest and enjoyed the feel of the steady beat of his heart. A languid drowsiness took hold of her. She could not have moved if her life depended on it. He left for a moment, and upon returning, he gently wiped her stomach clean with a damp cloth.

She yawned. "Might I sleep now?"

"Nay. Mayhap later."

Chapter Fifteen

A vague sound burrowed through the haze of sleep enveloping Alexandra. She wrinkled her nose, unwilling to rouse from her cozy cocoon.

"Capt'n?"

Alexandra's eyes snapped open and she shook the arm wrapped about her waist. "Derek, wake up."

"Ah, Lexi. Again?"

Warming at his amused tone, she rolled toward him. "Someone is at the door."

The rapping came louder. "Capt'n?" Obadiah called. "Are ye awake? I've brought your mid-day meal."

Derek sat up and swung his legs over the side of the bed. "Just a moment." He pulled on his breeches and crossed the room.

Alexandra scooted under the covers, embarrassed by the lateness of the hour and not yet comfortable with anyone seeing her in Derek's bed. A moment later a gentle swat on her behind brought her topside. "Why did you do that?"

Derek sat beside her and caught her mouth in a leisurely kiss. He handed her a sweet roll. "There is no need to hide. We have naught to be ashamed of."

Alexandra stared at the mole beneath his collarbone before allowing her gaze to slide across the breadth of his unclothed, bronzed chest. Aware her cheeks had pinkened from her prolonged perusal, she averted her eyes. "I suppose it will take time to become used to it."

"I've acquired quite a taste for it already."

Her startled gaze flew back to him. His response disconcerted her. "Do you regret marrying me?"

"Nay."

"And all that has followed?"

His eyes twinkled. "I wouldn't change a moment." His arms settled about her waist. "Care to share another moment?"

"'Tis morning, Derek." The heat of a blush rose to her hairline. "Besides, what if someone requires your services?" She forced herself to take a bite of the roll he had given to her.

"As captain I'm entitled to do as I please." He nuzzled a spot behind her ear. "And I must say, offering my 'services' to you pleases me greatly."

Alexandra swallowed her roll with difficulty and shivered at the tingling sensations spilling through her. "You're incorrigible, Derek."

He nipped her earlobe. "Aye, and you enjoy every minute of it."

"Heaven help me, but I do." She sighed. His laughter rumbled in her ear. She buried her face in her hands.

Derek moved her hands away from her face and tilted her chin. "There is naught wrong with admitting you enjoy the intimacy that has developed between us. You're a woman. I'm a man. 'Tis the way of the world."

Alexandra peered at him through lowered lashes. If he didn't think her brazen, perhaps he would answer a question she had been unable to ask. "Have you been with many women?"

Derek choked on his coffee. "Pardon me?"

"Never mind." She started to rise from the bed, but his hand closed around her wrist, halting her.

"I've been with a few women. Why do you wish to know?"

She shrugged and smoothed wrinkles from the blankets on the bed. "Curiosity." She pursed her lips in thought for a moment. "How do I compare to the other women?"

"There is no comparison."

"Oh." She twisted her wedding band round her finger, disappointed by his words.

"Lexi, I think you—" Another knock on the door interrupted him. "Yes?"

"'Tis Travis. We're entering the York River."

"Thank you. I'll join you momentarily." Derek turned back to Alexandra. "We shall resume this conversation later. For now, make ready your belongings. We'll reach Queen's Creek shortly."

She ambled to the windows and studied the autumn sky now completely void of the previous night's storm. The storm that had raged inside the cabin had dissipated as well.

Derek strode across the room and stood behind her. His hand rested on her hip. Warmth from his touch spread from her fingertips to her toes. She struggled to control her trembling.

He pressed a kiss to her cheek. "I will return for you soon."

She nodded, fearful her voice would reveal her emotional uncertainty should she speak. The cabin door closed and her shoulders lowered in dejection.

No comparison.

No comparison.

No comparison.

His words mocked her. He had found her lacking while she had been swept away by the heady tide of intoxicating pleasure from his touch. Could she learn to make it so for him? She couldn't bear to disappoint him.

She forced her thoughts to the coming hours. They would reach Williamsburg today. She packed her few belongings, then picked up her diary and poured out all her worries, her fears, her frustrations.

A light tapping caught her attention. Thinking Derek might have forgotten something, she hurried to open the door. Dr. Sebastian stood before her.

"M-may we t-talk?"

She inclined her head and opened the door.

"I've c-come...ask f-forgiveness."

Alexandra swallowed past the lump in her throat. He was still the same man who had befriended her. The truth of her identity could not change that.

She reached out and took his hand. "I'll forgive you, Dr...Grandfather, if you'll forgive me for failing to place myself in your situation." She drew the frail man close for a hug. "Considering the circumstances, I might have done the same thing."

They stared at each other for a moment. Their special bond wrapped itself around her heart. Would she be able to develop a similar closeness with her family? She hoped her parents would be as accepting as Dr. Sebastian.

"W-wish Daphne...here." His dark blue eyes misted and his brow wrinkled in consternation.

"Daphne?"

"M-my wife."

The warm feeling within her broadened. "I look forward to meeting her." A grandmother? She hadn't even thought about having a grandmother.

Dr. Sebastian shook his head. His sad expression tugged at her heart. "C-can't. D-dead."

Alexandra ached at the sorrow in his voice. She felt cheated. It wasn't fair to have found, and lost, her grandmother in the space of a minute. She longed to ask questions, needed to learn more, but she did not want to cause him more pain.

The doctor shuffled over to the windows and stared out over the sparkling water of the receding Chesapeake Bay.

"L-loved you...sh-she did." Unshed tears

glimmered in his dark eyes. Eyes so like her own. "N-never stopped...hoping." His gray moustache lifted in a wistful shadow of a grimace. "C-couldn't...s-save her."

Alexandra gave his thin shoulder a reassuring squeeze. "I'm sure you did all you could."

"H-had a v-vision. Sh-she...sent me...to you." A tender smile stole upon his face. He stroked her left hand with reverence, with love. "H-her...ring."

Alexandra's gaze dropped to her finger. The sapphires winked at her. "From the moment Derek slipped it on my finger I have felt a comforting presence, especially when I'm frightened or uncertain."

Dr. Sebastian beamed with joy. "Sh-she...found way...b-be with you."

"I wish I could remember her." Her voice lowered. "I wish I could remember something. Anything."

"N-no need...fear."

She shook her head "But I won't know them and they won't know me. Even my name is different." Her chin quivered. "I'm not their little girl anymore, and I fear I shall be a disappointment."

"Th-they...love you." He pressed a kiss to her cheek and left the cabin.

****

Alexandra sat across from Derek in a coach that swayed as it rolled along Capitol Landing Road. Dr. Sebastian had insisted on following in a separate coach. Ill at ease and uncertain about the coming hours, she kept her eyes focused on the countryside. She studied with pretended interest the homes and taverns they passed.

She pulled her woolen cloak tighter and smoothed wrinkles from her skirt for the twentieth time in the past quarter hour.

Derek caught her hands between his and raised

them to his lips. "You must calm your nerves, Lexi, lest you wear a hole clear through your petticoat."

"I cannot help it." She pulled her hands back into her lap. Every step of the horses carried her closer to her family.

One of the front wheels hit a rut in the road. Derek slipped a steadying arm around Alexandra and settled her on the seat beside him.

"Pardon me." She straightened her skirts.

The coach hit yet another hole. Derek cushioned her from the jostling. The fingers of his right hand traced the curve of her shoulder. His touch sent delicious tingles through her.

She chanced a peek at her husband and found herself caught in the snare of his burnished gaze. The air crackled with intense awareness.

With the fingertips of his other hand, Derek trailed a lazy path from her cheek to her chin. Her eyelids fluttered shut at the tender ache he wrought within her. A rush of warm giddiness left her breathless.

She tilted her head and branded his handsome features upon her mind. She memorized the pleat that appeared when he drew his brows together, the brown-gold blend of his eyes, the strong line of his jaw.

He outlined her mouth with his thumb, teasing her, promising her, tormenting her with the allure of delights yet to come. She stilled his movements with her hand. "We cannot do this. Not here. Not now."

He closed his fingers around her hand. "I understand your fear, but 'tis unnecessary. Your parents will welcome you with open arms and open hearts."

She blinked back a sudden rush of tears. "But—"

"No buts." He wiped away the moisture from her cheek. "I'll be with you. We'll do this together. You mustn't let this anxiety overwhelm you." He tipped her chin up. "Look to the future."

His lips descended upon hers, taking all she gave and returning it tenfold. She entwined her arms around his neck. Her heartbeat thundered in her ears as he explored her mouth.

She touched her tongue to his, enchanted by the reaction she roused in him. He ground his mouth into hers as if he could devour her whole. Shaken by the ferocity of the passion fusing them together, she clung to him and rode the heady wave as it swept her along.

She sighed as his hands moved beneath her cloak to cup her breasts. "You wouldn't be trying to distract me from my worries, would you?"

"Is it working?" He nipped the flesh swelling over her bodice.

She trembled from the wondrous sensations spilling through her. "Oh, yes."

"Then I shall continue." He blazed a fiery path up the curve of her throat, to her jaw, and over to her ear where he taunted her again with his tongue and his teeth.

Her fingers opened his shirt and splayed against the dark, crisp curls. She moistened her index finger and drew it down the center of his broad chest, down his trim, flat belly.

At his sharp intake of breath, she smiled wickedly and persisted in traveling her chosen path. She halted just above the evidence of his desire for her. Following a moment's hesitation, she placed her hands on his hard thighs, dangerously close to his manhood.

Derek uttered a low growl and hauled her onto his lap. "Would you have me take you here and now in the coach?" He delivered another soul-scorching kiss that left her gasping for air. His hand wandered beneath her skirts and caressed the sensitive skin of her inner thigh, then moved higher.

"You must stop, Derek. Someone might hear us."

"There's no one here." A devilish grin stretched across his face. He found her feminine place moist and ready, and expertly stroked and caressed her.

She clutched his shirtfront for support and writhed against his hand. An exquisite surge of joy shot though her and carried her higher and higher.

"We're nearing Montgomery Hall, sir," their driver called.

Alexandra tumbled back to reality. Her eyes locked with Derek's. He grinned against her mouth. "Welcome home, Lexi."

With a squeal, she moved off his lap and set her clothing to rights. She tried to pat her hair in place. What would they think? She glanced at Derek. "How do I look?"

He tweaked her nose. "Like a woman who has been thoroughly and enjoyably kissed."

"Derek!" She covered her flaming cheeks with her palms and felt the threat of tears. "It's all your fault. They'll never accept me now."

Derek chuckled. "Lexi—"

"Don't you make light of this." She pounded her fists against his chest and choked back a sob. "This is the most important day in my life and now look at me." She hit him one final time before taking refuge in the corner of the coach. She stared out the window and fought the trepidation and doubts assailing her.

The coach rolled along a wide driveway lined on both sides by trees. In the distance, she saw an imposing house and several smaller outbuildings.

Derek turned her toward him. "I was not teasing you and I'm sorry if I hurt you. 'Twas never my intention."

Alexandra pulled her cloak about her and allowed her gaze to slide past him. She caught a glimpse of people milling about the plantation. Her lower lip quivered. In a few minutes she would be face to face with her mother and her father.

"Lexi?"

She met his gaze. He held his hand out to her and she accepted it, drawing strength from him.

"I wasn't making light of you or of this situation. I, more than anyone else, know what this day means to you. I've been with you every step of the way, and I shall remain by your side for as long as you need me."

"I'm sorry." She held tight to his hand. "I shouldn't have—"

"Shhh." He pressed a finger to her lips. "'Tis forgotten."

The coach rolled to a stop.

Chapter Sixteen

As Alexandra alighted, the late afternoon breeze whipped her long skirts and cloak around her trembling legs. She exhaled a long breath and accompanied Derek and Dr. Sebastian up the wide path of flat stones to the front entrance of the large two-story brick home. The red Virginia creeper and cross vines along the house caught her attention. The cheerful white window and door frames eased her trepidation some.

Derek looked down at her. "Are you ready?"

She swallowed hard and nodded.

He knocked on the front door and smiled at her.

The door opened.

"Master Derek, is that you?"

Derek chuckled. "Yes, Harrison, it is."

A wide grin split the older man's wrinkled face. "And Dr. Sebastian, too? Come in! Come in! Mrs. Montgomery will be so happy to see you."

Alexandra took refuge behind her husband. Her heartbeat thundered in her ears. She placed an unsteady hand on her churning stomach.

She glanced up and saw a beautiful woman in a red silk gown descending the staircase. Alexandra ducked behind Derek again and twisted her wedding band around her finger.

Could this be the woman in Bartholomew's portrait?

She was older, but she still had long black hair and dark blue eyes. Her lips curved into a welcoming smile and she hurried down the remaining stairs.

"'Tis good to see you, Derek. And, Papa." She greeted her father with a hug and a kiss. "What kept you in Philadelphia for so long?" She wagged her finger at him. "I've been worried about you."

"I-I..."

The woman's smile faded. "Papa? What has happened to you?"

"I'm...f-fine."

She glanced toward Derek. "Tell me, please. What is wrong?"

"He's recovering from apoplexy."

"Apoplexy? Oh, my!" She took hold of the doctor's arm. "Come, you must lie down and rest. You poor dear. I'll take care of you."

He resisted. "S-stop, L-Laurel."

"But, Papa. You're not well. You must rest."

"I'm fine...R-rest later."

Laurel's brow furrowed. "Please, Papa."

He shook his head. "L-later...brought s-someone...to s-see you."

Her bewildered gaze searched the hall. "Who have you brought?"

Derek turned around and brought Alexandra to his side. She held her breath and awaited her mother's reaction.

Her mother. How odd those two words felt to her soul.

The smile on Laurel's face froze. She reached toward Alexandra, then pulled her hand back. Tears pooled in her eyes. "Is she...is it possible?" Her face paled and she swayed.

"Mother!" Alexandra reached for her.

Derek caught Laurel and carried her into an adjoining room where he settled her upon a settee. Alexandra sank down beside her and checked her breathing and her pulse. A lump thickened in her throat.

"Forgive me, Mother."

Laurel reached up to stroke the curve of Alexandra's cheek. "Forgive you? Whatever for?"

"I didn't mean to cause you a moment's distress."

"Distress?" Laurel shook her head. "'Twas joy, not distress." Moisture flowed from the corners of her eyes. "I'd given up hope you would ever come back to us." Fresh tears trickled down her cheeks.

A flurry of footsteps and rustling skirts sounded out in the center hall. A dark-haired young woman rushed into the parlor. "Mama, may I—" She stopped at the sight of her mother on the settee. "Mama?" Her gaze lighted on Alexandra. "What have you done to my mother? Get away from her!"

Alexandra gasped at her hostility. "I didn't—"

"Calm yourself, Jillian," Derek said. "Your mother is well."

"Derek?" Jillian hurtled herself into his arms. "You've come back!"

He set her on her feet. "That I have."

She stuck out her lower lip in a pout. "Is that the proper way to greet someone you've not seen for months?"

"We have much to discuss," he said. "Please be seated."

Derek moved to stand beside Alexandra. Jillian's features turned haughty and her eyes narrowed with suspicion. "Who is she?"

"Jillian." Laurel sat up. "Mind your manners and fetch your father and Marc. I believe they're in your father's office working on the accounts."

Jillian lifted her chin.

"Now, Jillian."

The younger woman left the room in a huff. Unsettled by the mixed reception she had received, and unsure of what to do next, Alexandra surveyed her surroundings.

Her breath caught at the elegant beauty of the

parlor decorated in shades of rose, hunter green, and ivory. The polished floor and dark walnut furniture gleamed in the candlelight from brackets on the walls and a brass chandelier. An exquisite embroidered rug covered the floor.

Her gaze swept past the rose silk damask chairs and curtains to the green paneled surface above the fireplace. She felt drawn across the room.

To the fireplace. Above the mantle hung a portrait—a larger, but identical copy of the miniature portrait in the cameo locket.

She turned and found Derek by her side. He took her right hand and placed the locket in her palm.

"'Tis really true, isn't it? I am Charlotte."

He nodded.

Frustration overwhelmed her. "Why can't I remember?"

"You will."

The front door opened and closed. Two men and Jillian entered the parlor. The older man appeared to be around fifty years of age. He smoothed his unruly thick brown hair, which was so dark it was nearly black, with a hint of gray at the temples. The younger man with sandy-blond hair did not resemble either of her parents or her sister. His penetrating green eyes scanned the room and rested on Alexandra.

The person she assumed to be her father went to Laurel's side. "Are you ill? I wasn't able to make any sense of Jillian's ramblings."

"I'm fine, Jared. 'Twas only a moment of weakness, but it has passed."

He frowned. "Weakness? Of what sort?"

Her lips curved into a smile. "The sort caused by an unexpected, though blessed, surprise."

"You're speaking in riddles."

Laurel turned him around and directed his

attention toward Alexandra. His mouth opened and closed twice in succession. He looked from Alexandra to Laurel, then back to Alexandra.

Alexandra met her father's gaze. She sought Derek's hand and held tight.

Jared's eyes never left Alexandra. "She looks like you did when we wed."

"Because she is our daughter."

Jared paled.

Jillian muffled a gasp and moved to her father's side. "It isn't true, is it, Papa?"

Alexandra took an involuntary step back from the vehemence spewing from her sister's eyes.

"Have you no shame, Jillian?" Laurel said. "Sit down. I want to hear how this miracle came to be."

The young woman lifted her chin, but before she could speak, her father said, "Obey your mother. Now."

In a swish of yellow satin and lace, Jillian flounced over to a cushioned window seat. Derek and Alexandra remained standing while Jared took his place beside his wife. Marc stood behind his grandfather's wing chair.

"How did you find Charlotte?" Laurel asked. "Where did you find her?"

"Your father found Alexandra living in Philadelphia," Derek said.

"Alexandra?" Laurel's face whitened. "Why do you call her that?"

"'Tis the only name she has known. She has no memory of her abduction. She has no memory of you."

"No memory?" Jared said. "Then how can you be sure she's Charlotte?"

"I'm sure."

"What proof can you offer?"

"Look at her." Laurel moved to Alexandra's side. "How can you doubt it?"

"I want to believe it." Jared looked into Alexandra's eyes. "I mean no disrespect, but if you have no memory of us..."

"Sh-she has...birth-m-mark," Dr. Sebastian said. "L-like mine."

"Show them the cameo, Lexi," Derek said.

She handed it to Laurel.

"Sweet merciful heavens. My locket." Laurel opened it and revealed the miniature of her eldest child. "It's been missing ever since you were taken."

"I found it," Alexandra said. "Before I ran away. I hoped it would lead me to my parents."

"Where have you been all this time?" Laurel asked. "How did you find out about us? Why were you running away?"

Jared placed a hand on his wife's arm. "One question at a time. Give the child a chance to answer."

Alexandra twisted her wedding band around her finger. "I lived in the home of Polly Taylor. She takes in children with nowhere else to go, and I had been told that I had been abandoned. It wasn't until I overheard Bartholomew—"

"Bartholomew!" Laurel and Jared said in unison.

Laurel's hand covered her mouth while Jared clarified, "Bartholomew Taylor?"

"Aye," Derek said. "Polly Taylor is his sister-in-law."

"Is she part of this?" Jared's mouth whitened around the edges.

"No," Alexandra said. "Polly would never stoop to such behavior."

Derek pulled a letter from his pocket and handed it to Jared.

Alexandra continued. "After I overhead Bartholomew's brother question him about my *abandonment*, I searched Bartholomew's office hoping to find information about my parents. 'Twas then I found the locket. I also found papers that appeared to incriminate him in illegal activities."

"Unbeknownst to her," Derek said, "she also took the letter you now hold. A letter from my mother to Polly Taylor, formerly Polly Smythe, one of my mother's friends from her school days. Bartholomew must have intercepted it, thus preventing Polly from learning the truth."

The sandy-haired youth spoke up. "Why are you called Alexandra, not Charlotte?"

"I know why."

Everyone turned toward Laurel. "It's the name he used to call me. I knew Bartholomew only slightly before I met and married Jared. Something about him frightened me. He persisted in calling me Alexandra, in spite of my protests. One afternoon he accosted me on the street and rambled of our marriage, of our new home, of our future. Nothing I said dissuaded him of his ludicrous notions."

A chill slithered down Alexandra's spine. "That's what he meant."

Realization dawned. She met her mother's pained gaze. "He must have thought I was you." She looked around the room at her newfound family and saw acceptance on all but one face. "The night I ran I heard Bartholomew tell his brother of our upcoming marriage. He vowed nothing would stop our wedding this time. He had never mentioned marriage to me once, let alone twice."

Laurel gathered her into her arms. "If only I had realized the extent of his madness all those years ago."

"Don't blame yourself, Mother. I don't."

Laurel wiped the tears from her cheeks. Her eyes glistened. "At least you're here now. I think it's high time you were properly introduced to the rest of your family."

She walked over to Jared. "Char—forgive me, Alexandra, this is your father, Jared Montgomery."

He stepped forward and engulfed her in a hug. "I'm so glad you're home where you belong. You have been sorely missed." His voice thickened. "I apologize for my doubts, but there have been so many false hopes over the years that I had to be certain. Rest assured, I have never been happier."

Alexandra rose up on tiptoe and pressed a kiss to his cheek. "You have naught to apologize for, Papa. When Derek first told me who I was I had a difficult time believing him. Sometimes I still do."

"What about me?"

She turned around and found herself in another embrace.

"I'm your brother, Marc. I'm glad you're here."

She stared up at him. "Me, too. I must say, though, it will take time to get used to having a younger brother who is taller than I am."

His green eyes danced with mischief. "I'll soon turn fifteen. Mother declares I grow an inch a week."

"You would think so, too," Laurel said, "considering the rate he outgrows his breeches."

"Mother." His cheeks reddened.

Laurel laughed and placed her hands on Alexandra's shoulders. "There is someone else I want you to meet. Jillian? *Jillian.* Come here now."

Alexandra watched her sister sullenly slide off the windowsill and shuffle over to her mother's side.

"Hello, Jillian," Alexandra said.

Silence.

She tried again. "I'm pleased to make your acquaintance. Derek has told me a little about you."

For just a moment, a light appeared in Jillian's dark, brooding gaze. Then it was gone. Alexandra glanced at Derek, uncertain how to proceed.

"Please forgive Jillian's bad manners." Laurel stared pointedly at her younger daughter before once again facing Alexandra. "'Twould seem she is going through a missish stage. Perhaps some time at the spinning wheel would remedy that."

Alexandra bit her lower lip and glanced sideways at Derek. He seemed to be having an equally difficult time containing his mirth.

"Speaking of manners, or lack of them, I have been remiss in my duties," Laurel said. "You must be tired and hungry. I do hope you'll stay the night, Derek. Once you're settled in your rooms, I will have Tildy bring you a light supper. Would you like some hot cornbread and cheese, or perhaps a dish of fruit compote and some nuts?"

"Mrs. Montgomery," Derek said. The silence thickened at his hesitation. After a nudge from Alexandra, he said, "There is something you should know."

"Yes?"

He drew a deep breath and continued. "Lexi and I are married."

"No!"

Chapter Seventeen

"No!" Jillian shouted again and stumbled backward. "You couldn't have." She ran to Derek's side and clutched his arm, her eyes awash with tears and raw pain. "It can't be true, Derek. Tell me it isn't true."

The familiar grip of guilt knotted his insides at the anguish he was causing Jillian. "'Tis the truth." He gently pried the distraught young woman loose from his arm and reached for Alexandra. Her face had paled from the very rejection he knew she had feared and expected. He drew her into the circle of his embrace and gave her a reassuring squeeze.

Tension permeated the air in the parlor and made the task of breathing uncomfortable. When and how should he explain to Alexandra that he had almost taken her sister as his wife?

"Married?" Laurel murmured, her expression dazed.

Jared rose from the settee, his features tight. "You'd best explain yourself. When and how did this come about?"

"We were married a sennight ago."

"And the reason for the rush?" Jared cleared his throat. "Was time a factor when you made this sudden decision?"

Derek saw Alexandra flush beneath her father's veiled question, and he clenched his jaw against a flash of anger. "Not for the reason you are implying, sir. I have the highest regard for your daughter."

"Why the rush? Why couldn't you wait until you

returned home?" Derek also heard his unspoken question. *What about Jillian?*

"Bartholomew took her again and planned to force her into marriage. After she escaped, I decided we should marry as quickly as possible. Before he could try again."

Alexandra trembled. Derek brushed his lips against her temple and held her tighter.

Jillian's lower lip quivered. "You will regret this," she said to Derek. She raked Alexandra with a final frosty glance, then turned and swept from the room.

Laurel stepped forward and gathered Alexandra into her arms. "Jillian's behavior will be dealt with. She knows I won't tolerate such goings on." Her warm gaze rested on Derek.

"Please don't be hard on her for my sake," Alexandra said. "I'm sure this...situation just took her by surprise."

Derek agreed with the doubtfulness Laurel tried to conceal. Jillian had always been willful. He regretted having to hurt her in this manner, but there hadn't been time to take her aside and explain his actions. To tell her they had never really been suited to each other. That in the end she would be happier with someone capable of loving her properly.

And Alexandra? Shouldn't she also be with someone able to love her properly, someone capable of protecting her? He dismissed the ramblings of his conscience and whispered into Alexandra's ear. "'Tis easy to see that disobedience runs in your family."

Under the cover of her skirts, Alexandra trod upon his toes. "I apologize for the distress I seem to have caused Jillian."

"Don't fret." Jared stared at Derek. "'Tisn't your doing. I shall have a talk with her."

Alexandra's lavender scent stirred Derek's senses. He slipped his arm between her cloak and her gown, and while appearing to listen to the conversation, his hand roamed along the small of her back and settled on the slight flare of her hips.

She stiffened beneath his touch and ground her heel into his foot with renewed vigor. Nearly chuckling aloud, Derek trailed his fingertips up and down her waist, inching ever nearer to the enticing curve of her full breasts. The rosy flush of her cheeks heightened, and he knew the vixen would pay him back threefold once they were alone.

"What do you think, Derek? Derek?"

"Hmm?" Derek's mind was filled with delightful images of Alexandra's revenge. He turned his attention to Laurel.

"Your marriage to my daughter changes things. I had looked forward to having her here so we could get to know each other. However, since she is your wife, do you plan to take her to your family's plantation?"

"I hadn't thought that far ahead." He glanced at Alexandra. "She will remain here for the time being. She has been separated from you too long as it is."

Alexandra turned her startled gaze on him. "Where will you be?"

"You're more than welcome to stay here," Laurel said. "We can put the two of you in the west wing where you can have your privacy, yet still be nearby."

Derek smiled his gratitude. "We appreciate your generosity. May we discuss this further on the morrow? Alexandra needs to rest."

"Of course. I shall show you to your rooms." Laurel turned toward Dr. Sebastian. "I'll return and see you settled."

****

Alexandra and Derek followed Laurel through the house. With every room they passed, Alexandra's eyes opened wider. The elegant atmosphere exuded warmth and hospitality. The wooden floors and trims gleamed. Not so much as a speck of dust or a tilted picture spoiled the effect.

"Here we are," Laurel said. "The bedchamber as well as the sitting room and study are for your use. If there is anything you need, please tell me. We want you to be happy and comfortable here."

Alexandra hugged her mother. "You have already made me feel more welcome than I dared dream."

"Tildy will bring you a light supper and Samson will bring your belongings." Laurel closed the door behind her.

Alexandra surveyed the large bedchamber, feeling awkward now that she and Derek were alone. The silence stretched and lengthened.

To cover her nervousness, she wandered about the chamber and admired the exquisite needlework of the four-poster's bed curtain. Its colorful theme of blue and peach had been carried to the oval braided rug on the floor at the foot of the bed.

Peach brocade curtains had been drawn against the fast approaching nightfall, while floral cushions on the window seats promised comfort should one desire to spend time reading or daydreaming there.

"Lexi," Derek said, only to be interrupted by a rapping on the door. He opened it to admit three servants.

Tildy, a middle-aged woman of ample girth, placed their supper on the round table near the fireplace. A younger female set to work building a fire. Meanwhile, Samson brought in Alexandra's valise and Derek's sea chest. Once the youngest of the servants had a warm, cheery blaze crackling and sending out rays of heat, she and Tildy put Alexandra and Derek's clothing into the dark walnut highboy and wardrobe.

Having never been coddled by servants,

Alexandra grew more uncomfortable by the minute. Curious about Derek's reaction, she peered sideways at him. When she realized he was watching her, a jolt of longing shot through her.

His brown-gold eyes had taken on the glow of the fireplace and held her mesmerized. Scarcely aware of the servants' departure, she somehow found herself standing before him.

Her heart fluttered and her skin tingled from his nearness. She moistened her lips with the tip of her tongue. They needed to talk, but her thoughts had been swept away by a whirlwind of conflicting emotions. Why did he have this effect on her?

He untied the fastenings of her cloak, one by one. Her gaze locked with his. The awareness she had experienced earlier in the coach returned full force. Why did she crave his touch so?

He slipped the cloak from her shoulders. Goosebumps rose on her exposed flesh. She stiffened her knees, hoping to force her trembling limbs to hold her upright. It wouldn't do to swoon at his feet.

Speak! Ask what the morrow will bring. Will he stay or will he go?

She parted her lips. "Derek—"

His mouth covered hers, absorbed her words, and sent waves of sensation coursing through her, overriding her will to think.

Derek's lips moved to her neck. She gasped at the feelings he roused in her. "We must talk."

"Later." He brought his hands to the bowknots of her bodice. His fingers grazed her sensitive skin.

She frowned and placed her hands against his chest. She fully intended to push him away. Instead, her fingers pulled his shirt from his breeches and crept up his heated skin. She marveled at the strength, the sheer power, beneath her fingertips.

Impatient to feel more of him, she removed his coat. His motions stilled. His gaze grew darker. She walked around him, removed his shirt by slow degrees, inch by tantalizing inch, and tormented him with her fingers and her mouth.

The image of them in the parlor a short time earlier flashed through her thoughts. He had dared to touch her intimately, albeit beneath the cover of her cloak. Still, he had not played fair.

She moved to stand behind him and gave her hands free rein. His sharp intake of breath delighted her. Her fingers trailed down his sides, past his trim hips, and along his thighs. She pressed her breasts full against his back and brought her hands up to his tautly muscled stomach.

Her fingers came together at the waistband of his breeches. They dipped in, then out, teased, taunted. Ever so softly, her hands continued their journey. She massaged his flesh until his hardness pulsed through the fabric of his breeches.

Alexandra abruptly straightened and walked over to the table where she seated herself and speared a piece of fruit with a bone-handled silver fork. She forced herself to ignore Derek's look of disbelief, though heaven help her, it was not easy.

Before the fruit touched her lips, Alexandra found herself yanked out of the chair, tossed over his shoulder, and dumped onto the center of the enormous bed.

Derek knelt over her. He pinned her hands above her head. Sparks from his gaze pierced her soul. "So ye mean to toy with me, eh, wench?"

"No more than you did whilst we were in the parlor with my family."

His lips curved in a sardonic grin. "So that's the way of it, is it?"

"Yes." Her breasts rose and fell with every breath she took. "If you will kindly let me up."

Derek paused as if to consider her suggestion. "I think not. I'm rather comfortable."

"Oooh!" She struggled against his grip of iron, and realized she had only succeeded in further opening the bodice Derek had somehow unfastened. "Get off!"

"Is that the proper way for a wife to treat her devoted husband?" He lowered his mouth to the shadowed valley, nipping and sampling, before working his way back up to her mouth and kissing her senseless.

He released her wrists and buried his fingers in her hair. His exploration of her mouth left her gasping.

Taking her by the hands, Derek pulled her up until she knelt before him. The will to protest had long since vanished. She closed her eyes in pleasure. His lips trailed a sensuous path down her throat while his hands slipped her bodice from her shoulders.

She helped dispense with her stays. He unfastened her skirt and petticoats and slid them past the gentle swell of her hips. Her fingers moved to his breeches. Before long their clothing lay in a heap on the floor.

They came together. Derek's hands and mouth were everywhere, caressing, stroking, kissing. Alexandra reciprocated on every count.

Derek's hands traveled ever lower until they came to the triangle of black curls concealing her feminine secrets. She parted her thighs to grant him freer access and clutched his shoulders. He plundered her depths. She trembled until she thought she couldn't bear it any longer.

His mouth fastened onto her breast. The tension inside her built until it became both exquisite and unbearable.

With a boldness she did not know she possessed, Alexandra pushed Derek onto his back. Her hand closed around his maleness. She stroked him until she felt a bead of moisture against her fingertip.

Straddling him, she lowered herself onto his rigid erection. Startled by how different he felt this way, she pressed on and accepted his length and breadth. He filled her so completely she gasped.

He moved beneath her. Her hair tumbled about her shoulders. She rode him with abandon, meeting and accepting thrust for thrust. As the sweet ache of fulfillment built to a fever pitch, the tide of passion swept her away.

Derek's hands moved to her hips. He held her immobile as he plunged up into her, time and time again. Tears coursed down her cheeks. Then he paused, looped his arm around her and rolled until she lay beneath him. He withdrew his length from her. Again, he spilled his seed, this time upon her thigh. She started to protest, but he parted her folds and gave her the most intimate of kisses, robbing her of conscious thought. His tongue delved deep.

Pressure built and consumed her. She was almost there. Almost there. Alexandra clutched his hair, scrambling, reaching, until he brought her to the zenith, then she tumbled back down through the darkness, falling, falling. She held onto him, unwilling to be separated from him, lest she disappear into the black pit of nothingness.

Her racing heart slowed bit by bit, until it beat in time with his. For a moment, contentment flowed through her. All seemed right with the world. She had escaped the clutches of Bartholomew. She had found her parents. With her thumb, she stroked the tanned skin of her husband's broad chest and teased several crisp hairs. She had Derek. Her thumb stilled.

Or did she?

Uncertainty usurped contentment. How long would he stay?

Chapter Eighteen

How long would he stay?

Alexandra pondered the disturbing question, then frowned at the unfavorable answers which came to mind.

"Lexi?"

Derek's voice vibrated against her ear and she smiled in spite of her dark thoughts. She had grown fond of the brief interludes following their lovemaking when they lay wrapped in each other's arms.

"Lexi?"

"Hmm?"

"What is troubling you?"

She shrugged. "Why do you think I'm troubled?"

His breath fluttered the wisps of hair near her forehead. "We've been together well nigh day and night for several weeks. I've become skilled in reading your moods."

"My moods?" Alexandra pushed herself away from him and sat up. She covered herself with the embroidered coverlet. "I don't have moods."

He sat up beside her. "You're not fooling me. What is worrying you?"

She stared across the darkened room, into the fireplace. Orange flames tinged with red and blue danced along the logs and cast shadows onto the walls. She was hesitant to tell him, frightened of what his answer might be. "What will happen now?"

"We go to sleep."

She jabbed him in the ribs with her elbow. "That

is not what I meant."

"What do you mean?"

"I'm safe from Bartholomew, and I've been reunited with my family." She twisted her fingers in her lap, unable to look at him, afraid to hear what she feared he might say.

"Go on."

"My mother wants me to stay here, and I must confess, I want to get to know my family."

"And so you should."

"But what about you? What are your plans?"

Derek pulled her against him and rested his chin on her head. "First of all, we are married and I don't take my responsibility to you lightly. Since our marriage has been most thoroughly consummated there will be no annulment. Second, I agree you need to become acquainted with your family. I'll be with you as often as I can, but I also have a responsibility to my family which requires me to be away for periods of time."

"I understand."

Responsibility.

The word echoed through her thoughts. She stroked the underside of his forearm and snuggled closer, but could not shake a sense of foreboding. Even the soft, easy cadence of Derek's breathing as he slept failed to keep the night shadows at bay. Instead, fingers of fear for her new life, for her rediscovered family, crept into her mind and dragged her toward the ever-widening chasm of nothingness awaiting her.

Alexandra eased out of bed so as not to wake Derek. She found her diary and padded across the room to a window seat. Moonlight streamed through the parted curtain and she delved deep inside herself. She drew forth the strength necessary to get through the next few hours until the break of day. She struggled to ward off the dark and dangerous demons lying in wait should she allow herself to sleep.

She poured her thoughts, her doubts, her worries onto paper, and hoped the act would either make them clear or exorcise them from her mind. How long before Derek was called away? Would he take her with him or would he welcome the time apart? How long would the strange, uneasy tension exist between Derek and her parents? She had seen the strained looks pass between everyone in the parlor at the announcement of their marriage. Something was terribly wrong.

Alexandra wrote until exhaustion overtook her and her head rested against the cushion of the window seat. Vaguely aware of two strong arms sliding beneath her, she nestled into the haven carrying her across the room. Her sleepy smile became a moue of protest as he placed her back in bed. She wished back the warmth and security that had surrounded her.

It returned when Derek drew a coverlet over the two of them and settled her against the length of his body. Throughout the remainder of the night, he held her close. Whenever a nightmare dared encroach upon her sleep, he whispered endearments and words of comfort and soothed the restless wandering of her mind back into a gentle, peaceful slumber.

****

Embarrassed by the lateness of the hour, Alexandra forced herself to enter the spacious dining room. She wondered where Derek had gone and why he hadn't wakened her.

"Good morning, dear," Laurel said. "Did you sleep well?"

Alexandra tried to force back the blush warming her cheeks. "Yes, thank you. Please forgive my tardiness."

"No need to apologize. You were tired. Make yourself comfortable and have something to eat."

Alexandra seated herself across from Laurel and took a slice of the cold ham Tildy offered. "Has everyone eaten already?" She stirred milk and sugar into her tea.

Laurel nodded. "Your father and Marc left for their daily round of the plantation. Derek should be returning at any time. I do believe he has a surprise for you."

Her curiosity piqued, she said, "Do you know what it is?"

Laurel's eyes twinkled. "Um-hmm."

Alexandra lowered her voice and whispered across the table. "Will you give me a hint?"

Her mother shook her head.

At that moment Derek strode into the dining room and dropped a kiss on Alexandra's shoulder. He heaped his plate full and sat beside his wife. He looked so utterly handsome she couldn't help but stare.

His cheek dimpled from his amused grin. "Is something amiss, Lexi?"

"Nay." She exchanged glances with her mother, and forced herself to chew and swallow a forkful of ham. Every time his arm brushed against hers, her stomach quivered. Would the time ever come when she became less conscious, less aware of him? All he had to do was glance her way and she became giddy, her insides turned to mush.

Derek turned his gaze upon her. Tremors raced up and down her spine. "I'll be riding into Williamsburg. Would you care to join me? We could have you fitted for new gowns."

"I—"

Jillian swept into the dining room. "It sounds perfectly lovely." She sat in the empty chair on the other side of Derek and turned large brown eyes on him. "May I go with you?"

"Jillian," Laurel said in a low tone.

Alexandra witnessed the challenging glare Jillian sent her way and placed a hand on Derek's shoulder. The tenseness of his muscles surprised her. "I don't mind. It will give us time to become better acquainted."

He met her gaze. "Are you certain?"

"Yes. I'm looking forward to it."

Jillian placed her hand on Derek's arm. "We'll have a grand time."

Alexandra's stomach lurched at the familiar way Jillian touched her husband. Each time Derek began a conversation with her, Jillian found a reason to disrupt it and garner his attention. Perhaps her decision to allow Jillian to accompany them had been rash.

The three of them rose from the table.

"Don't forget your wrap, Alexandra," Jillian said. "I would hate for you take a chill." Somehow the sincerity of her voice never reached her eyes.

Alexandra hurried toward her room. The trill of her sister's laughter sent warning bells clamoring through her. Even as she quickened her steps, she chastised herself for her unwarranted jealousy.

She slipped her cloak about her shoulders and fastened it as she hastened toward the front entrance. She saw Jillian standing close to Derek.

Too close.

Jillian looped her arm through his and tried to pull him through the opened door. He turned toward Alexandra and held his other hand out to her. She slipped her hand into his, answering his squeeze with one of her own.

The driver opened the door of the coach and helped her inside. Jillian managed to wedge herself beside Derek.

"Would you not be more comfortable on the

other seat?" Derek asked Jillian.

"No. This suits me just fine."

Alexandra glanced sideways at Derek and was rewarded by the clenched line of his jaw. It seemed he was not happy with the situation either. His hand sought hers and brought a secret smile to her lips.

She leaned her head against his shoulder and closed her eyes. She inhaled his scent and pretended they were alone. Excited by the prospect of a new gown or two, she scarcely heard Jillian's chatter during the hour-long ride along the Capitol Landing Road.

Polly had showered them with love and attention, but there had never been excess coin for new clothes. Fortunately, Alexandra had been skilled with needle and thread.

By the time they entered the town and were traveling down the Duke of Gloucester Street, Alexandra was sitting on the edge of her seat, peering out her window. In all her life, at least the part she could remember, she had never traveled outside Philadelphia.

Derek pointed out the general stores and the specialty shops, such as the milliner, a silversmith, and an apothecary. Many of the houses she saw served as shops, stores, and taverns, as well as residences, just like in Philadelphia, though on a smaller scale.

The rattling of the carriages and wagons along the street filled her ears. She heard bells ringing. Most likely from the College or the Capitol, Derek told her.

The coach rolled to a stop in front of a millinery shop. Derek assisted both women from the coach and escorted them inside.

Everywhere she looked her eyes met a colorful array of finery and frills as well as necessities. Soaps, buttons, muffs, fans, caps, and knitting needles filled the counters. Brightly colored ostrich plumes suspended from the ceiling caught her eye. Through a door in the center of the shop, a woman decorated a hat.

A middle-aged woman approached them. "Good morning, Miss Montgomery. And Mr. Tremaine, your presence in my shop is a pleasant surprise. A pleasant surprise indeed."

"Thank you for your kind words, Mrs. Brooks. May I introduce my wife, Alexandra Tremaine."

The milliner's eyes widened and her glance darted between Derek and Jillian. "M-my. What a pretty little thing you are."

Alexandra lowered her eyes, warming at the woman's compliments, though confused by her flustered manner. Was there something so terribly wrong with her that made everyone's mouth drop at the mention of her marriage?

"How may we be of service?" Mrs. Brooks asked, her demeanor once again calm and collected.

Derek drew Alexandra close to his side. "I wish to order a complete wardrobe for my wife."

Alexandra's gaze flew to Derek. "You're being far too generous. I have no need for so many clothes."

"Nonsense. If I choose to spoil my wife, then I shall do so." He turned back toward the milliner. "We're ready to begin."

Jillian sniffed a bar of sweet-smelling soap. "Is the gown I ordered ready for the final fitting?"

Mrs. Brooks tilted her head sideways and frowned. "Ah, yes. I believe so. Martha, please attend to Miss Montgomery."

With that, the older woman swept Alexandra and Derek off to a private fitting room. Before she knew it, Alexandra stood in the center of the room clad only in her stays and chemise while her measurements were taken. Derek sat in an upholstered wing chair while Alexandra turned page after page of the pattern books.

Her head began to whirl. So many choices! Mrs. Brooks and her assistants held bolt after bolt of fabric up against her. And such an array of fabrics—damasks, silks, satins, brocades, dimities, cambrics.

"What a treasure you are," the milliner said. "With your hair and coloring, you can wear well-nigh anything."

Jillian entered the room attired in a manner similar to Alexandra. She carried two bolts of fabric and sauntered over to Derek. "Should I choose the lemon silk or the emerald satin?"

Derek cleared his throat. "The, uh, green, I think, would suit you."

Jillian moistened her lips and leaned over the seated Derek. Her breasts nearly spilled from the confines of her stays and low-cut chemise. "Are you certain?"

Alexandra clenched her hands together. How dare Jillian put so much of herself on display. Had she no shame? Why, she had a mind to scratch her sister's eyes out. And to think she had felt sorry for the chit. She would not stand idly by for such goings on. Not with *her* husband.

She started to move toward Jillian, but Mrs. Brooks halted her. "Permit me to handle this, my dear. I have dealt with the young lady on several occasions over the years.

"Miss Montgomery, the green satin will look beautiful on you." The milliner placed firm hands on Jillian's shoulders and guided her from the room.

Alexandra plucked at her chemise and nodded her approval of the finely striped pink and blue silk the assistant showed her. She could not look Derek square in the face. Why hadn't he done something about Jillian?

She felt his eyes on her. Well, she would not give

him the satisfaction of seeing her squirm. With a shake of her head, she vetoed the white damask covered with large red flowers. At a light touch on her elbow, she glanced down to see Derek at her side.

"There is no need, you know." He brushed the tender skin of her forearm with his thumb.

"No need for what?" She nodded at the cream dimity strewn with tiny pink rosebuds, still refusing to meet his eyes. She girded herself against the tingles flowing to her toes.

"No need to feel jealous. She was merely vying for attention. She won't come with us next time."

Alexandra lifted one shoulder in a shrug. "It matters not to me."

Mrs. Brooks swept back into the room. "How are we doing in here?"

"Fine, thank you. You have so many beautiful fabrics. 'Tis difficult to choose." Alexandra tried to cover her agitation with a smile.

Perhaps she had misjudged Jillian. Could she have been trying to garner a bit of attention for herself in an attempt to compete with the sudden arrival of her long-lost sister?

Alexandra grew weary. So many choices. Gowns, chemises, stays, hats, caps, bedgowns. Her mind whirled.

Derek appeared by her side. "Tired?"

She nodded.

"This will be all for today, Mrs. Brooks. Please have these gowns delivered to Montgomery Hall before the week's end." He indicated the rose silk, the cream dimity, and the sapphire satin gowns. "I would like the rest delivered by the following week."

"Oh, but Mr. Tremaine, 'twould be impossible."

Derek turned his most charming smile on the middle-aged woman. Alexandra's own knees weakened at his devilish grin. "I will make it worth your time and effort, I assure you."

Mrs. Brooks blushed. "I-I shall do my best, sir." She and her assistants excused themselves.

Alexandra dressed under Derek's watchful gaze. Her cheeks grew warm. He helped tie the bowknots on her bodice. Her pulse quickened at the slight pressure from his fingers against her flesh.

"Thank you."

His hands stilled. A mischievous grin quirked his lips. "'Tis my pleasure." He arched an eyebrow and trailed a finger down her arm. "'Tis even more a pleasure to help you undress."

Alexandra swatted his hand. "Pshaw. That isn't what I meant."

"Oh?" His hand slid around her waist and pulled her against him. His mouth hovered above hers. "And what, pray tell, were you thanking me for?"

Her mouth turned dry, and her words came out in a whisper. "For bringing Jillian."

Derek's eyes widened, then narrowed. "Jillian?"

She nodded. "I'm afraid she doesn't like me very much, and I would so much like to be her friend."

He tweaked her nose, though his mouth looked tight around the corners. "Silly goose. Of course she likes you. You're her sister." He brushed his lips against hers. "Hungry?"

She nodded again, yet her eyes remained fastened on his inviting mouth. He tipped her chin. Their eyes met.

Yearning coursed through her. She allowed her fingers to creep up his shirtfront. The heat from his chest scorched her fingertips, but she cared not. The rapid beating of his heart exceeded hers.

She parted the opening of his snowy white ruffled shirt and pressed her lips there. Intrigued by the pulse beating in the hollow of his throat, she continued her ascent until she reached his sculptured jaw. He turned his head and captured her

193

mouth.

"Derek, I'm famished," Jillian said as she entered the fitting area and came to an abrupt halt.

Alexandra pushed herself away from Derek, as if she had been caught doing something wrong. What a ludicrous notion. Derek was her husband. Yet she could not contain a shiver at the rage emanating from Jillian.

"You've come at the perfect time, Jillian," Derek said. "And I'm glad to hear you're hungry. Lexi and I were on our way to collect you."

The three of them strolled to a nearby tavern where they dined on ham, a salad of mixed greens, and sweet potatoes, followed by apple pie.

Each time Alexandra tried to draw her sister into conversation, Jillian rebuffed her. She spoke only to Derek. A great sadness washed over her. Were she and Jillian destined to remain sisters, without the added joy of being friends, as well?

Chapter Nineteen

18 November 1752
My parents have worked hard to help me feel at ease here. Mother includes me in her daily activities, and Father seeks me out several times a day. The sense of wonder and joy in their eyes when they look at me makes me feel all warm and soft inside.

When Marc isn't working with Father or entertaining me with a fanciful tale, he is with Dr. Sebastian, whose health continues to improve daily.

All would be perfect, or nearly so, if Jillian would allow me to be her friend, but all my efforts have come to naught. If we are amongst a group of people, she remains on the side of the room opposite me. If I enter a room and find her alone, she leaves without acknowledging my presence. I know I must be more patient, but 'tis terribly difficult.

Will Derek return this day, as I have been wishing? I have been lonesome for him. Our bed has felt over-large the endless nights we have been apart whilst he attends to family business.

My first meeting with his family was awkward, tho' not much diff'rent than my parents' reaction upon learning of our marriage. After recovering from the unexpected shock, his parents, too, made me feel welcome. Except for Jillian's continued disdain, my time here has been more than it seemed prudent to hope for.

With a heavy sigh, Alexandra placed her diary in the drawer of her dressing table. After checking her image in the looking glass and smoothing her cream dimity skirt, she fastened her cloak around her shoulders and left her bedchamber.

Laurel had extended an invitation to join her while she made her daily round of the plantation, and Alexandra looked forward to this time with her mother. As she neared the front door she heard what sounded like an argument coming from the small sitting room opposite the dining room.

The door was ajar.

It didn't bode well for her to remain in the hall. She knew she should leave.

But she could not.

Instead, she moved toward the small room, her eyes focused on the open door. The closer she got, the louder the voices became. She recognized her sister's voice.

"You cannot deny it, can you? You want me. I know you do."

"Jillian."

Alexandra's eyes widened. Derek? With hesitant steps, she approached the slight opening between the door and its frame and peered through it. Derek's back was toward her, but she could see Jillian. Jillian stood so close to Derek that a whisper could not have passed between them. Her hands roamed over Derek's chest, across his shoulders, and encircled his neck. She pulled his mouth toward hers.

A sharp pain stabbed Alexandra's heart. She couldn't move, couldn't look away from the shameful display between her sister and her husband.

Twin tears rolled down her cheeks.

Derek caught Jillian's wrists and lowered them to her sides. Alexandra could not hear his murmured words.

"How could you do it, Derek? You were supposed to marry *me!*"

Alexandra froze. An icy coldness took root deep

within her. A loud buzzing in her ears blocked out further conversation between the two traitors. The walls closed in on her. She blindly stumbled from the hall and fled to the sanctuary of her bedchamber.

The moment she stepped inside, she realized her error. The room wasn't a sanctuary at all, not with all the signs marking Derek's presence—his papers on the desk, his clothing, his shaving items.

She reached inside the wardrobe and withdrew one of his shirts. Pain, sharp and searing, ripped through her. She clutched the soft linen to her chest and inhaled his lingering scent. Deep, shuddering sobs spilled past her lips.

Why hadn't he told her he had been promised to another? To her own sister, no less? She drew a ragged breath and lifted her teary gaze. Fabric glistened from the corner of the clothes cupboard.

A low moan stuck in her throat. With trembling fingers she touched the ivory silk and pulled it toward her until she held the full length of her wedding gown against her. Agony reverberated throughout her body, doubling her over.

Hot tears coursed down her cheeks. The gown must have been intended for Jillian. How else could Derek have acquired it so quickly?

The looks of stunned surprise. The whispers. The strange behavior. All of it became clear.

Derek's decision not to have children wasn't because he didn't want children. He just didn't want hers.

Alexandra died a little more inside. He loved Jillian. A pure and virtuous love. A love now to be forever denied him.

Because of his honor.

Because of his sense of responsibility.

Because of her.

The joy she had found in his arms dimmed with the knowledge he hadn't felt what she had. With her he satisfied his baser needs as he would with any doxy he might find along the waterfront.

Aboard the *Wind Spirit* she'd overheard the crew discussing their own amorous pursuits. Not once had any of them mentioned love. She had allowed herself to believe Derek was different.

She had been a fool.

How many people knew Derek and Jillian had planned to marry? She tightened her hold and twisted the silken fabric in her hands. She tried to summon anger, anger at Derek for loving Jillian, and at Jillian for having his love, but she could not. Each day must be an ordeal for Jillian, must bring fresh reminders of her betrayal.

Which was worse? Loving someone legally bound to another, or being married to someone whose heart belonged elsewhere?

Her fingers tingled and burned. Alexandra dropped the gown. She must talk to Jillian, must try to make her understand what had happened.

And why.

She made her way back to the sitting room. Empty. She tried Jillian's bedchamber. With trembling fingers, she smoothed the skirt of her floral gown and knocked.

"Come in."

She stepped inside. From the stark whitewashed walls to the pristine ruffled curtains and bedhanging to the delicate alabaster figurines displayed in the corner cupboard, everything about the room suggested aloofness.

"This is my room. Get out."

Alexandra's head snapped around. Jillian advanced toward her. Alexandra stepped back, startled, but not surprised, by her sister's venomous expression.

Jillian pointed a tapered finger toward the door. "Leave. Now."

"I had hoped we could talk."

"I've no desire to talk to you."

"I know we can't be friends, but—"

"Friends?" Jillian gave a derisive laugh. "For as long as I can remember all I have heard is 'Charlotte, this' and 'Charlotte, that.' 'Charlotte, Charlotte, Charlotte,' 'til I'm fair sick of it. Mama and Papa never forgot about you. Never. No matter what I did, *you* were uppermost in their thoughts."

"Our parents love you."

Jillian's eyes narrowed. "You're calling me a liar?"

"Nay. 'Tis not what I meant. I never intended to disrupt your life."

"You haven't *disrupted* my life, you've ruined it." Jillian clenched her hands into tight fists. "Go back from whence you came."

Alexandra flinched, but pressed forward. "I understand why you hate me. I've given you good reason."

Jillian's dark eyebrow arched. "Hate you? Hate doesn't even begin to cover it. Given the choice, I'd see you dead, but soon it won't matter. I've tired of this conversation. Leave, or have you claimed my chamber for your own as well?"

"I don't want to take anything else from you. I wouldn't have taken Derek from you had I known about your plans to marry."

"You haven't taken Derek from me. He may have married you to protect you, but he's still mine. Naught has changed between us. And you'll soon be gone. If not—" She lifted her shoulder in a shrug. "It won't matter. He still prefers my bed to yours."

She turned her back on Alexandra and sat in front of her looking glass. She pulled a silver-handled hairbrush through her black locks. Morning sunlight glinted off the back of the rapidly moving brush. "Leave me in peace. You're not welcome in my chamber."

Stunned by her sister's blatant admission of improper intentions toward Derek, Alexandra slipped from the chamber and fled the house, unmindful of where she was going. She willed her hands to stop shaking and wiped the moisture from her face before she entered the spinning house.

Several slaves greeted her. She responded with a slight nod and threaded her way to an idle spinning wheel. Leaning slightly forward on her left foot, she picked up a long slender roll of soft carded wool from the wheel's platform and wound the end of the fibers on the point of the spindle. All the while, the image of Derek and Jillian locked in a passionate embrace burned itself into her memory.

Nudging a spoke of the wheel with a wooden peg, she seized the roll of carded wool with her left hand and held it a distance from the spindle. She drove away the painful remembrance and focused instead on the hum of the wheel. Quickly stepping backward three steps, she held the yarn high as it twisted and quivered. The familiar chore soothed her. Taught by Polly at an early age, Alexandra enjoyed spinning, particularly during times of worry.

She glided forward with an even, graceful stride and allowed the yarn to wind on the swift spindle. If only Polly were here to counsel her now. She took another pinch of the wool-roll, a new turn of the wheel, and repeated the process. She kept her thoughts centered only on the feel of the coarse wool between her fingers, on the quick backward and forward steps, determined to work to the point of exhaustion where troublesome concerns dared not intrude.

"I thought I might find you here."

Alexandra glanced up, and seeing her mother standing in the doorway, she forced a smile and joined her. They walked along the lane. As they passed the wash house, singing tinged the late autumn air with a soulful melody.

"I'm truly glad you're here," Laurel said.

Alexandra glanced sideways at Laurel. Sadness once again crept through her. "Me, too." She noticed the cameo around her mother's throat and her footsteps faltered. Dark, unsettling sensations she had not allowed herself to feel for some time assaulted her anew. With great strength of will she forced them away. "I see you've had the chain repaired."

Laurel's fingers rested on the locket. A tender smile lit up her eyes. "Yes, a jeweler in town replaced the clasp." She stopped and placed a hand on Alexandra's shoulder. "I cannot tell you how much it means to me to have it back. Your father gave it to me as a wedding gift." Her brow furrowed with a frown. "I wish I knew how it came into Bartholomew's possession. It must have happened when he took you."

Alexandra lowered her gaze to the ground. She traced the ribbing of her dimity skirt with her finger.

"Alexandra?"

She lifted her gaze.

Her mother's eyes softened. "Discussion of your abduction makes you uneasy."

"I cannot remember anything about it. Ofttimes, when I held or wore the locket, I would experience a terror such as I have never known. It was as if memories lurked, hovering on the fringes of my mind, yet unable to surface."

"Perhaps 'tis less a matter of can't and more a matter of won't."

"Will you tell me about that day?"

Laurel shook her head. "My father has cautioned me against it. He feels you will remember when you are able."

"I find this entire situation so unnerving. You

are my mother, but deep down I don't feel like your daughter, no matter how much I desire it. This is my home, yet I feel like a stranger waiting for something to happen and snatch it all away." Her heart ached with the knowledge that her marriage, precarious at best, was a sham.

Laurel pulled her into her arms and hugged her. This single action reminded Alexandra of what she had been deprived of most through the years—her mother's touch. They clung to each other for several minutes.

"Give it time, my child. 'Twill work itself out."

Alexandra hesitated. "Is it hard for you to call me Alexandra?"

"I must admit it was difficult at first. You had been Charlotte to me for so long, and indeed, I associated the name with Bartholomew. But you are you, and the name suits you. It is your middle name and mine, as well as my mother's before me."

Alexandra caressed her wedding band. "Grandfather gave this to me. He said it belonged to my grandmother."

Laurel smiled. "It did, and I know she would be pleased for you wear it. I'm sorry she can't be here with us today."

"I feel as though she is."

The two women continued their walk arm in arm toward the slave quarters. Laurel stopped before a cabin. "A babe has been born. Would you like to see her whilst I check on her mother?"

"Yes. 'Twould be nice to hold a baby again."

They entered the one-room cabin. It was simple but immaculate, with whitewashed walls and a clean interior. Alexandra's gaze took in a plain table with two stools against the wall. A handmade cradle sat before the small fireplace.

Laurel proceeded across the room to the rough bedstead. "How are you feeling, Bridget?"

"Jes' fine, Miss Laurel. I sho' do want to thank you fo' the new wool blanket. 'Twill keep her plenty warm this winter."

Laurel's grin dimpled her cheeks. "I'm glad you like it."

Alexandra gravitated toward the cradle. She peered down at the sleeping infant and marveled at the sweet vision presented by the dark-skinned baby with a cap of black curls and extraordinarily long lashes.

A painful need squeezed her heart. Would she ever have a babe of her own? She brushed a finger back and forth against the baby's cheek. So soft. So precious. She blinked back the sudden prick of tears.

"You can hold her if you like."

Alexandra glanced up and found the infant's mother watching her.

"Bridget, this is my daughter, Alexandra."

"Pleased to meet you, Miss Alexandra."

Although Alexandra read exhaustion in the other woman's dark brown gaze, she also read sincerity. "The pleasure is all mine, I assure you." She took great care to support the baby's head and cradled the warm bundle in her arms, swaying back and forth.

Alexandra lost track of time, so entranced was she by the miracle of life held snug against her body. She never tired of looking at the sweet child and smiled each time her tiny mouth moved in a sucking motion.

"What is her name?"

"Cara."

"'Tis a lovely name. You are indeed fortunate to have such a beautiful little girl."

"Yes, ma'am. That I am."

Alexandra squeezed her eyes shut and tried to etch this feeling in her mind. She wanted to carry it with her everywhere she went. She must have squeezed Cara a bit too tight because the baby grimaced and burst into an ear-splitting wail.

"Oh, my." Alexandra put the infant up to her shoulder and patted her back, but it didn't help. If anything, her cries worsened. "Are you hungry, little Cara?" She carried the baby to Bridget and watched in amazement as she clasped the babe to her breast.

Silence.

Laurel placed an arm around Alexandra's shoulder and gave her a hug. Their eyes met and they shared a smile.

"Babies are something special."

"Yes, they are," Alexandra said.

As they strolled past the shoemaker's house, Laurel said, "'Twill be lovely when our home is once again blessed with the pitter-patter of little feet. It has been so long."

Alexandra smiled at her mother's dreamy expression, then steeled herself against the recurring pain in her heart caused by the doubtfulness and uncertainty of her marriage. "I know about Jillian and Derek."

Laurel sighed. "I had hoped to keep it from you a while longer. Who told you?"

"It doesn't matter how I found out. I feel horrible for causing Jillian so much pain. Did they...were they...close?" The word *love* stuck in her throat and would not be dislodged.

"Derek has spent a great deal of time here during the past years." Laurel chuckled out loud. "When you were very little you used to follow him around everywhere he went. He never seemed to mind, though. Why, I remember on your fifth birthday, you publicly announced your betrothal to Derek."

"I didn't!" Alexandra covered her mouth with her hand. "What did he do?"

"Oh, he took it all in stride. I suppose he didn't

have the heart to hurt your feelings. Perhaps he married the right sister after all."

Alexandra's smile faded. Perhaps he still didn't want to hurt her feelings. She forced herself to ask the question that tormented her. "How long have they intended to marry?"

"As I said before, Derek has been here whenever possible. Perhaps, in part, it was because of guilt."

"Guilt? Whatever for?"

"After you were taken from us, he came to me and vowed to find you. He was a young man of only sixteen or seventeen years, yet he took it upon himself to return you to us. When he realized he could not carry out his promise, he became very protective of Jillian and his own sisters, apparently determined such an incident would never occur again. Jillian reveled in all the attention he gave her. They never made a public announcement, but somehow we all came to expect they would eventually marry."

"How did she react when he traveled to Philadelphia in search of me?"

"None of us knew where he had gone or why. She moped around for a short time, but she had become accustomed to his absences during his coastal trade and his visits to the West Indies."

From the corner of her eye, Alexandra saw Derek coming toward them, accompanied by Max. Her heart began its usual staccato rhythm. Why did her body continually betray her whenever Derek was close by? Why couldn't she be immune to the yearning he stirred within her?

"Good morning, Lexi." He pressed a kiss to her forehead that made her toes curl despite her inner protests. He slipped his arm around her shoulders and nodded to her mother. "Good morning to you, Mrs. Montgomery."

Alexandra held herself stiffly.

"I've been looking for you," he said.

She squirmed beneath his penetrating gaze and leaned over to pet the Newfoundland. "When did you return?"

"A short while ago. I've been looking for you ever since."

"I will leave the two of you alone," Laurel said. "I must see to the sewing house. However, since I have both of you together I would like to discuss something with you."

"Yes?" Alexandra said.

"Your father and I would like to give a ball celebrating your return and your marriage."

"Wouldn't that be a lot of trouble? And expense?"

"Oh, pooh. You're our daughter and we want to express our joy about your return."

"We would be honored," Derek said.

"Wonderful. We shall begin planning it this very afternoon. Enjoy your time with your husband, my dear." Laurel headed in the direction of the sewing house.

Alexandra stood near Derek, uncomfortable with his presence. When she lifted her gaze and found him watching her, she warmed at the intensity of his perusal.

He held his hand out. Following a moment's hesitation, she slipped her hand into his. He gave her hand a warm squeeze. Tingles spread through her arm.

At that moment Alexandra came to a decision. Whether there had been an agreement between her husband and Jillian or not, what was done was done. She would do her best to ensure that Derek would not for one moment regret marrying her. Her spirits lifted. She turned a brilliant smile on him and squeezed his hand in return.

"What have you and your mother been doing this morning?"

"We visited the slave quarters. I held a newborn baby girl." She sighed at the memory. "I love babies."

Derek gave her a sharp look. "My sister Hannah's former husband complained quite a lot about their two children. Said they were always howling about one thing or another."

Alexandra thought back to her meeting with Derek's family. Hannah Tremaine Morgan had been recently widowed. Alexandra had found three-year-old Tessa and one-year-old Brandon a source of delight. Little Tessa had favored her with many toothy grins. How could anyone complain about those charming children?

A troubling thought occurred to her. How would Derek react if they were to have children in spite of the precautions they were taking? She needed to gather the courage and ask him what those precautions were.

Chapter Twenty

22 November 1752
What am I to do about Jillian? Every day she finds reasons to see Derek, to touch him, to whisper in his ear. I cannot allow her to snare him in her web of seduction.

27 November 1752
Jillian has taken unusual pains with her appearance. A slight smile hovers around her lips. Her eyes are illuminated from within. What will she do next?

I must fight her effect on Derek. He is blinded by love for her, unaware she isn't good for him. I will love him so thoroughly, so completely, that mayhap he will learn to love me in return.

2 December 1752
Jillian disappears each day between dinner and supper, as does Derek.

Have my greatest fears been realized?
****

Alexandra lifted a forkful of tangy Virginia ham to her mouth and glanced at Jillian who had dressed in an exquisite gown of heavy green silk. Her black hair had been swept up. Three long curls rested on her bared shoulder. Secrets sparkled in the depths of her brown eyes.

This day Alexandra planned to find out where her sister had been keeping herself. She would follow her and discover, for better or worse, the object of Jillian's affections. Alexandra bit into her biscuit, scarcely aware that it melted in her mouth.

"Laurel tells me you have given your consent for the ball." Jared poured wine into his glass.

Alexandra licked the butter from her lips. "You and Mother have been far too generous."

"Ball?" Jillian said. "You're giving *her* a ball?"

Alexandra recognized the petulant look narrowing her sister's eyes. A sick feeling of dread knotted her stomach.

Bewilderment flickered across Laurel's expression. "Didn't I tell you? We're having a party to welcome Alexandra home and celebrate her marriage to Derek."

Jillian's eyes flashed with anger. Alexandra schooled her features to reveal naught of the torment caused by the scorching heat of the younger woman's wrath. Instead, she said, "I do hope you will be there."

"Humphh." Jillian pushed herself away from the dining room table and flounced from the room.

Shaken by the outright rejection, Alexandra excused herself, and ignoring Derek's questioning gaze, followed the route her sister had taken. She stepped onto the front steps and closed the door behind her. Max rose from his resting place beside the steps and moved to her side.

"Max, stay."

The Newfoundland flicked her fingertips with his tongue. She patted his head and hurried down the steps. The dog followed.

"Max, stay."

With something akin to a sigh, he obeyed her. A cool breeze rustled her amber brocade skirt and sent a shiver through her. If she fetched her cloak, she would lose sight of her sister.

She pulled her wool shawl closer about her shoulders and struggled to keep up, yet stay far enough back so as not to be noticed. They passed most of the plantation's outbuildings. Where could Jillian be going?

Despite the chill in the air, Alexandra wiped perspiration from her brow and trudged along. At times she barely kept her sister in view. They neared a cluster of trees. "Oh, no. Don't let me lose you now."

When Jillian remained near the edge of the wooded area, Alexandra breathed a sigh of relief. Then the younger woman stopped. Alexandra darted behind a tree and peered around its enormous trunk.

A small cloud of dust in the distance grew larger. Alexandra waited, her breath caught against the anticipation of the moment. Finally, she would discover the cause of Jillian's odd behavior.

She could make out the shape of a coach now, but not any details to help identify its passenger. If only she could move closer without alerting Jillian to her presence.

The carriage came to a stop in front of Jillian. A man dressed in black alighted. He kept his back toward Alexandra. Something about him seemed familiar, frighteningly so, and froze her in place. *Turn around.*

She watched him help Jillian into the coach. He turned in Alexandra's direction for a split second.

A loud roar buzzed in her ears and her knees grew weak. Stricken by a soul-deep fear, she clutched the tree in front of her to steady her trembling limbs.

It could not be.

But it was.

Bartholomew.

The coach door slammed shut, and the driver guided the team of horses back the way they had come. Alexandra snapped to attention.

"No, Jillian!"

The autumn breeze tossed her words back at her. She gathered up her skirts and ran toward the carriage, but it increased speed and put more distance between them.

Alexandra continued to run. She held her hand against the stitch in her side and tried to ignore the stab of pain. Her slippered foot stepped into a small hole.

Shards of white-hot agony splintered through her ankle and shot up her calf. With a cry, she fell to the hard ground. She remained still for several minutes until her breathing slowed and the pain dimmed.

Placing her palms against the grassy surface, she pushed herself up into a semi-reclining position and pressed probing fingers to her ankle. She bit her lip against the acute soreness.

Drat it all.

She had really done it this time. Miles from home and no one knew where she had gone.

By slow degrees, she dragged herself over to a tree and pulled herself up. She gingerly placed weight on her right foot. Another flash of agony rippled through her. She clutched the tree and gasped for air.

A glance about for something she could use for a crutch revealed a fallen branch nearly three inches in diameter. She lowered herself to her knees and crawled over to it, paying little heed to the stains and tears in the skirt of her gown.

Her fingers closed around the branch. She placed it on end and pulled herself upright. After several practice steps, Alexandra collapsed behind a large tree and decided she would try again later. For now she must rest and conserve her energy until Jillian returned.

What was Jillian doing with Bartholomew? Did he know Jillian was her sister? She prayed it was not so, for he would surely use that knowledge against all of them.

How had he known where to find her? Had he followed them from Philadelphia? She winced against the throbbing in her ankle and leaned against the tree. She eased her woolen shawl off her shoulders and wrapped it around her ankle, binding it snugly, and settled herself against the tree to await Jillian's return. She must make her sister see reason. She must make her understand the danger.

Alexandra stared up through the netting of crimson and gold leaves, rubbed her hands up and down her arms, and refused to dwell upon the bite of the autumn chill. She must think about something else, something warm.

Someone warm.

Derek.

Her lips curved upward. A sudden realization broadened her smile.

Jillian was not seeing Derek.

Just as quickly, shame and self-loathing tugged the corners of her mouth down. She should have known Derek would not sneak off for a tryst with Jillian. Though he might love her sister, he was too honorable to act on his feelings. His innate sense of responsibility would not have allowed it. She would make it up to him by being the attentive, dutiful, obedient wife he deserved.

Dutiful?

Obedient?

She grimaced at the reminder of her character flaws. If naught else, she would be attentive. He had admitted to being fond of her. Perhaps she could coax his fondness into something deeper, fan the embers into something lasting.

Into love.

Her memory evoked the warm and the tender, the powerful and the passionate moments they had shared. With a sigh of satisfaction, she closed her eyes and relived them one by one.

****

A crunching sound and the whinny of a horse intruded upon Alexandra's dreams. The slamming of a door and more crunching jarred her awake. She blinked in confusion at the darkening skies, unable to remember for a moment where she was. And why.

Jillian.

Alexandra scrambled to her feet, instantly regretting her hasty impulse. "Oh." She clutched the tree as pain shot through her leg.

"Who's there?" Jillian said.

Alexandra grabbed her makeshift crutch and hobbled out of the trees. "It's me."

"What are *you* doing here?"

"What were *you* doing with Bartholomew Taylor?" Alexandra inched closer.

"'Tis none of your concern." Jillian turned to leave.

"Wait! I have something to say to you and you *will* listen."

The younger woman stopped and stared at Alexandra, her mouth open. "You have no say in what I do."

Alexandra shuffled toward her. "I do if you're involved with Bartholomew Taylor."

Jillian turned away.

"He's dangerous. Don't you know who he is? He's—"

Jillian advanced toward her. "He is kind. He's charming."

"He is using you to get what he wants. Me."

"You? Bah! Not everyone in this world wants you. You have Mama. You have Papa. You have—" Her voice broke. "Derek."

"Bartholomew is the man who abducted me. He tried to force me into marriage."

Jillian held her hands over her ears. "I won't listen to you. He loves me. I know he does. He's mine and you can't have him." With a sob, she turned and fled.

"Stop, Jillian. You can't leave me out here."

"You found your way here. You can find your way back. I hope you never come back."

Alexandra stared in astonishment as her sister disappeared into the night. Thunder rumbled in the distance. A cold wind chilled her to the bone. She lifted her disbelieving gaze to the heavens. "Why now?"

Another volley rolled across the sky.

She scowled. "Sorry I asked." Muttering beneath her breath, she began the long journey home.

Move the crutch forward. Lean onto it. Take a step. Move the crutch forward. Lean onto it. Take a step. She repeated this process over and over, centered her concentration on every step, and refused to acknowledge the throbbing in her ankle.

Home. She must get home. Derek would be worried. No one knew where she had gone. She doubted Jillian would reveal her whereabouts.

No. If she were going to get home, she would have to depend on herself.

Alexandra stared at the darkness spread out before her like a never-ending ocean of black. A flutter of fear stirred within her. She had never explored this part of the plantation.

She lifted her chin and squared her shoulders. She had overcome too much to allow something as minor as a sprained ankle, a little bit of thunder, and the dark to stop her from making her way back home, back to Derek.

Move the crutch forward. Lean onto it. Take a step.

****

Derek glanced at the tall-case clock. Half-past

nine. He slammed his fist on the mantle. Where could she be?

The front door opened, then closed.

"Lexi? Is that you?" Derek ran to the entry hall. His rising spirits deflated. "Oh, it's you."

Jillian arched an eyebrow and swept past him. "I feel the same way, I assure you."

He closed his hand around her elbow and brought her to a halt. "Have you seen Alexandra?"

Jillian shook free and spent an inordinate amount of time smoothing her long skirts. "Am I my precious sister's keeper now? Isn't that *your* duty?"

Her nervous demeanor and sharp, sarcastic tone suggested all was not as it appeared. He placed his finger beneath her chin and forced her to meet his gaze.

"Where is she?"

Emotions he could not quite identify flickered through her large brown eyes. Wariness perhaps? Jealousy for certain. Ear-splitting thunder boomed overhead. He gripped her chin more harshly than he intended and quelled the desire to shake the truth out of her.

"Tell me what you know. If you have allowed anything to happen to her—"

Jillian jerked free. "Your little spy should be here soon. Why did you have to bring her here?"

Derek advanced a step closer. "What do you mean 'spy'? Where is she?"

"Don't get your tail feathers in a knot. She followed me to the wooded area near the northeast boundary dividing your property from ours."

After delivering a blistering glare at the sullen young woman before him, Derek hurried out into the rain and raced toward the stables.

Chapter Twenty-One

An ominous crack of lightning split the sky. After a bit of a struggle, Alexandra tugged open the door of the large outbuilding and staggered inside. Leaning against the interior wall to catch her breath, she pushed a sodden mass of hair from her eyes and surveyed what she presumed to be a tobacco barn or warehouse. A number of hogsheads, most likely packed with tobacco and waiting to be shipped, filled the spacious building.

At least she would not be struck by lightning in here. Her ankle cried out for a respite from the strength-sapping walk. She hobbled farther inside the barn and lowered herself to the floor so she could rest against a hogshead.

Her wet clothing clung to her. Shivers traversed the length of her slight frame. She clenched her chattering teeth together and rubbed her hands up and down her arms to restore warmth. As was her recently acquired habit, she moved her wedding band back and forth across her finger. The subtle motion eased her anxiety.

She closed her eyes and pictured a fireplace aglow with a dancing fire, radiating heat, precious heat. The flickering tongues of red, blue, and orange flames beckoned her closer. The heat flushed her cheeks a rosy hue.

In her imaginings a man stood beside her. A tall, handsome man.

Derek.

An inner warmth suffused her body. She slipped

her hand into his and lost herself in the depths of his promise-filled gaze.

"Lexi!"

Alexandra smiled up at Derek. Then his image faded.

"L-lexi-i!"

She reached for him. Her fingers passed through nothingness and brought her back to awareness with a startling pang of disappointment. He had seemed so real.

"L-lexi-i!"

Alexandra lifted her head and listened. The wind whistled through the eaves of the barn. She must be hearing things.

"L-lexi-i!"

There it was again. Someone *was* calling her name.

She grabbed the rim of the hogshead and pulled herself up. With the aid of her crutch, she limped toward the entrance, where she pushed and strained against the door until it gave way and allowed her to slip through the opening.

"L-lexi-i!"

She pivoted around on her crutch. Which direction was his voice coming from? The cold wind buffeted her heavy, wet skirts and threatened to send her atumble.

"I'm here!" She peered through the rain and tried in vain to see through the dark thicket of trees. "Please let him be there."

A bright flash of lightning illuminated the sky. A deafening crash of thunder followed. Alexandra jumped at the unexpected noise.

She clenched her hands into tight fists. "'Tis only a little bit of rain." She found a small measure of comfort in the sound of her own voice.

An answering volley of thunder contradicted her self-assurance. In its wake, powerful arms closed around her. Terror tripped through her. Reacting on sheer instinct, Alexandra screamed. She clawed at the vise-like grip and kicked with every ounce of strength she could muster. She abruptly found herself turned and hoisted into the air before settling against a chest too broad to be ignored.

"It's me. Derek. I'm not going to hurt you." He cupped her chin with his hand and stroked her cheek with his thumb.

Alexandra ceased her struggles. Her ears absorbed his words, but her eyes scanned his features, first in disbelief, then with joy. "It *is* you." Her fingers traced the path her gaze had taken and caressed his eyes, his nose, his mouth.

Derek lowered his mouth to hers for the sweetest, most glorious of kisses. She parted her lips and allowed him complete, full access. All too soon the kiss ended, and Derek set her on her feet.

Her mind still atwitter from his touch, Alexandra took a step toward him. With a sharp cry, she pitched forward and clutched his rain-dampened shirtfront.

He caught her. "What is it, Lexi?"

"My ankle. I sprained it."

In one fluid motion, Derek scooped her up against him. Their gazes locked and her heart fluttered. For this moment, all seemed right with the world and there wasn't any other place she would rather be.

"I must get you home before you catch your death." Derek carried her to his stallion.

She glanced down. The Newfoundland pranced beside them and wagged his tail. She looked back at Derek. "Did Max find me?"

"He helped." Derek placed her on his horse and swung up behind her. He slid his arm around her waist and drew her against him before urging Storm forward.

The wind and rain slacked off, leaving behind a drizzle that might have been annoying under different circumstances. Instead, Alexandra barely noticed. All rational thought had fled her mind. Her entire awareness was centered on the sensations roused by Derek's touch, by his close proximity.

She indulged in the luxury of leaning against her husband's broad chest. His firm, powerful thighs pressed intimately against hers. The steady pressure of his forearms beneath her breasts as he guided Storm stirred such a longing, such a sweet yearning, that she could scarcely sit still.

"What were you doing out here, Lexi?"

Alexandra listened to the pleasant rumble of his chest, then her smile faded.

"Lexi?"

"I-I went for a walk." How would he react to the news about Jillian and Bartholomew? Perhaps she shouldn't tell him the woman he loved was meeting another man. She wanted to spare him the pain she had been enduring. Yet she must find a way to prevent Bartholomew from inflicting further harm on her family.

"Why did Jillian leave you out here in this weather, in your condition?"

Alexandra stiffened and stared straight ahead. "Jillian?"

"Aye, Jillian. No one knew where you had gone. When Jillian returned, I asked if she knew of your whereabouts. She finally told me where to look. I cannot fathom why she left you here. The chit has much explaining to do."

Alexandra shifted in the saddle. "'Twas my fault. I angered her."

Derek chuckled. "What did you do? Beat her in a horse race?"

"No, I—"Alexandra faltered. "I followed her, or more specifically, I spied on her."

"Spied on her?" He crinkled his brow in thought. "Come to think of it, she did call you my little spy. Whatever for?"

"I had to find out for certain who she has been meeting the past few afternoons."

"Why didn't you just ask her?"

"Jillian hates me. We don't have sisterly conversations. In fact, she seldom acknowledges my presence."

"Who did you think she could be meeting? She turns away every suitor who comes calling."

Alexandra moistened her dry lips with the tip of her tongue and responded in a small voice. "I feared she might be meeting you."

Derek pulled Storm to an abrupt halt. "Me?" He placed his hands on her shoulders and swiveled her around until she faced him. "You thought *I* was meeting Jillian?" The muscle in his jaw jumped. "For what, pray tell, illicit assignations?"

Alexandra blanched at the raw fury sparking from his brown-gold gaze and leaned back as far as possible on the stallion to escape Derek's searing wrath.

He closed his hands around her slender shoulders once again. His fingers bit into her sensitive flesh and he dragged her against him. "*You* are my wife. Do you believe I take my wedding vows so lightly?"

Alexandra's heart twisted at the shadowed depths of his eyes, at the harsh rasp in his voice.

He shook her. "Answer me. Tell me where your distrust comes from."

Tears sprung to her eyes. "You're hurting me."

He dropped his hands, but his piercing, expectant glare remained fixed on her. She rubbed her arm with a trembling hand.

"Jillian has been behaving oddly. She has had a secretive, mysterious look about her, as if she were in love. In addition, she has disappeared after dinner every day for the past sennight."

"Why did you think she was meeting me?" he asked, his voice now devoid of emotion.

A terrible emptiness settled upon Alexandra like a weighted mantle. She studied her hands. "I overheard the two of you talking. Jillian said you—" She cleared her throat and forced herself to meet Derek's cold stare without flinching. "Jillian said you were to wed her."

Derek stiffened and, though he hadn't moved, he distanced himself from her. He drew within himself and closed his expression. "I meant to tell you."

"Did you?" Pinpricks of tears burned the backs of her eyes. "Before or after every person in Williamsburg cast speculative glances my way? Before or after you realized you couldn't stay away from her?"

He clenched his jaw.

She didn't want to listen to his reply. She couldn't bear to hear the words spoken aloud. It wouldn't take much to shatter the remaining remnants of her already broken heart.

"Lexi—"

She held up her hand. "Keep your excuses. I don't care to hear them."

Without a word, Derek turned her around and urged Storm forward. The arms that rested around her waist were impersonal in their touch. They merely served the purpose of keeping her anchored to the saddle.

During the remainder of the ride, Alexandra held herself rigid. She deprived herself of the longed-for luxury of leaning back against him, of melting into the comfort of his arms, of pretending naught was wrong between them.

Her ankle throbbed most of the journey back to the plantation, but she refused to voice her distress.

Instead, she endured it and used it as a means to pass the interminable length of time it took to reach Montgomery Hall.

****

Menacing, whirling images. Large, looming shadows.

Evil laughter. Muted pleas.

Gunfire. Stillness.

Thick, suffocating darkness closed in around Alexandra. Strong hands gripped her shoulders. Breathing hard, she pushed at the faceless demon and struggled to rid herself of his touch.

Terror swirled in the pit of her stomach and welled up. It threatened to suck her entire being into the vortex of a maelstrom from which she would never escape.

She opened her mouth, but no sound emerged. Her heart pounded. A roar sounded in her ears. She couldn't catch her breath.

She was going to die.

"Lexi, wake up."

A gentle voice called her back from the depths of despair. Her anxiety diminished.

"That's it, Lexi. Open your eyes."

Her eyelids fluttered open. A moment later, her vision cleared and revealed Derek leaning over her, worry etched on his handsome features. She sat up and threw her arms around his neck.

"Tell me what you remember from your nightmare," he said against her tousled hair.

She shook her head. "Nay. I don't want to. I cannot."

He unlocked her hands from his neck and propped her against the pillows. She soaked up the sight of him and turned her cheek into his palm.

"You must try to remember." He placed a finger to her lips and halted her refusal. "Do you want to banish these nightmares and regain your memory, or do you prefer to live the remainder of your life in this manner?"

She tilted her chin in stubborn defiance. "I cannot do what you are asking of me."

His gaze softened. "I'll be here. No harm shall come to you. Whatever you're afraid to face will continue to have power over you until you allow yourself to unbury it and deal with it."

"But what if I cannot face it? What if I lose complete control of my sanity? You will be forever saddled with a lunatic wife."

He took her hand into his and lifted it to his lips. "Nay. 'Twill not happen. I won't allow it."

The corners of her mouth tipped up in a wry half-smile. "*You* won't allow it? What an arrogant man you are, Captain Tremaine. Do you command the seas and the heavens as well?"

He grinned. "Close your eyes, wife, and mind your saucy tongue."

With a sigh and a wrinkle of her nose, she did as he requested.

"Relax." He stroked her hair. "Tell me about your dream."

"I don't recall anything."

"Try again. What do you see? Or hear? Or feel?"

"Fear. And a laugh. A wicked laugh." An involuntary shiver shook her body. "It was dark. The shadows hid his face." Alarm quickened her breathing. She snapped her eyes open.

"Whose face?"

She clutched the satin coverlet in her hands. "I don't know. It was too dark."

"How do you know it was a man?"

"I don't know. I just do." She hugged her arms around her midsection. "I don't want to think about this anymore." Her bottom lip quivered. "I can't do it."

He pressed a kiss to her forehead. "You've done

well. We'll try again another time." He moved to lie beside her and drew her into his warm embrace. The steady rise and fall of his chest and the strong thump of his heart against her ear soon lulled her into a drowsy state.

Derek threaded his fingers through her long tresses. "I wonder what induced this last nightmare. You haven't had one since the evening we set sail."

The image of Bartholomew racing along the Philadelphia wharf, calling her name, flashed through Alexandra's mind. She sat up with a start.

Derek knelt beside her. "What is it, Lexi?"

"I just remembered." She turned her anguished gaze upon him. "I saw him this afternoon."

Derek arched an eyebrow in confusion. "You saw who this afternoon?"

"Bartholomew."

Chapter Twenty-Two

Derek gripped Alexandra's shoulders. "You saw Taylor?"

She nodded, her sapphire eyes rounded.

He dropped his hands. "Where did you see him?"

She moistened her lower lip and revealed the tip of her pink tongue. "This afternoon. He's the man Jillian left with."

Derek pulled his gaze from Alexandra's tempting mouth and stared at her. His eyes narrowed in disbelief. "Are you certain?"

Her mouth set in a grim line, she said, "I watched a man step out of his coach and assist Jillian inside. He turned in my direction for only the briefest of moments, but I know it was Bartholomew."

Derek raked his fingers through his hair. He eyed Alexandra in the silvery moonlight streaming through the parted curtains. "Surely she knows of his actions toward you. Doesn't she realize the danger he poses for you, for your family?"

"She won't listen. She despises me."

Derek frowned. "It doesn't sound like the Jillian I know."

"There is quite a lot you don't know about your precious Jillian."

Derek scrutinized her suspiciously bright eyes. "She isn't 'my Jillian.'"

With jerky movements, he rose from the bed and walked over to the window. He had nearly blurted out that he had married the only woman he wanted.

Why had he stopped short? He glanced sideways at Alexandra. Tears shimmered in her eyes. A force within him demanded he go to her, take her in his arms, and tell her everything would be all right.

No, damn it. She didn't have faith in him. She believed him capable of infidelity. A vise closed around his heart. The fate of their marriage was in her hands. She was the one filled with doubt, not he.

He drew a long, slow breath against the constriction in his chest and fixed his gaze upon the stables visible outside the house. "Whether or not you believe me when I tell you naught will happen between Jillian and me is beside the point. For the time being we must decide how to handle this situation."

He turned away from the window. Her ebony veil of silken hair shielded her expression from his view as she stared at her hands. He clenched his jaw and steeled himself against the powerful urge to toss aside the hurt and anger her suspicions caused and lose himself in her beauty.

She lifted her gaze to his. "What should we do? We must stop her involvement with Bartholomew."

Derek nodded. "I agree. We'll tell your parents on the morrow and proceed from there."

"Jillian won't like it."

He climbed back into bed. "She'll get over it." He pounded his fist into the pillow several times before he settled into the mattress with his back toward Alexandra. Every nerve ending pulsed in awareness of the woman a few scant inches away. Yet those same scant inches seemed as broad as the Atlantic Ocean, as unbridgeable as the deepest abyss.

****

Derek scarcely noticed the early morning light that poured through the opened rose silk curtains and bestowed a false sense of cheer to the parlor. He and Alexandra stood before her parents and awaited their reaction to the unpleasant information.

Laurel's colorless countenance spoke volumes, whereas Jared's face grew more mottled by the minute while he clutched the arm of the rose damask settee. "You are certain of this, Alexandra?"

"I would give anything for it to be otherwise, but I saw them together."

Laurel wrung her hands in her lap. "I don't understand how this could have happened." Her bottom lip quivered. "Will we never be free of him?"

Jared slipped an arm around her shoulders and pulled her close. "Shhh, now. Don't fret, dear. He won't take another daughter from us."

Alexandra knelt before her parents and placed her arms about them. Footsteps in the hall caught Derek's attention. Jillian entered the parlor in festive spirits, oblivious to the presence of her family. Her dark eyes twinkled and her mouth curved in a lighthearted grin. She twirled around the room.

Then she saw her parents and Alexandra wrapped in a tight embrace. Her steps faltered and the light in her eyes faded.

Derek took careful note of her changed demeanor. Intense resentment, nay, enmity, flared upon her features. He would not have been surprised if sparks had shot out of her narrowed eyes. Her pursed lips transformed her face into an unbecoming bitterness.

Alexandra had been correct. Jillian hated her. How had she been so adept at concealing her feelings that only Alexandra had been aware of them? How could he have thought he could have married her? From the corner of his eye, he saw Jillian clench her hands into small fists and turn to leave the room. He caught one of her wrists.

She struggled against his iron grip. "Let go of me."

Jared rose from the settee and strode over to Jillian. "You will remain here. There is a matter of importance we must discuss."

Derek released her and took his place beside Alexandra.

Jillian lifted her chin in defiance and glared at the four people in the parlor. "Well? What is this important matter we have to discuss?"

"You must stop seeing Bartholomew Taylor," Laurel said. "At once."

Jillian whirled and advanced toward Alexandra. "You told them. 'Twas none of your concern."

Derek started to step between the two sisters, but Alexandra placed her hand on his forearm.

"From the moment Derek told me I had a sister I looked forward to meeting you. I sincerely hoped we would be friends. However, regardless of your feelings for me, I care so very much about you. For your sake, you must stay away from Bartholomew."

"Don't tell me what to do." Jillian stomped her foot. "I won't listen to you."

"Jillian, he's using you."

"Nay. I won't let you talk about him in such a manner. He wants me, not you. You can't have him."

Laurel stepped between them. "Bartholomew Taylor has brought nothing but misery and heartache to this family, Jillian. You will have no further association with him. Do I make myself clear?"

Jillian's eyes glistened with unshed tears. "It isn't fair. She gets everything she wants. I wish she had never come back."

"Enough!" Jared's voice thundered. "Remove yourself to your bedchamber at once. You will remain there until your manners and good sense return."

Without so much as a backward glance, Jillian gathered her long skirts with her hands and flounced from the parlor. She stomped her way up the stairway toward her chamber and muttered loudly about injustices running rampant through the house.

****

Propped against several large pillows, Bartholomew Taylor drew a deep, satisfied breath and watched the young woman asleep beside him snuggle closer.

He curled his lip in a smug sneer and congratulated himself on the speed with which his plan was coming together. Soon, very soon his lifelong dream would become reality. His thoughts wandered back twenty-two years, to another place, another time.

At twenty-three years of age, Bartholomew was a carefree young rake. Freed from the controlling thumb of his once domineering father, dead from a most unfortunate accident, Bartholomew fancied himself in love with Laurel Alexandra Whittaker, whom he called Alexandra.

He spent most of his time envisioning his life with the sixteen-year-old black-haired beauty and planning their home. It never occurred to him that his plans might go awry. Just when he was on the verge of asking for Alexandra's hand, bold, handsome Jared Montgomery caught her fancy.

Although Bartholomew's hopes were temporarily dashed, he refused to admit defeat. Instead, he continued to prepare for his betrothal to Alexandra, confident of his ability to win her heart and her hand.

A short time later, he glimpsed his beloved through the window of the milliner's shop. While he waited for her, he conjured images of her in the bridal gown he had commissioned, a breathtaking confection of satin, lace, and pearls.

The moment she stepped outside he looped his

arm through hers. "My dear Alexandra, 'tis a stroke of good fortune you are here. I intended to call on you this eve."

"P-please call me Laurel." She stepped back.

Pleased by her maidenly shyness, he drew her closer. "I prefer to call you Alexandra. 'Tis my own special name for you. Mine and no one else's. It's what I shall call you every day, every blissful night after we are united in marriage."

"Marriage? You are mistaken, sir. I am to wed Jared Montgomery."

Bartholomew refused to hear what she was saying. "They can't make you wed him. I won't let them. You'll be the most exquisite bride anyone has ever seen. I cannot wait to have you all to myself in our new home."

She pulled away. "Listen to me. I will not marry you. I cannot. Not now, not ever."

He swept her up into his arms, intending to carry her away, but Jared Montgomery and Everette Tremaine rounded the corner of the shop and interfered.

"Release her, Taylor." Jared's hand rested on his pistol.

Everette drew his sword. "You heard him."

Bartholomew tightened his hold on Alexandra. She cried out in pain. Instantly contrite, he put her down. He placed a finger under her chin and tilted her face. "I would never harm you, Alexandra. My heart can barely contain the love I have for you."

She wrenched free and ran to Jared's waiting arms.

"Laurel is going to marry me," Jared said. "If you value your life, you'll stay away from her." He led her to his waiting carriage. Everette mounted his steed and followed close behind.

A few weeks later they were wed.

Bartholomew had vowed to make Montgomery

and Tremaine suffer for taking his Alexandra from him and forcing her into marriage. That burning vow had dictated every moment of his life thereafter. A soft feminine sigh brought him back to the present. He stroked the young woman's ebony locks, then slid down beside her and awakened her with a harsh, ravaging kiss.

Her dark eyes fluttered open in surprise, but she did not protest. Instead, she opened her mouth to him and matched his ardor. He slaked his lust quickly and took secret delight in the flicker of disappointment she hastily concealed.

Jillian pulled the scarlet satin coverlet over her nude form and rested her head on his chest. She traced a random path along his ribcage with her fingertip. "D-do you love me, Bartholomew?"

He rolled his eyes toward the ceiling and forced himself to answer in a soothing, patient tone, despite his irritation. "Now, Jillian, we have discussed this at length, on more than one occasion."

"I know. It's just that—"

"It's just what?"

Her finger halted its journey. "Alexandra knows about us. She saw us yesterday afternoon."

Bartholomew's flagging interest suddenly revived. He bit back a smile. His good fortune and patience were rewarding him handsomely. When he arrived in Williamsburg and discovered Alexandra had a sister, an insecure chit who thrived on the attention he so diligently lavished upon her, he had carefully planned step by step how he would use her to get Alexandra back.

"Because of her interference, Mama and Papa won't let me be with you. But I don't care. You and I are meant to be together." Jillian tipped her head and met Bartholomew's gaze. "When shall we be married?"

"Soon. Very soon."

Jillian settled her head back on his chest. "I can't wait. Our wedding will be the most spectacular event of the year. The ball Mama and Papa are giving Alexandra will pale in comparison. Alexandra this, Alexandra that. I hear Alexandra, Alexandra from dawn to dusk until I'm fair sick of it."

"What ball are you referring to, my pet?" Bartholomew's mind was already spinning another plan, one even better than the first.

Jillian gave an unladylike snort. "'Tis a ball to welcome Alexandra home and to celebrate her marriage to Derek."

Bartholomew clenched his hands into tight fists at her mention of Alexandra's marriage. His mind ticked off the various ways he would make her groom pay for his actions.

"...at the ball."

Bartholomew shook his head and stared at Jillian with unseeing eyes. "What did you say?"

"Let's announce our engagement at the ball. Imagine the look on her face when we arrive together and tell everyone present about our decision to wed. She will be so envious because I will have what she wants. 'Twill be delightful."

A slow smile spread across Bartholomew's face. Wicked glee rose within him. "Yes. It will be a surprise none of them will soon forget."

Soon, Alexandra, soon. You will once again be mine.

Forever.

Chapter Twenty-Three

Alexandra placed the sleeping infant in the cradle and turned to pick up the year-old child clutching her long skirts in an age-old battle for balance.

He lost and landed on his backside with a solid thunk. His eyes rounded in surprise for but a moment before he wrinkled his face and prepared to deliver a mighty howl.

"Oh, no, you don't." Alexandra scooped the dark-skinned child into her arms and made funny faces at him.

He blinked. His long black lashes swept onto his dusky cheeks, and he stared solemnly at her.

"That's a good boy. You don't want to cry, do you? No. Baby Cara just went to sleep and you mustn't undo all my hard work."

A smile touched Alexandra's lips as a glow of contentment almost filled an empty spot in her heart. This feeling had bought her to the nursery for the slaves' babies every day, ofttimes twice a day, ever since holding Cara three weeks earlier.

Thankfully, the mothers did not begrudge the time she spent with their children, and though they had been shy with her at first, she now knew most of them by name. The children had taken to her right away. She shifted Caleb to her other hip and tucked a loose strand of hair behind her ear.

Sudden tingles traversed the length of her spine and invigorated her with awareness. She drew a deep breath to steady her trembling insides and lifted her gaze.

Derek's potent masculinity reached out and caught her in its powerful grip. It speared her with an ache of such bittersweet longing that it hurt to look at him. Caleb squirmed and she clasped her arms tighter around the wriggling child.

Derek stepped through the doorway. His presence filled the room. "Your mother told me I might find you here."

Alexandra struggled to tamp down the excitement flooding through her. "You were looking for me?"

"Aye." He closed the distance between them in several long strides. "'Tis nearly time for dinner."

Alexandra winced and caught her breath at his disturbing nearness. "I suppose I lost track of time."

A mewling sound at her side drew her gaze down. The babe Cara moved fitfully, then launched into an earsplitting wail.

"Oh, dear." Alexandra glanced up at Derek and frowned at the strange look in his eyes. Unable to reflect further upon its meaning, she handed Caleb to him.

"What are you doing?"

Alexandra rolled her eyes heavenward. She bent over the cradle and brought the crying baby to her shoulder, murmuring in consoling tones.

"Be you daft, woman? I'm not accustomed to holding children."

Alexandra bit back a grin as she watched the man capable of handling bears in the woods and vessels on stormy seas brought to his knees by a mere child. "I can't very well hold the two of them at once. Would you prefer to trade?"

Derek's eyes rounded. He opened his mouth, but no sound came forth. In the end, he settled for an emphatic shake of his head.

"I thought not." Alexandra stroked the silky

curls of the babe nestled against her shoulder. She closed her eyes and reveled in the softness of the cherub. She never tired of this bubbling joy, this peaceful contentment. Her smile slipped. Derek would not welcome the news she continually delayed telling him.

"Lexi!"

Her eyes snapped open at his alarmed tone. With a thundercloud settled squarely upon his features, Derek held Caleb out before him with stiffened arms. A wet area on Derek's snowy shirtfront grew larger.

"Look what this...this person did to me!"

Her heart sank at the look of disgust on Derek's face. Caleb reached out to her. His lower lip quivered, indicating a rapidly approaching eruption.

"You needn't frighten him so. He's but a child." She placed Cara in her cradle then took the tearful boy and changed him into dry garments. After relinquishing the little one to his mama, Alexandra placed her cloak upon her shoulders and swept past Derek into the frosty winter afternoon. Max rose from his place of repose outside the door and followed her.

Derek quickly caught up with them. "Where are you going in such a hurry? If you aren't careful, you'll re-injure your ankle."

"My ankle has healed quite nicely, thank you. You *did* come to call me for dinner, did you not?"

"Aye. I wanted to tell you of the dinner guests."

Alexandra had gradually grown accustomed to the ever-changing number of people present at the dinner table. Planters took hospitality very seriously and never turned a soul away at mealtime, be he friend or stranger. Consequently, their friends and family felt little need to wait for an invitation. "Who will be dining with us?"

"My family."

Alexandra stopped midway to the house and stared at her clothing in dismay. She fingered her hair. "I must look a sight."

"Aye, a fetching sight indeed." He slipped his hands through the cloak and settled them upon her hips.

She brought her head up and studied him through narrowed eyes. The scorching heat from his touch traveled through her skirt and petticoats. Her cheeks grew hot.

An invisible string held her steadfast, unmindful of her mind's commands to step back and widen the all too meager distance between them. Gentle puffs of Derek's breath feathered across her forehead. Goose bumps rippled along her flesh.

Her gaze followed the outline of his well-formed lips. She watched spellbound as he lowered his mouth to hers. For a moment, Alexandra allowed herself to fully experience the tender, roving touch of his lips, the thorough exploration of her mouth. Then common sense intruded and brought with it an acute awareness of her surroundings.

She gathered her scattered wits and placed the palms of her hands firmly against his broad, muscular chest, intent upon pushing him away. But her fingers began an upward sojourn of their own accord.

She took a shaky step backward. Her pounding heart echoed in her ears. "This is not the time or place for...for this. If we do not hurry and change, we will be late for dinner."

To her surprise, Derek merely bowed his head in acquiescence and looped her arm through his. Her stomach fluttered the entire walk to the house. The fluttering grew more pronounced as they crept through the west wing and entered their bedchamber.

Alexandra hastened to the wardrobe and

withdrew a gown of winter weight sapphire silk. She ran her fingertips over its smooth surface and reluctantly acknowledged the reason for her choice—it was Derek's favorite. The day he had purchased the fabric he had whispered in her ear how it matched her eyes and set off her ebony tresses and fair skin to perfection.

Her cheeks warm from the memory, Alexandra's fingers fairly flew over the fasteners of her serviceable gray dress in her haste to slip into the other gown. How much longer would she be able to wear it?

"Drat it all!" She tugged at a knotted ribbon. "Why must this happen today of all days?"

"Patience, Lexi," Derek said from behind her. He slipped his arms around her and stilled her jerky movements.

Unable to speak past the lump in her throat, Alexandra willed her wobbly knees to bear her weight while she stood quietly during her husband's ministrations. The maneuvering of his hands under her breasts sent flickers of need surging through her. Lost in his subtle spicy scent, she bit back a moan. His breath teased the sensitive curve of her neck and she shivered.

At last the ribbon came unknotted and Derek opened the gray bodice. He lowered it to reveal her shoulder. She turned her head a fraction of an inch and cast a sideways glance at him. The burning intensity of his brown-gold gaze caught her hesitation and melted it away by slow degrees.

He dropped his lips to her bared shoulder and fired her blood with nibbles that traveled up the slender column of her neck. From the outer edges of a sensual haze, she felt the garment fall from her other shoulder, slide down her arms, and pool at her feet, leaving her clad only in her chemise. He gathered her against him and carried her across the chamber toward the four-poster bed.

Alexandra rested her head against Derek's chest, utterly buoyant and carefree now that she was back in his arms. How she had missed him. She brushed her fingertips across the wisps of dark hair peeping through the opening of his shirt.

A knock sounded on the door.

Derek halted mid-stride and pressed a finger to her lips. On impulse, she flicked his bronzed finger with the tip of her tongue. He shifted her in his arms and gave her an exasperated frown. He shook his head in an apparent signal to remain silent.

"Derek? Alexandra?" Jillian rapped with greater intensity. "I know you're in there."

Derek gave a disgruntled groan and plodded toward the door, still carrying his bride. Alexandra reached down and opened the door.

"What do you want?"

"Dinner is ready." Smug satisfaction glimmered in Jillian's eyes.

"We are well aware of the time."

She lifted a shoulder and turned to leave. "Makes no difference to me." From down the hall her parting words drifted back to them. "Perhaps you'd prefer Mama or Papa come for you."

Derek kicked the door shut.

"Please put me down."

His eyes narrowed with something she couldn't quite identify. Derek sought her mouth, and his scorching kiss robbed her of all rational thought. He lowered her feet to the floor and held her against the hard length of his body. "Family or not, I hope you don't intend to tarry over dinner."

Alexandra's power of speech deserted her. Even after they had dressed and were on their way to the dining room, it still refused to return. The slight pressure of his hand against the small of her back continually renewed her awareness of him.

His last words rambled through her mind and intertwined her emotions in a perplexing muddle of confusion. She wanted the man beside her. She loved the man beside her. But their future as husband and wife remained unsettled.

The hum of conversation and the clink of china floated through the open door. Alexandra pushed her concerns to the back of her mind. Derek found her hand, and with an encouraging squeeze, they entered the room. The gentlemen present rose from the handsome mahogany table while Derek held her chair.

Seated between her grandfather and her husband, Alexandra acknowledged the greetings of their combined families. Beneath the cover of the damask tablecloth, Derek pressed his leg against hers. The heat from his touch penetrated the many layers of petticoats and skirts. Her skin tingled and her breath quickened. Shivers of intoxication surged through her and mingled with her disjointed thoughts.

Try as she might, she could not focus on the conversation. She managed an affirmative, if vague, response to Derek's sister Jo's question about the upcoming fair, but most of the meal passed in a blur.

Despite her firm resolve, her eyes kept straying to Derek. The promising glimmer in his gaze roused within her pulse an erratic rhythm and fired her with bittersweet longing.

Servants came and went. They placed tantalizing dishes before her, then removed them with scarcely a bite eaten.

Her hunger was not for food.

She watched Derek sink his teeth into a biscuit. The sensual way he captured a drop of melted butter with the tip of his tongue deepened the ache consuming her. His eyes met and held hers. The suggestive warmth of his gaze, the enigmatic tilt of his mouth caught and held her fast.

A loud cough broke the spell. Her glance flickered sideways, then halted. At the hate and triumph spewing from Jillian's eyes, a chill raced along her spine.

"Ignore her."

Alexandra turned at the murmured words.

Derek placed his fingers beneath her chin and caressed her cheek with his thumb.

"She is jealous. Don't let her ruin this for you. For us."

His statement confused her. Don't let her ruin what? She wanted to ask, but feared his answer would be the dinner, not their ambiguous relationship.

She knew he wanted her in the physical sense. That much had been apparent for quite some time, but it wasn't enough.

Could it be that he truly cared for her, mayhap was even learning to love her?

Alexandra yearned to be his wife in every possible way, to share the joys and the sorrows of wedded life. Had she eased her way into his heart, past the ingrained sense of responsibility that had spurred him to propose marriage?

The molasses-spiced aroma of sweet Indian pudding wafted past her and brought with it a sudden wave of nausea. With her fingers splayed over her abdomen, she held her breath and waited for the unpleasantness to subside.

"Lexi?" Derek whispered. "Are you ill?"

She shook her head and pasted on a false smile. "'Tis nothing. I think perhaps the ham didn't settle well."

Derek continued to cast concerned looks her way, despite her efforts to appear hale and hearty.

After the queasiness ebbed, sad uncertainty took its place.

Time was running out.

She must discover the true extent of Derek's feelings.

Before he learned of the babe.

Chapter Twenty-Four

Derek entered the darkened bedchamber. He stood among the concealing shadows and watched Alexandra pull the silver-handled brush through the lustrous length of her hair. His fingers tingled with the desire to participate in the routine task, to feel her silken tresses slip through his fingers. The flickering light from the candles on her dressing table bathed her creamy complexion in a soft glow.

Alexandra's behavior of late baffled him. Earlier in the day he had thought they were regaining the closeness they had achieved before she had learned of his past involvement with Jillian, an involvement which now seemed incomprehensible to him. Jillian, with her peevish, spiteful ways, couldn't be more different from his gracious, generous Lexi. His decision to marry Alexandra had proven wise.

Derek's thoughts drifted back a few hours to the nursery for the slaves' babies where he had indulged his need to fill his gaze with her gentle beauty. He had witnessed the love pouring out from her as she tended to each child.

He had also seen the naked longing.

He had seen and recognized it because the same ache, the same need gnawed at him, twisted and knotted his stomach. He'd give his right arm to have a baby daughter who looked like Alexandra, who had her laughing blue eyes and infectious smile.

But he could not.

He had failed to keep Alexandra safe. Not once, but twice. He would not risk failing his own child.

The nightmarish image of his daughter in the hands of someone like Taylor gripped him, chilled him to the depths of his soul, haunted his dreams of having a family with Alexandra.

His own pain he could bear. His own need he could deny. He would not bring a babe into the world. He shifted this attention back to the vision reflected in the looking glass.

His wife.

Somehow, some way, he would demonstrate how happy, how successful their marriage could be. He would convince her he wanted *her* for his wife.

Not Jillian nor anyone else.

Only her.

She lifted the hairbrush to the crown of her head and counted off the ninety-ninth stroke. The fabric of her lace-trimmed bedgown softly outlined the generous swell of her breasts and kindled a liquid fire within his blood.

He crossed the floor in noiseless strides and closed his hand around the brush handle. He slowly pulled it through her ebony locks. "One hundred."

With a small gasp, Alexandra glanced up into the looking glass. Derek caught her sapphire gaze and held it. He willed her to share her thoughts, her hopes, her desires. The physical attraction flowing between them could not be denied. But he wanted more.

He wanted love.

Derek held his hand out to her, palm up. A flash of hesitation flickered across her expression. Then her mouth curved in a demure smile. She slipped her hand into his and rose from the maple armchair to stand before him.

He circled his other arm around her waist and urged her closer. His body tensed at her touch. He took a deep breath to calm the flood of desire raging through him. He wanted to prolong this night of rediscovery.

For both their sakes.

They moved together in slow, unhurried steps, in unison to a silent melody known only to the two of them. Derek inhaled the lavender scent of her hair. He reveled in the feel of her in his arms, in communicating without the encumbrance of words.

He slid his hand up Alexandra's back degree by degree and traced lazy, languid circles with his thumb. A contented sigh drifted to his ears and did strange things to his insides.

He bent his head and brushed her lips with his, then he nuzzled the corners of her mouth and the delicate line of her jaw. She pulled his snowy linen shirt free from his breeches and slipped her fingers under the hem. They crept along the taut muscles of his stomach. Ablaze from her feathery touch, he drew in a sharp breath.

Alexandra halted her movements as though uncertain she should continue. Her mouth trembled beneath his. Stirred by a strong need to return the pleasure, he cradled her face between his palms and pressed teasing kisses to her closed eyelids and the tip of her nose before returning to her tempting, honeyed lips.

She opened to him. Elation and joy filled him. She felt so damned good, so damned right in his arms. He truly was the most fortunate of men because she was his wife.

He had never felt this way with another woman.

Derek deepened his kiss. He delved his tongue into her mouth and sought out the hidden, sweet recesses. His hands glided down her slender form and explored her hollows and curves.

Alexandra burrowed closer. The exquisite pressure of her body against his drove him wild with need. His lips traveled to the curve of her throat. She tipped her head back and arched against him.

He continued his quest along her collarbone, along the lace edging of her bedgown.

He caught the end of the ribbon between his teeth and untied the bow. He trailed his tongue over the swell of her breast. A moan came from deep inside her. Burning in torment, needing to feel her flesh against his flesh, he slipped it off her shoulders. The sheen of her skin in the candlelight further whetted his appetite.

Alexandra shrugged free of the sleeves. With a soft whoosh, the gown drifted downward and revealed her rosy flesh. Side-stepping the puddle of fabric, she took his hand and led him to the side of their bed. He lifted his eyebrow, surprised, yet pleased by her actions.

Their eyes locked. He witnessed a hint of shyness in her gaze. She worried her bottom lip with her teeth and touched the waistband of his velvet breeches.

He could see the uncertainty returning. Unwilling to give up their renewed closeness, he placed his hands upon hers and helped her remove his garments. He swept her into his arms and tenderly placed her among the pillows. Taking care not to crush her beneath his weight, he covered her body with his.

He wanted to please her. He wanted her to remember the passion they shared. The reasons for their estrangement of the past two weeks faded from his memory as he cupped her satiny breast and rolled the nipple between his thumb and finger. He smiled at her intake of breath, determined to make this night perfect, a night she would never forget.

It had been too long, seemingly a lifetime, since he had held her, touched her. He found her waiting nipple and suckled, bringing forth quivers from her body. She arched against him, her lips parted in a silent sigh.

Derek captured that sigh with a plundering kiss and filled his hands with the length of her burnished hair. Its fragrant scent further inflamed his senses. Intent upon exploring Alexandra from the top of her head to the tips of her toes, he released one hand from the curly tendrils. His fingertips grazed the undersides of her swelling breasts and stole down the plane of her stomach.

He paused in his journey, suddenly aware of subtle differences in her body. Her breasts seemed fuller and her stomach... He frowned. Her flat, trim stomach had changed since the last time they had been intimate. With a slight shake of his head, he gave his hands and mouth over to the welcome task of paying homage to the sheer exquisiteness of the beauty beneath him.

He nudged her knees apart and trailed a path of adoring nips along the sensitive skin of her inner thighs. He moved ever closer to the wellspring of her femininity. With his tongue he probed the soft folds and feasted on her sweet nectar. She wriggled beneath him.

Derek rose over her and waited. He waited for her to open her eyes. When she did, joy spiraled through him. He held her passion-darkened gaze and slipped his throbbing length into her velvet sheath. How good it felt to be home.

He moved within her, slowly at first, ever aware of the clouding of her gaze, of the perspiration glistening on their bodies. Unable to hold back any longer, he quickened his thrusts. As the moment of his satisfaction approached, he slowed his movements and withdrew from her hot moistness.

"Please." Alexandra pulled him closer. "I need you within me."

Derek caught her mouth and feasted on her sweetness. "Let me pleasure you this way."

Tears shimmered in her gaze. "You...you do not

wish to be inside me?"

He caressed her cheek. "Lexi, sweet. I cannot spill my seed within you."

Confusion marred her brow, then cleared. "All this time, you withdrew early, 'twas not because you did not want me? You denied yourself...completion?

Derek guided her hand to his length. "Does this feel like I do not want you?"

She shook her head.

"My need for you exceeds my need to breathe. Being inside you is heaven."

She stroked his erection. Her face pinkened. "No child will come from this night's union. So, if you please—"

Derek's restraint broke. He plunged into her warmth. Alexandra wrapped her legs around his waist. She raked her fingernails along his back, matched his rhythm, gripped him tight within her. Her muscles contracted and increased his pleasure to the point of pain. They moved as one toward the ultimate pinnacle, clinging, straining, surging.

Tensed and trembling, Derek forced himself to wait until the greatest convulsion claimed his wife before he sought his own release. His nostrils flared and heat surged through him. She pulsated around his hard length, pulling him deeper, milking him until he came and spilled his seed deep within her. Together they reached the zenith. Together they hurtled over the precipice, and together they plummeted back down.

Still buried deep within her, Derek held her in a fierce, shielding embrace. Together they rode out the lingering vestiges of their exquisite union and their racing pulses and ragged breathing slowed. As the minutes ticked by in the pre-dawn hours, sleep wrought from exhaustion claimed his wife. He inhaled her essence and allowed his eyes to drift shut.

****

The early morning's light streamed through the parted curtains and roused Alexandra from her brief slumber. Her eyelids fluttered open and revealed a bronzed chest sprinkled with dark hair. Its spicy scent filled her nostrils and brought with it a familiar unsteadiness.

She cleared the cobwebs from her drowsy mind and became aware of her position. Two brawny arms held her flush against the bronzed chest, so close a feather could not pass between them. One of her legs lay over Derek's hip.

She swallowed a disconcerted groan and struggled to gather her scattered wits. What must he think of her wanton behavior? The bronzed chest before her rumbled. The rumble developed into unchecked laughter. Before she had time to consider this turn of events, she found herself sitting astride her handsome husband.

Her body moved in rhythm with him. She closed her eyes and gave herself over to the wild sensations rippling along her nerve endings. Her head fell back as Derek's hands roamed along her thighs and moved ever upward. He teased her nipples and brought them to pebble hardness. Her breasts swelled and ached for his attention. At long last, his hand closed around the full mounds, kneading, stroking, caressing, until she thought she would surely die from the rapture.

Derek pulled her forward and feasted on her breasts while gripping her hips. He held her immobile and thrust up into her. She clutched his forearms for support lest she tumble into nothingness.

Alexandra lost all sense of time and place, conscious only of the man beneath her. She gloried in the wondrous feelings only he could create.

The pressure began at the center of her being

and built. She bit her lip, wanting to remain united with this man. A rush of heat suffused her body and carried her to dizzying heights.

She steeled herself against the contracting shudders of her body. In a quick movement, Derek rolled. He placed her beneath him, and with a final thrust, hurtled them both over the brink, into the realm of exploding stars. A scream echoed throughout her head.

Had she died?

Her heart thudded against her ribs, or was it Derek's heartbeat she felt? The oneness they had achieved both exhilarated and frightened her. What if it never happened again? She dragged a deep gulp of air into her bursting lungs.

"Lexi."

At Derek's murmur, she looked up. The emotion revealed in his eyes reached out to her, soothed her. He had experienced it, too. She gave him a tremulous smile. "Good morning."

"Good morning, Lexi."

She knitted her eyebrows in a small frown. "Why are you laughing?"

"I'm not laughing."

"Yes, you are."

Derek tweaked her nose. "I am grinning, not laughing."

"You look like a cat who just cornered a defenseless mouse in the corner of a barn and is pondering the infinite varieties of meals to be made."

He caught her mouth in a heady kiss. "'Tis only because I'm happy." His hand retraced its path and settled on her stomach. "Even if you are filling out a bit."

"Filling out?" Alexandra grew still. Her gaze followed Derek's arm to her stomach. Prickles of unease stole her breath.

His fingers stroked her skin. "Perhaps it's a

249

combination of rich Virginia food and a lack of a certain activity."

Alexandra swallowed hard. "Activity?"

"Mm-hmm." Derek caressed the length of her thigh and left a scorching trail in its wake. "I would be happy to remedy the problem."

"My *filling out* troubles you? Y-you do not wish to have a fat wife?" Her mouth went dry in dread of his response.

He nuzzled a certain sensitive spot behind her ear. "I want your enticing body to stay just the way it is."

Alexandra's heart slid to her toes and landed with a thud. She opened her mouth to tell him the truth, but she could not push the words past her lips. He had already stated his position on having children in terms too clear to be misunderstood. And last night she had been less than honest. All this time he had thought they were protected from conception. Apparently, withdrawing before he achieved release hadn't been enough, and his seed had been most thoroughly planted. Tears stung the back of her eyes. She eased off the bed, slipped into her chemise, and padded over to the wardrobe, all the while blinking back the hot tears.

"What are you doing, Lexi?"

Alexandra selected the first thing her fingers touched, a long-sleeved gown of rich red brocade, and forced false cheer past the tightness in her throat. She willed her voice not to betray her by trembling. "Why, I'm dressing for the fair, of course. It is today, is it not?"

"Aye."

"Then we have no time to waste. Everyone will surely be gathered in the main house and we mustn't keep them waiting. I'd also rather not have my loving sister come fetch us again." She struggled to keep the strain out of her words. How had she gone from the heights of happiness to the depths of despair in mere minutes?

Alexandra heard Derek rise from their bed and chanced a sideways peek at him. His pained frown brought a swift ache to her heart. If he found her roundness troubling now, how would he feel in a few more months?

She readjusted her stays for a looser fit and stepped into the gown. She tied the bow-knot fastenings and tried to take a deep, cleansing breath, but the gown wouldn't allow it. She rested her palms on her stomach and bit her lower lip in the agonizing knowledge that perhaps her time was running out more quickly than she had anticipated.

She caught an unexpected glimpse of herself in the ornate looking glass and felt distanced from the woman staring back at her. At first glance the image in the mirror looked the picture of health. Thick, glossy black hair tumbled over her shoulders. Her skin had a special quality about it, a radiance enhanced by the deep red of the gown.

But Alexandra knew better. An air of sadness, of melancholy, surrounded her reflection and was painfully evident in her sorrowful gaze. A gaze devoid of happiness, of joy, of serenity. All the emotions she had always associated with impending motherhood.

It wasn't supposed to be this way.

Chapter Twenty-Five

Alexandra accepted Derek's hand and stepped from the coach, eager for her first glimpse of the Williamsburg fair. Jillian pushed past them. Alexandra toppled against Derek and Max.

Derek caught Alexandra in the circle of his arms and drew her close. "I'd like to toss that bit of baggage across my knee and instill some manners in her."

Tempted to agree with him, Alexandra tipped her head up and saw the muscle working in his clenched jaw. "Please don't. I'm not hurt and I can't force her to accept me, much less like me. Let us make the most of this day."

Derek took her hand in his and pressed it to his lips. His anger-darkened gaze softened. "If that is your wish, I'll say naught to her today."

"It is." She welcomed the warmth filling the void created by Jillian's rudeness.

"Very well." He looped her arm through his and bent close to her ear. "But I make no such promise for tomorrow."

Alexandra's brother, Marc, headed toward the soaped pig chase. Derek's mother and sisters invited Laurel to see the latest fashions from London. The four women set off in a whirlwind of chatter, punctuated by the shrieks of glee emitted by Hannah's children as a company of players from the theater strolled by. Derek and Alexandra's fathers hurried to view the horses and cattle offered for sale.

Alexandra and Derek ambled along the busy

streets. She watched the people milling around them and surmised the country folk came from miles around to sell their produce and have a good time in much the same way as the Pennsylvanians who attended the Philadelphia fairs.

Everywhere they walked, Alexandra saw people engaged in contests and games of strength and skill. In one area, men wrestled for a pair of silver buckles. Nearby, fiddlers competed for a violin.

Alexandra noticed a cluster of young women. When she spotted Jillian and Jo in their midst, her interest grew. "What are they doing?"

"A contest for the most beautiful maid, I believe."

"Our sisters are there." She grabbed his hand. "Come on. I want to see who wins." She ignored his stifled groan and pulled him through the throng of onlookers to the front row.

A small glow of pride welled inside her. The cut of Jillian's gown revealed her flawless figure while the emerald silk enhanced her creamy complexion. Her chocolate brown eyes sparkled with excitement.

Alexandra glanced toward her sister-in-law. Jo smoothed her rose gown of satin and lace while taking surreptitious peeks at the young women around her. She met Alexandra's gaze. The flush upon Jo's delicate cheekbones deepened, and her movements stilled. Her shy smile illuminated her green eyes and turned them the color of polished jade.

"Might I have my hand back?"

"Hmm?"

Humor danced in the depths of Derek's gaze. "Would you care for my other hand? I believe you've well-nigh squeezed every drop of blood from this one."

Alexandra grimaced and loosened her grip. "Forgive me. I didn't realize what I was doing."

"I was only jesting, Lexi." He tweaked her nose and favored her with his endearing grin.

Her heart did a double thump and her insides turned liquid at the sensual undertones of his playfulness. She suppressed a sigh of contentment, wanting desperately to prolong this moment of camaraderie.

The noise and activity of the fair faded away and left the two of them wrapped in a magical spell. Wondrous emotions rose inside her. She longed to shout her love.

But she did not. She could not.

She could not risk courting disaster.

She could not face his possible rejection.

She could not bear to see the laughter leave his eyes.

For now it was enough to know she loved him. She would confront his feelings for her another day.

A tug on her arm shattered the moment of magic. With a confused frown, she stared at the unfamiliar, gray-haired man beside her.

"Please, miss. Come with me."

She glanced sideways at Derek. He merely grinned in that infuriating manner of his.

"Miss?"

She shrugged free. "Who are you? What do you want?"

"I'm the judge, miss, and I wish to award you first prize." He placed a pair of silk stockings in her hand.

Prickles of unease skittered along her nerves. A chill slithered down her spine. With great strength of will, she turned and encountered the full force of the fury emanating from Jillian, a rage so tangible that Alexandra took an involuntary step backward and sought the shelter of Derek's presence.

Understanding dawned on her. She placed the stockings back in the judge's hand. "I am not a participant in the contest, sir. I am a married woman."

The older man flushed. "Forgive me, ma'am." He glanced up at Derek. "You are a fortunate man."

Derek squeezed Alexandra's shoulder. "Indeed I am."

Her pleasure at her husband's response lasted until the moment the judge awarded the silk stockings to Jillian.

Jillian remained still until the crowd dispersed. Anger glittered in her dark eyes. She strode toward Alexandra and dropped the stockings at her feet.

Alexandra picked them up and searched for the words to ease the embarrassment she had unwittingly caused. "Jillian, I—"

"Quiet!" Jillian's voice hissed. "I'll hear naught of your protestations. Never again will I be held up to ridicule because of you. I'm weary of the never-ending chorus of your attributes. I'll soon begin my new life, a life in which you will have no place. I no longer have a sister."

"That is quite enough," Derek said.

Jillian swept past him, her head held high. He started after her, but Alexandra stopped him.

"Leave her alone." She pulled her cloak around herself against the soul-numbing declarations of her sister. "She has every right to feel this way."

"It matters not to me if she is kin. I won't stand by while she berates you in such a beastly manner."

"Put yourself in her place, Derek. She lived most of her life in the shadow of her missing sister. Then I returned, wed to the man she was supposed to marry."

"We've already discussed this."

"I'm only explaining the reasons for her behavior. After all she has endured, today must have been more than she could bear. Another embarrassment because of me. I'll never be able to get through to her now. I had hoped we could find a way to lessen the tension between us."

"Stop chastising yourself. 'Tis not your fault the judge thought you were the prettiest one here. I've known it for some time."

Pleased by his statement, Alexandra bit her lower lip. "Surely you jest, kind sir."

"Nay. Not about this. I have been blessed with the comeliest of wives." He brushed her lips with his.

She beamed at him, giddy from his compliment. Perhaps even more from the whisper-soft kiss.

He smoothed a loose wisp of hair near her ear. "I shall find a way to keep that glow of happiness upon your face. You have been far too somber of late."

Alexandra's smile froze. Doubts niggled away at her once again. He knew something was amiss.

Derek clucked his tongue. "Is that gloom I now see? Come. We will find a way to bring the sparkle back to your eyes. Are you hungry?"

She nodded. "A little."

Within minutes they were sitting side by side, feasting on meat pies and sipping cider. Derek fed her a morsel of cake. With the tip of her tongue she took tentative swipes at the crumbs on her lips, conscious of his penetrating gaze. He seemed capable of reaching into her soul and discerning her innermost thoughts.

She fussed with her skirt and twisted her hands in her lap, uncomfortable with his scrutiny. She was not ready for him to learn her secret yet. She fidgeted with the sapphire-laden band of gold round her finger and sought the solace it usually afforded.

This time the solace did not come.

Derek popped the last bit of cake into his mouth and stood. He held his hand out to her. "The foot race is about to begin. Would you care to watch?"

She placed her hand in his and accepted the thrill that always accompanied his touch. "I-I would like that very much," she said, annoyed with herself for stammering like a timid maid.

Derek tucked her hand in the crook of his arm and they made their way to Duke of Gloucester Street where they found the ideal place to watch the men race from the College to the Capitol.

Alexandra's eyes traveled up the length of her handsome husband. Her pulse quickened. "Have you ever competed for a prize?"

His eyes turned a molten gold. The suggestive tilt of his mouth and his raised eyebrow sent an aching, almost unbearable need through her. She was powerless to resist the force that pulled her to him.

He slid his hands beneath her cloak and blazed fiery paths along her arms. She shivered and moved closer. Under the cover of her outer garment, he explored her back and sought out her curves and contours with slow, deft strokes. Her body cried out for more.

His hands traveled upward until they rested on her shoulders. He bent his head and took possession of her lips. She clutched his arms, lest her wobbly knees give way.

A cheer rose from the crowd. Mortification surged through her. Her face burning with embarrassment, she slid her hands over to the broad wall of his chest and pushed away from him.

He caught her by the wrist and pulled her back against him. "Relax, Lexi."

"Relax? How dare you tell me to relax!" Her voice dropped to a hissing whisper. "We made public spectacles of ourselves." She averted her eyes.

Without saying another word, Derek turned her around. A few feet away, the winner of the race was receiving his prize, a pair of silver buckles, amid more cheers from the crowd. Two other men stepped forward to claim the second and third place prizes, a pair of shoes and a pair of gloves.

Appalled by the shameful way she had overreacted, Alexandra closed her eyes against the heat rising in her face. Lately, it seemed her judgment had been impaired. She placed her palm on her stomach. Would she continue in this manner until she was delivered of this babe? Did pregnancy affect other women in this disturbing manner?

Derek stroked her hair. The tenderness of his touch brought tears to her eyes. She squeezed her eyes shut and commanded her wayward emotions to come under control before she further disgraced herself. She would not cry. She would learn to react in a rational manner, with her head, not her heart. Women had babies every day. If they could sail through their pregnancies, she could, as well.

Alexandra slipped her hand into Derek's, and they wandered among the tents and booths. The afternoon passed quickly as they admired the handiwork displayed by numerous craftsmen. Nearly every type of merchandise imaginable could be purchased at the fair.

She smiled back at the old men and women who were grinning for a cheese. The ballad singing contest alternately charmed and amused her. One of the more bawdy tunes brought a flush to her cheeks.

They passed two events Alexandra did not care to watch, a cockfight that drew a boisterous, enthusiastic audience and a slave auction. The sight of the bloodied, frenzied gamecocks sickened her, as did the obese man who prodded unwilling Negroes forward to be inspected by prospective buyers.

Struggling against the compulsion to cover her ears against the sound of someone crying, she shuddered at the cruelties she was witnessing and walked away from the distressing sights as quickly as her legs would allow.

A persistent squealing finally edged its way into

her disturbed thoughts. Her gaze focused, then centered on the comical sight coming toward her. The corners of her mouth turned up as she watched her brother half-drag, half-carry a wriggling pig.

"I suppose this means you won the contest," Derek said.

Marc nodded and flashed them a triumphant grin. "I'm taking him home." Pride glinted in his green eyes as he shifted the weight of the animal and hurried past them.

Alexandra and Derek shared a moment of spontaneous, companionable laughter. A minute later the irate animal's squeal echoed through the air and renewed their mirth.

"Do you think Marc will be able to get his prize home?"

Derek shrugged his shoulders. "If not, he'll have another chase on his hands." He smoothed a stray lock of her hair before trailing a finger down her cheek and over to her chin. "Do you want to watch the horse races?"

She shook her head. "You go. I want to look for my mother."

He frowned. "I don't want you to be alone."

She opened her arms in an expansive gesture. "Look around you. How can I be alone when I'm surrounded by all these people? Besides, Max is here."

The worried expression remained entrenched upon his face. "Still—"

"Go. I will see you in a short while."

After Derek left for the racetrack adjacent to the town, Alexandra scanned the crowd for a glimpse of her family. She saw only unfamiliar faces and decided to explore a bit on her own.

She paused to watch a young boy dance and caper upon a straight rope. She held her breath and thought he would surely fall numerous times as he appeared to misstep, yet he never faltered.

Next, a woman walked upon the rope with a wheelbarrow in front of her, followed by dancing a lively courante and a jig upon the rope. Alexandra applauded with the rest of the audience. A dancing master could not have done it better on the ground. She ended her performance by dancing with baskets upon her feet and iron fetters upon her legs.

A bone-numbing chill from deep within Alexandra obliterated the pleasure she had derived from the show. She knew a sudden, wrenching fear. Her feet remained rooted to the ground as her mind raced with disjointed thoughts. She struggled to slow her thinking, to discover the source of her anxiety.

Someone was watching her.

Alexandra forced herself to move in a calm manner. She reached for Max and took surreptitious glances around her. No one returned her stare. No one avoided her gaze.

Still, she felt the force of someone's eyes boring through her. She pulled her hood upon her head and clutched the ends of her cloak together to shield herself.

She began walking, trusting Max to stay close. She didn't know her destination, but she hurried along, scarcely able to prevent herself from breaking into a run. She must keep moving.

He was coming closer. She sensed it and did not attempt to dispute her feeling. Instead, she quickened her pace.

A colorful tent beckoned her closer. Without a moment's hesitation, she lifted the flap and stepped inside. She blinked against the dimness of the interior.

"Sit down. I have been expecting you."

Chapter Twenty-Six

A dizzying rush of blood roared in Alexandra's ears. How could he have been expecting her?

"Come closer. You have no need to fear me."

Alexandra took several cautious steps and peered into the solemn face of the young man seated at a small table. She searched his eyes for a sign of his intentions. The glow from the small, flickering candle revealed dark gray eyes, eyes that bespoke sincerity, not evil. She sat in the chair across from him. Max settled at her feet.

"You wish to have the cards read."

She almost refused, but upon remembering her purpose for entering the tent, she decided to stay. "Yes." She would listen to what she had always considered foolish prattle. Perhaps her pursuer would tire of waiting and leave.

The man placed a card in the middle of the table. "Concentrate on the question you want answered while you shuffle the cards, then cut them to the left three times with your left hand."

Feeling silly, Alexandra closed her eyes and thought for a moment before deciding on her question. *What must I do to ensure a successful, happy marriage, one blessed by children?* After she followed his instructions, she leaned forward to hear the words he spoke as he positioned the top ten cards face up on the table.

"This covers you. This crosses you. This is beneath you."

Alexandra had never had the cards read before.

She watched him form a cross with the first six cards, then place the last four in a vertical line beside the cross. He studied them. Of what significance were the swords that appeared on most of the cards?

"You are surrounded by conflict," he said. "'Tis a question of sorrow and separation versus conquest and victory."

She looked up and frowned. Sorrow? Separation?

He touched the card showing a blindfolded and bound maiden surrounded by swords. "You experienced bondage in your past."

Her chest tightened against the unwanted assault of memories of life with Bartholomew, of her flight from him.

"A man recently came into your life. He is brave, is he not?"

The image of Derek filled her mind and gave her strength. "Yes. Very brave."

"I see the possibility of pain and misfortune in your future. Alas, I also see death."

"Who?" Alexandra stared at the card he slowly tapped with his long, slender finger. The picture of the woman sitting in despair with her head in her hands frightened her. "Who is going to die? You must tell me."

He shrugged. "'Tis difficult to say. Someone close to you, perhaps. A dark-haired man."

Tremors of paralyzing fear spiraled through her. She could not let it happen. "How can I change what you have seen?"

He turned his impenetrable gaze upon her. "You fear losing what you have found. Beware of pride."

Alexandra placed her trembling hands on her stomach. Unable to breathe, she gasped for air. Had she ordained Derek's death?

The reader's full lips curved in the semblance of

a smile. "You have begun a new family. You hope for a happy family life."

In the dim light, his eyes turned the color of smoke and steel. They held her captive. His voice lowered, yet he spoke intently. "For love to triumph over hate, you must have faith. You must believe love is stronger than hate or you will not defeat the force, the conflict that surrounds you."

A lone tear slid down her cheek. "I cannot let him die."

"In the abiding constancy of your faith, in the steadfastness of love, dwells the power to direct your destiny."

Her mind reeled from all she had been told. Alexandra left the tent on unsteady legs followed by Max.

"Aunt Ally!"

Alexandra turned to see Tessa break free from Hannah. She lowered herself to her niece's level and caught her in a hug. "Are you enjoying the fair?"

"Yes'm." Dark ringlets spilled about her elfin face. "We're going to the puppet show." She pointed to a colorful booth. "Will you come with us?"

Not wishing to intrude, Alexandra glanced up at Hannah, who shifted Brandon to her other hip. "Perhaps you should ask your mama."

"We would be delighted if you would accompany us." Hannah's hazel eyes echoed the smile curving her lips.

Tessa slipped her tiny hand into Alexandra's and led her to the stage where two male puppets crossed sticks in a longstaff bout to earn the favor of the young maiden standing to the side.

Two powerful arms slipped around Alexandra's waist. She jumped and scarcely muffled a scream before she realized her husband had sneaked up on her. "You frightened the very life out of me."

"Why?" He dropped a kiss on the curve of her

neck. "Do many men take you into their arms?"

Alexandra stiffened and recalled the terrifying feel of eyes upon her. She opened her mouth, then clamped it shut, feeling foolish. She had no proof. No one had actually accosted her. Perhaps she had imagined it.

Tessa pulled on the hem of Derek's midnight blue coat. "Me can't see."

He swung her up through the air and settled her on his shoulder. "Better now?"

"Better now," the child said.

Derek threw his head back and laughed.

For love to triumph, you must have faith. Perhaps they could have a true marriage. One of love, not of perceived duty. She must be honest with him. She must take the ultimate risk and reveal her love for him.

And she must tell him about the babe.

He deserved to know he would soon be a father. She would tell him tonight, when they were alone.

"Lexi?"

Alexandra grinned at the antics of marionettes. "Yes?"

"I must leave this evening."

Separation and sorrow.

Fear lanced her heart and her smile faded. "Leave? Why?"

"A pressing matter requires my attention."

Have faith.

"What about the ball?"

Derek lowered his head and brushed her lips with his. "I will return in less than a fortnight. I promise."

I also see death...a dark-haired man.

Panic rose. Should she beg him to stay or allow him to go without question? How could she best protect him? She could tell him of the babe. Perhaps he would not leave if he knew. But what if he truly did not want children and decided not to come back?

She chided herself for her selfish behavior. He had left on business several times since their marriage. He was a sea captain by profession. She could not react in such an illogical manner every time he set sail. Deep in her heart, she knew he would not abandon their child. She twisted her wedding ring around her finger and sought guidance.

Believe love is stronger to defeat the conflict that surrounds you.

Applause for the presentation of "Children of the Wood" broke through her thoughts. Moved by the tale of the two starved children who died and were buried by a robin, she blinked back her tears and summoned all her courage. "I wish you a safe voyage and a speedy return."

Beneath the cover of her cloak, she clenched her hands into fists until her nails dug into her palms. She would not prey upon his sense of responsibility by telling him of their babe to keep him by her side. She would trust his decisions.

****

15 December 1752

These past days without Derek have been a torturous eternity of waiting. Fear for his safety plagues my every thought.

17 December 1752

The ball and Christmas are fast approaching. Mother flits about, efficiently overseeing the preparations for the coming week. She scarcely needs my help. I pray Derek returns soon.

20 December 1752

All of my efforts to rid my mind of worry have come to naught. I miss him more than I thought possible. Cook has been trying to tempt my appetite

*with an array of tasty morsels she and her helpers
are preparing for the ball.*

22 December 1752
*The ball is tomorrow. He promised me he would
return in time. Please let him be alive and well.*
****

Alexandra stood at the staircase landing's large
multi-paned window, bathed in the golden glow of
the setting sun. She waited and worried. Waited for
Derek's schooner to appear at the plantation's wharf.
Worried about his reaction to her confession.

She placed her hand on her abdomen and
wondered if she would look different to him. Within
weeks her condition would be apparent to all. Would
he turn away from her in disgust? She wouldn't be
able to bear it.

"Alexandra?"

She leaned over the balustrade looped with
spruce garlands. "Yes, Mother?"

Laurel stood at the foot of the stairs. "Our
guests are arriving."

"I'll join you in the ballroom in a few minutes."
With a heavy sigh, she cast one more longing glance
out the window, then gathered the folds of her
burgundy velvet skirt and descended the stairs in
slow, unhurried steps. Her brow knitted in concern.
Derek had said he would be there. Something
terrible must have happened.

"Why, wherever could your husband be, sister
dear?"

Alexandra turned to see Jillian emerge from the
shadows of the hall. The jubilant expression in the
younger woman's dark gaze put her on guard.

"Do you suppose he has tired of you already?"
Jillian shook her head and clucked her tongue. "I
can see why. You look a bit dreadful. I fear that color
doesn't suit you. Did you do your own hair? Your

secret's safe with me. I shan't tell anyone."

Alexandra resisted the urge to smooth her hair. The slight movement would only serve to reward her sister's desire for revenge. Instead, she stood confident. Derek had often remarked he liked her hair unbound and he had chosen her dress himself. "I won't fight with you. Nothing you can say will spoil this day for me." With quiet dignity, she walked past the younger woman.

"I do believe the purpose of this ball is to celebrate your marriage. Won't that be a trifle difficult without your roving husband?"

Alexandra's footsteps faltered for but a moment at the venom in her sister's voice. Then she squared her shoulders and continued on her way, struggling to shut out the echo of Jillian's mocking laughter.

"Derek has *not* left me," she whispered. "He will come back. He must." She lifted her chin a notch and entered the ballroom.

Festive splendor greeted her. Christmas finery decked the large room and brought a hint of a smile to her troubled heart. The fragrance of pine and bayberry mingled in the air. Garlands of box and bay added touches of gaiety. Sprigs of holly had been tucked behind the mirrors. In one corner, fiddlers played a romantic ballad that tugged at her already fragile emotions.

She forced back the sudden onslaught of weepiness and moved forward to greet her guests. Many of the prominent planters of the area accompanied their wives in wishing Alexandra well with her marriage and asking after Derek. After each congratulatory offer, the scorching heat of Jillian's triumphant gaze bored through her back.

Where are you, Derek?

Behind her she heard the doors open. The curtains fluttered, and a hush fell over the room.

She turned.

There stood Derek. Dizzying joy swept through her.

Her husband caught her up against his lean, muscled form. "I claim the right of kissing the fair maiden standing beneath the kissing ball." He lowered his mouth to hers and stole her breath.

Alexandra entwined her arms around his neck and reveled in the sweet sensations. "I thought you'd never arrive."

He pressed a final kiss to the tip of her nose. "I always keep my promises. Don't you know that by now?"

A lump in her throat thickened her speech. "I'm sorry I ever doubted you." A frown gathered on her forehead and she gave his chest a sharp poke. "Where *have* you been?"

His eyes alight with a merry twinkle, Derek turned and signaled to a house servant. Within seconds, Polly Taylor and the children swarmed around her, talking and hugging all at once.

The children had come. Tears spilled down her cheeks as she pulled them close, touching each and every one of them to assure herself they were really there.

She looked up. Derek stood outside the circle of children, his grin wide. "Is this the pressing matter you had to attend to?"

He nodded. "You are pleased with your Christmas gift?"

"Pleased? I'm more than pleased. It was more than I dared to dream for." No wonder she loved him so. She arched an eyebrow and wagged her finger at him. "Why didn't you tell me?"

He lifted a broad shoulder in a shrug. "You've seemed pensive these past weeks, and I thought perhaps you were missing Polly and the children more than you cared to let on, so I decided to surprise you and bring the sparkle back to your eyes."

Guilt for the true reason of her melancholy tweaked her conscience. She slipped her hand into his and pulled him closer. "You are truly the dearest of men, Captain Tremaine. After the celebration, there is something I must tell you."

Derek brushed her lips with his. "Is this something I should look forward to?"

Uncertainty laced her voice. "I hope so." *Please, let it be so.*

"Then I shall count the minutes until we are alone. For now, may I have this dance, Mrs. Tremaine?"

"I shall have to check my dance card, sir."

"Fie on your dance card. I'm claiming all your dances." He turned and bowed toward Polly and the children. "Enjoy the party. If you'll excuse us, my wife and I are going to dance."

Alexandra cast a longing glance at Polly and the children.

"Be off with you now," the older woman said. "There will be plenty of time for visiting later."

The next two hours passed in a blur of cotillions, minuets, and reels. Instead of tiring, she abounded with energy, conscious only of the man holding her in his arms. He smiled at her with tender warmth and promised an evening of delight. She cleared her mind of all worries and gave herself over to the joys of the moment, confident the future would take care of itself.

During the elegant supper that followed, Alexandra's appetite returned with a vengeance. She feasted on fragrant baked ham, roasted turkey, plum pudding, baked sweet potatoes, and cranberry relish. A tempting slice of minced pie and a cherry tart rounded off her meal. She pushed her plate away and leaned back against the chair, unable to believe she had eaten so much.

She glanced sideways at Derek and caught the mischievous glint he quickly concealed. She sniffed and gave him a look of haughty disdain. "Something amuses you, sir?"

He held his hands up in a signal of surrender. "I shan't say a word."

"Wise move, kind sir. Shall we continue dancing?"

His eyes crinkled at the edges in suppressed laughter. "If you wish."

"I wish." She couldn't hold her haughty demeanor a moment longer and collapsed in peals of laughter. "If you do."

His expression smoldered with the promise of the night to come. "Most definitely."

They rose from the table in unison and joined the other couples in a lively country dance. A short time later, the sound of tinkling glass brought the dancing to a halt. Jared and Laurel invited Alexandra and Derek to accompany them to the center of the room. Servants bearing trays of amber-colored wine circulated among the guests.

"As you know," Jared said, "we are gathered here this evening for two reasons. First, the Lord above finally saw fit to return our beloved daughter to us." He lifted his glass of Madeira high. Those present followed suit.

"And, second, we are here to celebrate the marriage of Alexandra to Derek Tremaine. May your union be blessed with happiness and good fortune."

Jillian stepped forward. "I, too, have an announcement to make."

A hush fell over the room.

Jillian's dark gaze glittered with defiance. "At this time I wish to announce *my* betrothal."

Alexandra looked up at Derek in dismay. She shook her head. "It can't be."

"Yes. It can and it is."

At the familiar masculine voice, she clutched Derek's arm in dread.

Bartholomew Taylor stepped from his place of concealment among the guests. "I've come to take you home, Alexandra." His malevolent gaze pierced the delicate hold she had on her emotions.

"Nay! I won't go with you."

Bartholomew grabbed Jillian by her hair and she shrieked. With his other hand, he drew a pistol from beneath his coat. Startled gasps echoed around the room.

Both Laurel and Alexandra stepped forward. "No!"

"Let her go," Laurel pleaded. "I'm the one you want."

Annoyance flickered across Bartholomew's face. "Of what foolishness do you speak? 'Tis my Alexandra I want."

The fear in Jillian's eyes beseeched Alexandra, who murmured, "Shhh, Mother." She edged toward the mad man. "Release my sister, Bartholomew. I will do as you bid."

"No," Laurel said. "I'm the one he first called Alexandra."

"You lie!" Bartholomew's face purpled.

"Come here, Lexi," Derek said from behind her.

Unleashed fury blazed in Bartholomew's eyes. "Stay out of this, Tremaine. I won't allow you to keep her from me again."

"Alexandra is *my* wife." A dangerous undercurrent wound its way through Derek's voice. "It's time to admit your defeat, Taylor, and make a graceful exit."

Visibly shaking, Bartholomew lifted his firearm and aimed it toward Derek.

Two shots rang out.

Chapter Twenty-Seven

The sound of the gunshots paralyzed Alexandra.

A chasm split open. An invisible force dragged her over the edge of the abyss into the shadowy darkness of the past where she once again became five-year-old Charlotte. She saw her mother jump in front of her father. She watched them both fall to the ground.

The shifting wisps of the gray, cloying fog pressed against her, suffocated her. Shards of memories pierced her one after another.

Her mother's crumpled dress.

Her father's hands, limp and lifeless.

Blood mingled with the dirt. So much blood.

The splintering fragments swirled around her and forced her to relive the terrifying moments she thought she had successfully forgotten. The mighty vortex swelled and swallowed her whole.

She remembered closing her fingers around her mother's cameo necklace. The stranger had snatched her up and the chain had broken, leaving the necklace in her small hand. Seated before her abductor, she had twisted and turned in the saddle and tried to escape. Through her tears she had seen a young man racing to save her.

The young man had been Derek.

The stranger had been Bartholomew.

Alexandra shook off the numbing grip of the memories. Her vision cleared, and she focused on the two men lying on the ballroom floor.

Derek and Bartholomew. It had always been

Derek and Bartholomew.

She dragged great gulps of air into her lungs and took faltering steps toward her husband, fearful of what she might find. Dr. Sebastian knelt over him. She sank down beside Derek, distressed by his pale face and shallow breathing. Fighting back tears, she averted her eyes from his wound and ran shaking fingers through his hair. She willed him to open his eyes and look at her. She had so much to tell him. Would he have a chance to hear it?

"Is he..."

Laurel took Alexandra into her arms. "No, my child. He's unconscious, not dead."

Jared and Everette carried Derek from the ballroom with the aid of several guests. Alexandra moved to follow them.

"Alexandra."

She glanced down, surprised to find herself standing beside Bartholomew. Sparks of anger gather force and erupted into full-blown fury. She clenched her hands into tight fists and ignored the person trying to staunch the blood streaming from Bartholomew's abdomen. "How could you have done it? Time after time you have connived to ruin our lives. I'll have no more of it! 'Tis the end of the madness."

"Calm yourself," Laurel murmured from behind her. "Think of the babe."

Alexandra's heart skipped a beat and she fixed startled eyes on her mother. "You know?"

"Of course, I know."

Bartholomew turned his pale face toward Alexandra. Contentment shone upon his face. "A babe." With obvious effort, he lifted his hand and touched the hem of her skirt. "We shall have a perfect life. You'll see. You, me, and our child. 'Tis what I have been dreaming of all these years."

A grimace distorted his features as he doubled

up and writhed in agony. He drew a ragged breath. "I'll make you happy, truly I will. Perhaps Father will finally be proud of me."

Alexandra folded her arms around her midsection, chilled by his ramblings. She started to move away. She needed to be with her husband, but Bartholomew clutched her skirt. "Please stay. Don't leave me again."

The healer in her realized Bartholomew had been mortally wounded, and her anger slowly abated, replaced by pity. He would never experience or understand the true love shared between a man and a woman. The wistfulness in his eyes, the never-to-be-fulfilled hope for his father's love, sorrowed her.

His eyes glazed over and his skin turned clammy. "We belong together, you and I. You're my life. No one shall separate us again." He gasped for air. "You'll never leave me again, will you?" His voice faded into a murmured plea. "Forgive me."

Alexandra stared at the dying man, incredulous at his request. "God will have to. I cannot."

Bartholomew's grip relaxed. He closed his eyes and breathed his last breath.

Alexandra remained frozen in place, not quite sure she believed what she was seeing. Had the nightmare ended? Had Bartholomew's hold on her been broken?

The glorious realization finally penetrated her dazed thoughts. She was free! She never had to fear him again.

Hannah came forward and placed a comforting arm around her shoulders. "Derek has been calling for you."

Her euphoria shattered. Worry spilled through her chaotic thoughts. Frightened by the sympathetic murmurings of the departing guests, she followed her mother and Derek's sister from the ballroom.

What if his condition had worsened?

She stopped outside her bedchamber. "I can't go in. Not until I know if he, if he..." She choked back her rising fear and stared into Hannah's somber eyes, searching for truth, not kindness.

Hannah reached out and took Alexandra's icy hands into her own. "He is not dead, but his injury is serious. I understand how you feel. The memory of my husband's illness still brings an ache to my heart because there was naught I could for him, save share my strength and my love with him. 'Tis what you must do now. Go to him. Love him. Help him fight his way back to you."

Alexandra blinked back stinging tears, unable to find adequate words. "Thank you." She drew a steadying breath and entered the bedchamber.

In the dim light of the flickering candles, Derek reclined against the pillows, bare from the waist up, with the exception of the bandage on his shoulder. He looked as though he might awaken at any moment. She rushed across the room and knelt by his side. "Has he regained consciousness yet?" she asked, grateful her grandfather had almost completely recovered from his illness.

Dr. Sebastian finished rinsing his hands in a basin. "No. S-soon."

Laurel squeezed her daughter's shoulder. "You mustn't be alarmed. Perhaps you should lie down for a bit of a rest yourself."

She shook her head. "I need to stay with him." She glanced toward her grandfather. "Did you have to operate?"

"No. The b-bullet passed all the way through. It missed the humerus and s-scapula."

She exhaled in relief. "Thank goodness it's only his shoulder." She looked up at her mother. "I remember, Mama."

"What do you remember?"

"You and Papa and Bartholomew. I remember seeing him shoot you. I-I thought you and Papa were dead." Shudders ripped through her. "I thought you were dead."

Laurel stroked Alexandra's hair. "Shhh. 'Tis over now."

"I thought so, too, but it isn't. Not until Derek is back with me." She shivered at the frightening images still lurking within the depths of her mind. "Mayhap not even then."

Laurel patted her hand. "You have faced it and now you can put it behind you. Since you're no longer running or hiding from the past, I doubt your nightmares will return. You needn't fear for Derek. He will soon be well."

Alexandra reached over and smoothed the dark lock of hair from Derek's forehead. "He tried to tell me the same thing, but I wouldn't listen. I pray my foolishness does not cost him his life."

"This wasn't your doing, and I'll hear no more of such talk. Rest now. I will return in a short time." Laurel pressed a kiss to the top of her daughter's forehead and left the room with Dr. Sebastian.

Alexandra rested her forearms on the bed and covered Derek's hand with her own. Max settled himself at her feet. Fatigue seeped through her bones.

Her thumb moved back and forth across his hand in small, feathery strokes. "Open your eyes, Derek. Come back to me. Don't let him defeat you, defeat us."

Unexpected anger rushed through her and drove her to her feet. She paced in front of the bed. "I won't let him beat us. We endured much at his hands, but we survived."

She stopped and clutched the bed's rail. "Oh, Derek—" Her voice broke. "We've so much to look forward to. You can't leave me now." The thought of the coming years without him by her side stole her breath away and threatened to rip her soul from her body.

She climbed up onto the four-poster bed and settled herself beside him. "I have enough strength for the both of us," she whispered fiercely. "For all three of us. You are going to be a father. Can you hear me?"

Taking pains to avoid his wound, she rested her head on his chest and placed her arms around him. "Can you feel me here beside you? You're mine and I won't let you leave me now." Teardrops ran unheeded down her face and spilled onto his bare chest. "I won't let you go."

****

Alexandra awoke with a start. She must check on Derek. She pushed herself upright and realized someone had pulled the coverlet up over her. Her gaze traveled to the armchair.

Jillian?

She rubbed her eyes and looked again. Jillian lay curled up in the chair, fast asleep. How long had she been there?

Alexandra slipped out of bed, careful not to disturb Derek. She shivered in the chilled air and padded over to the fireplace. She stirred the banked coals and coaxed them back to life before adding another log. Several minutes later, satisfied with the warming blaze, she turned back toward the bed, intending to check Derek's bandage.

Jillian stood beside the chair. "I wanted to make sure Derek was all right." She traced a pattern on the floor with the toe of her slipper. "'Tis all my fault."

Alexandra frowned. "What is?"

"If it hadn't been for me, Derek wouldn't have been hurt."

Alexandra wanted to shout her agreement and

shake her sister, but who would that help? She swallowed her anger. "Derek would not want you to blame yourself."

Jillian hugged her arms around her middle and paced in front of Alexandra. "I brought Bartholomew here."

"No." Alexandra placed her hands on Jillian's arm, stilling her movements. "Bartholomew used you, just as he used our family all these years. Even if he had never met you, he would have sought a way to hurt us."

Jillian lifted her shimmering gaze. Alexandra ached from the agony she saw. She wanted desperately to draw her sister into her arms and offer comfort. Yet she feared rebuff and hesitated.

"I've been a fool, Ally. A blind, jealous fool." Jillian sniffed and dabbed her eyes with a rumpled handkerchief. "Can you forgive me?"

Alexandra's eyes filled. "I'm not the one who has been harmed."

"I've been wretched to you. I should be lying there, not Derek."

"I'll hear no more of such talk. I have not the energy to cast blame. With my husband's life in danger I need all my strength to pull him through this. What happened between you and me is in the past. Once Derek is healed, mayhap we can be sisters."

Jillian's lips curved in a shy smile. "And friends, perhaps?"

"We shall see. Go back to bed. The day has been long. We can talk again on the morrow."

"Come back, Lexi," Derek moaned.

Alexandra hurried to his side and placed her hand on his brow. Dismay flooded through her. "He's fevered. Please fetch the water and cloths from the washstand."

While Jillian hastened to do as she had been

bid, Alexandra touched a taper to the flames in the fireplace and lit the candle on the table beside the bed. A large stain widened on Derek's bandage.

Alexandra accepted the basin. "His bandage needs changing, too. Please bring me more water."

"Should I call Grandfather?"

"Yes."

Jillian hurried from the room while Alexandra moistened a cloth and placed it on her husband's forehead. He jerked his head and dislodged the cloth. "Now, Derek, don't be difficult."

"Lexi?"

She leaned down to better hear his faint words. "I'm here." She wiped the perspiration from his face.

He opened his eyes. Their glassy appearance brought a frown to her forehead. She replaced the scrap of fabric on his brow, alarmed by how quickly it grew warm to the touch.

"My beautiful Lexi." Derek lifted his arm, but it fell back to the bed.

"Lie still. You've already opened your wound once. You mustn't do further damage."

"Taylor..."

She cradled his face between her hands, disturbed by his pallor. "Bartholomew is gone. He's out of our lives forever. You must rest now."

"Have to tell you...before I die."

"Shhh," she whispered past a lump in her throat. "You are not going to die. I won't let you."

His eyelids fluttered shut.

She turned at a touch upon her shoulder and saw her grandfather, her mother, and Jillian. She wiped away the moisture on her face. "He's fevered and—" She drew a ragged breath. "And his bandage needs to be changed. I fear an infection has set in."

"Come with me." Laurel guided her to the armchair. "Father will take care of him."

Unable to take her eyes off Derek, Alexandra

watched her grandfather cleanse the wound and apply a healing salve. When Derek flinched, she flinched. "We can't let him die, Mama."

"We won't."

Jillian knelt beside her. "You must have faith."

Have faith...death of someone close to you. The fortune-teller's words came back to her. Had he meant Bartholomew would die, not Derek? She stroked her wedding band with her thumb and leaned back against the chair, somehow knowing in her heart that he would recover. He would not be taken from her.

The four of them kept a vigil for the remainder of the night. When the first light of day streaked across the sky, Derek's fever broke and he settled into a healing sleep. Alexandra refused to leave the chamber, insistent upon being there when he awoke.

She passed the eve of Christmas by the side of the man she loved. Derek's parents and sisters took turns sitting with Alexandra, as did Polly. Jillian visited often, seemingly content to sit by Alexandra's side.

Derek opened his eyes for a moment to smile at her before slumber once again claimed him. The clarity of his eyes and the lack of infection lifted her soul with gladness.

Dusk shaded the bedchamber.

The boom of a cannon in the distance heralded the holiday season and reminded Alexandra that it was Christmas Eve. A snippet from a song ran through her thoughts. "On the first day of Christmas my true love gave to me."

The only thing she wanted was for her true love to open his eyes and grin at her again. Fatigued from the strain of the past two days, she prepared for bed and snuggled against Derek. She needed the strength and warmth he emitted even while sleeping.

Struck by a sudden inspiration, she pressed her trembling lips to his cheek and told him a tale he had once told her. "Once upon a time a king and a queen were finally blessed with a baby. A baby daughter. They gave her a fine christening. She had for godmothers..."

****

Small currents of air skipped along Alexandra's arm, raising goose bumps and invading her dreams of love and laughter. With a slight shiver, she burrowed closer to the source of heat, disinclined to awaken to the realities of her first Christmas as a married woman without her husband.

A feathery movement heightened the sensitivity of her skin and brought her reluctant eyes open and a sharp retort to her tongue. Her astonished gaze absorbed the wonder before her and her angry words faded away.

"Good morning, Lexi."

"You're awake!" She placed her hand on his brow and found it cool to the touch. She continued to touch him to assure herself of his health. Her smile broadened with each passing moment. "Tell me I'm not dreaming. I couldn't bear it."

Derek grinned. "Does this feel like a dream?" He brushed his lips against hers.

"'Tis pure heaven." She sighed and stroked the corded muscles of his arm, unable to get her fill of him. "I'm so glad you're better." She glanced at his bandage and was relieved to see that his wound had not re-opened. "I have much to tell you."

He cupped her chin with his hand. "Me first. I don't want to waste another minute of our time together on misunderstandings. I love you, Lexi. Only you. I've loved you for so long I can't remember a time when you didn't occupy my heart, my soul. Together we shall banish your nightmares and your fears about your past. I want only to love you and be loved by you."

Alexandra's heart swelled in untold delight and she pressed her finger to his lips. "I love you with all my heart, yet I thought you married me only to protect me. I couldn't allow myself to believe you loved me in return. Instead, I doubted your integrity and foolishly indulged my silly notions about you and my sister. For that I beg your forgiveness."

Derek closed his hand around hers with a gentle squeeze. "You have it."

She swallowed hard. "You no longer have to worry about my nightmares. They've gone. When you were injured, my memory came back." She took a deep breath and plunged on. "And...and I'm ever so grateful you'll be here for the birth of our child." There. She had said it. Unable to breathe, she awaited his reaction.

A slow smile spread across his face. "I know."

"You do? How?"

"I heard you talking to me, calling to me. You told me of the babe. You also told me the tale of the Sleeping Beauty, but you didn't kiss me."

"I did so!"

"Are you sure?"

With a happy smile, she accepted his challenge and kissed him with every ounce of strength in her.

"That's better."

"And the babe?"

"I couldn't be happier."

"You're truly glad?" A slight frown pulled her brows together. "But you do not want children."

"Because I was afraid."

Alexandra blinked. "You? Afraid? You're not afraid of anything."

He shook his head. "On the contrary. I failed to protect you, Lexi. Twice. I couldn't let the same thing happen to our child."

"But it was never your fault, Derek." She cupped

his jaw with her palms. "*I* raced away from you in the wood all those years ago. *I* left your ship on my own. And you have protected me. From the river. From Bartholomew."

He pressed her left hand to his lips. The gems on her wedding band winked and danced in the light streaming through the window. "We are as this ring," he said, his voice clear and strong. "United in a love as brilliant as the blue fire of these sapphires, as enduring as their golden foundation. We will be as one for all time."

Derek caught her mouth in the most tender of kisses. He lowered her to the pillows and placed his hand on the slight rounding of her abdomen. "May I pay homage to the woman I adore more than any other?

Knowing she was the most blessed of women, Alexandra smiled and led him home.

Epilogue

29 August 1753
As dawn broke this morn I was delivered of two beautiful babes, Jessalyn Alexandra and Lucas Montgomery Tremaine.
Derek is holding the children in front of the window, telling them of the ships which will one day be theirs, speaking to them of the future.

About the author...

Penny Rader, born and raised in Kansas, fell in love with reading from the moment she learned to read, and quickly made the library her second home, enjoying stories with strong heroines, biographies of women, and mysteries.

Penny discovered romance novels in the eighth grade and knew she'd read these empowering books for the rest of her life. Years later she decided to learn to write her favorite kind of books.

She discovered Romance Writers of America, which she quickly joined. Realizing she needed a writing support system she set about organizing the Wichita Area Romance Authors.

If Penny isn't working, reading, or writing, she's probably watching a movie or one of her favorite TV shows or enjoying her family.

Thank you for purchasing
this Wild Rose Press publication.
For other wonderful stories of romance,
please visit our on-line bookstore at
www.thewildrosepress.com.

For questions or more information,
contact us at info@thewildrosepress.com.

The Wild Rose Press
www.TheWildRosePress.com

Other Historical Roses to enjoy
from The Wild Rose Press

from Vintage Rose (historical 1900s):
DON'T CALL ME DARLIN' by Fleeta Cunningham: In Texas, 1957, Carole the librarian faces censorship. Will the County Judge who's dating her protect or accuse her?
SOURDOUGH RED by Pinkie Paranya: At the end of the Klondike gold rush, Jen and her younger brother search for her twin, lost and threatened in Alaskan wilderness.

from Cactus Rose (historical Western):
OUTLAW IN PETTICOATS by Paty Jager. Maeve had her heart crushed; it won't happen again. Zeke has wanted Maeve since he first set eyes on her...
SECRETS IN THE SHADOWS by Sheridon Smythe. Lovely widow Lacy had taken in two young children—and the rambunctious little angels wasted no time getting her into trouble with Shadow City's new sheriff.

from American Rose (historical U.S.A.):
EXPEDITION OF LOVE by Jo Barrett. An up-and-coming scientist in the world of paleontology collides heart first with an unconventional suffragette who has no desire to marry. Can they resolve their differences?
WHERE THE HEART IS by Sheridon Smythe. Orphan Natalie Polk steps into the shoes of the errant orphanage house mother. The new owner not only accepts her as capable of running the home but falls in love with her, with obstacles galore. How can they have a future?

from English Tea Rose (non-American):
HIGHLAND MOONLIGHT by Teresa Reasor. Seduced by the warrior to whom she is betrothed, Lady Mary flees to sanctuary. But she is forced to wed him, to save him from the executioner. Was her dream as elusive as Highland Moonlight?
THE RESURRECTION OF LADY SOMERSET by Nicola Beaumont. An age-old mystery, a risky assignment, a marriage devised to suppress a secret... Lark has been hidden most of her life. With the death of her mentor comes the command to marry the new Lord Somerset. Without this marriage, the estate falls to his wastrel brother. Can either suitor satisfy the lady?

Printed in the United States
220059BV00004B/4/P

9 781601 544759